An eye for an eye, blood for blood.

UCLA student Cass Turner was hoping to move on from the family business—but when the business is professional assassination, that's easier said than done. And sleeping with the man she was supposed to kill only complicates things. Her relationship with Nick Kosta, a lieutenant in LA's largest crime family, was supposed to be no-strings-attached fun. But if the two of them want to stay alive, they'll have to keep each other close.

Nick's traitorous cousin, Isaiah, is out for blood, so Cass can't afford any distractions as they try to hunt him down. Yet she can't help puzzling over Nick's motives—does he really share her deepening feelings or does he just feel responsible for her? And if their relationship is for real, will they even have a future? Because with their enemies several steps ahead of them, one false move could bring disaster for everyone Cass holds dear... and in this game of cat and mouse, no one will leave unscathed.

Books by Amanda K. Byrne

Game of Shadows
Game of Vengeance

Published by Kensington Publishing Corporation

Game of Vengeance

Amanda K. Byrne

LYRICAL PRESS
Kensington Publishing Corp.
www.kensingtonbooks.com

Lyrical Press books are published by
Kensington Publishing Corp. 119 West 40th Street New York, NY 10018

All Kensington titles, imprints, and distributed lines are available at special quantity discounts for bulk purchases for sales promotion, premiums, fundraising, and educational or institutional use.

To the extent that the image or images on the cover of this book depict a person or persons, such person or persons are merely models, and are not intended to portray any character or characters featured in the book.

Special book excerpts or customized printings can also be created to fit specific needs. For details, write or phone the office of the Kensington Special Sales Manager:
Kensington Publishing Corp.
119 West 40th Street
New York, NY 10018
Attn. Special Sales Department. Phone: 1-800-221-2647.

Kensington and the K logo Reg. U.S. Pat. & TM Off.
LYRICAL PRESS Reg. U.S. Pat. & TM Off.
Lyrical Press and the L logo are trademarks of Kensington Publishing Corp.

First Electronic Edition: October 2016
eISBN-13: 978-1-60183-649-6
eISBN-10: 1-60183-649-X

First Print Edition: October 2016
ISBN-13: 978-1-60183-652-6
ISBN-10: 1-60183-652-X

Printed in the United States of America

Acknowledgements

Big, *big* thank you to my editor, Corinne DeMaagd. You helped me make this book all shiny and pretty, and I've loved working with you.

Thank you so much to the team at Kensington and Lyrical Press for your support and enthusiasm!

To my critique partner, the wonderful and amazing Liv Rancourt, your feedback (and your willingness to listen to whatever crazy happens to pop out of my head) is greatly appreciated.

And to the BF, Aaron, for helping me come up with new and interesting ways to murder someone. Some people might say that's not the best dinner conversation. Whatever. I love you, and thank you for listen to me babble on about the merits of knives versus guns.

Chapter 1

"No."

I huff out a breath. "What else am I supposed to do? Sit at home, twiddling my thumbs?"

"Nah. You'd be sitting on the couch in my office twiddling your thumbs." Nick's trailing his fingers over the scar on my stomach as if he's trying to reassure himself it won't split apart at the slightest provocation.

"You can't force me to come into work with you every morning. Unless you're planning on handcuffing me and tossing me in the trunk of your car." I try to scoot away from his touch and almost fall off the bed, biting back a sigh when he tightens his hold.

I liked my little beach hut when it was just me, and I could walk around in my underwear because it was too damn hot to wear any clothing. For the last three days, I've liked it even better, but two full-grown adults crammed into a double bed isn't exactly my idea of a good time. There's not a lot of action happening in said bed, though I have to admit I've slept a lot better tucked against his side. My libido's taking a vacation while I recover, and Nick hasn't so much as hinted at sex.

"You remember the handcuffs?" he asks, a lazy smile on his face. It's distracting, that smile, causing my brain to misfire even as I want to smack him for it.

I shoot him a death stare. "Do *I* remember the handcuffs." He cuffed me to the door of his car with a set of fuchsia fuzzy handcuffs a few days after we'd met. It's pretty hard to forget those things. "You're not seriously saying you'd use them?" I pull his hand off my waist. "I can't keep the rest of my life on hold, Nick. I want to go back to class."

He slips his hand free and glides it over the curve of my hip. "It's only for a little while longer."

A little while longer could easily turn into *not just yet*, and the next thing I know, I'm a college dropout, forced to either work a dead-end job or continue killing people for money. I struggle to keep my annoyance in check. He's worried. I can work with worried. I roll off the bed and pad across the room to the miniscule kitchen for a bottle of water. "You can't know that. I'm not made of glass, and I can't live in a bubble."

He gets to his feet and stalks toward me, brows lowered as he glares. He nicks the bottle from my hand and drains it. "You died. Twice. I don't want to find out if the third time's the charm."

Point to him. I stroke a hand up his chest, his enticingly bare chest, and curve it around the back of his neck, letting my fingers play through the ends of his hair as I consider my words. Isaiah hasn't been found, and as long as he's out there, Nick and I both have targets on our backs. At the same time, though, forewarned is forearmed, especially in this case. "Isaiah took me by surprise," I say softly. "He's not going to be able to do that again. Campus is crowded. If I'm not on campus or with a friend, I'll come straight to your office and hang there until you're ready to go home." The UCLA campus, where I'm trying to finish my last year, is a sprawling complex, and during the day, full of students. The student body is *huge*.

"It'd take some mad skills and serious *cojones* to pull something off there. I'm more likely to get jumped in the parking garage again than on campus."

He threads his fingers through my hair, rubbing the muscles of my neck until I want to purr with contentment. "You're not helping, love."

My heart sputters at the endearment. I went a month without hearing him say it. A month where I hadn't heard *anything* from him, and as the days bled into weeks, the doubts started creeping in. He's ten years and a world of experience older. I wouldn't blame him for not wanting to be tied to someone as young as me.

Yet every day since he's been here, he's proving it's not just heat and blind lust between us. The things we went through together and the forced proximity have thrown us directly onto the *this is more than just sex* track, and I'd be foolish to think the connection we forged isn't strong enough to withstand a few weeks apart.

It's not love. But it's getting closer every day, and it's scaring the poo out of me.

"C'mon. You've seen the campus. You'll have a copy of my schedule. You can have someone pick me up instead of letting me drive myself." I tip my head back. I hate the glimmer of fear in his dark eyes, hate that it makes me question his motivations, because it's the one doubt he can't lay to rest. A part of me is convinced this protective bent he's got is because someone in his family tried to kill me.

Not because he cares about me.

Whenever I stumble down that rabbit hole, though, I claw my way back out, determined to give him the benefit of the doubt. *He came for me.* He could have ushered me onto a plane as soon as he arrived or moved us to a hotel where we could have separate rooms. Instead, he stayed. I lost a lot of strength and stamina confined to bed for two weeks in the hospital, then off and on over the past month recovering from plastic surgery. So all we've really done is wander at a snail's pace through Phuket, trying to get the other to eat the fried grasshoppers from the various food carts. And that's only when we're not staying out of the heat of the day in my hut.

Honestly, those are my favorite times. The times when we're just sitting here, talking. The times that mimic the evenings in his condo in Manhattan Beach, where he distracted me from my guilt enough to eat.

It might have come out eventually that Nick's favorite food is an In and Out burger, but because we're here, with little else to do, I learned it earlier. Like I learned his favorite color is green, his favorite movies are *Stand and Deliver* and *Billy Madison*, and that he and Constantine grew up like brothers, much like Marc and Isaiah.

He presses his thumb into my lower lip, then lets it slip down to my chin. "How many classes?"

I can't stop the giddy joy rising in my chest and smile. A normal life. I get to go back to a normal life. Or as normal as I get. "Four. If they have the last courses I need to graduate during the summer term, I'll be done by September." Then I have to worry about getting a job, what to do with the rest of my life, and my lack of work history. Somehow I don't think putting *assassin* on my resume will score me any interviews.

His hand drifts farther, brushing over my neck and along the faint scar left by Josef, a member of the family who tried to kill me on Isaiah's orders. The doubts stir from their slumber at Nick's constant touch tonight. His attention should make me happy. I *am* happy. I step back and tell those doubts to shut up.

He studies me a minute more, the light on the little porch buzzing when another fly gets trapped. It's so damn loud, that buzzing, filling the silence. "Fine," he says. "I get a copy of your schedule?"

The worry line between his brows makes my heart sputter just as badly as when he calls me "love," only in an entirely different way. "Yes. A copy of the schedule, and anything else you think I need to stay safe. *Except* a babysitter. I've still got Josef's knife." Somewhere. It's probably buried in a bag at Nick's.

"I'm getting you your own. Something that fits your hand better." He picks up my hand, holding it palm out, and uses his thumb to trace the creases.

My excitement dims a smidge. Carrying my own weapon is permanent, one that speaks of Nick's faith that I can handle myself and the scrapes I get into. It's also part of the life I'm trying to leave behind, if only Isaiah would pop up from whatever rock he's hiding under.

And I wonder, not for the first time, if staying with Nick means I can't shed that identity. If it'll dog my steps like an unfriendly ghost.

Nick's phone rattles angrily across the table. He kisses my palm, drops my hand, and reaches around me to pick it up. "Kosta."

Knowing the call could take anywhere from a couple of minutes to an hour or more, I grab another bottle of water and wander out onto the porch.

The sticky heat of the night drops over me like a wet blanket, smothering me in its weight. The humidity around here is insane, giving the air a tangible quality, like I can squeeze it between my fingers and watch it ooze out like syrup. The hut is at the end of a row of other huts just like it, some with their porch lights on, some dark. This close to the beach, there isn't much of a bug problem, and I lean on the railing, staring out over the black water.

Funny how oceans are the same no matter which one you're looking at. People earn their living on them. Swim in them, play in them. The color is different. So's the temperature, and the creatures swimming through them.

The ocean's always changing too. The way it breaks apart and reforms, holding on to most of the old stuff that keeps it recognizable as a salty body of water, letting in enough of the new that scientists either scream with delight over previously undiscovered species or moan about the fate of the planet as its levels rise.

It's also not mine.

My ocean is the one near the Santa Monica pier. The place I go after a job, a kind of meditation that allowed me to slip back and forth between Cass the College Student and Cass the Assassin. I miss my ocean. I miss Los Angeles, I miss my friends, and I miss my mother.

I miss Turner something fierce.

The door opens behind me, and Nick steps onto the porch. He props his elbows on the railing. Our bare shoulders touch, the only body parts that do, and out here in the messy heat it's almost too much. "Good news? Bad news? Indifferent news?"

"Har." He shifts to wrap his arm around my waist, pulling me to his chest, ignoring my half-hearted protests that it's too hot to cuddle. "That was Con. LAPD raided one of the escort agencies, and the manager's being brought up on charges. Con's concerned he'll talk."

"You let a man run that service?" In the movies, it's always women who run those businesses.

"He did a good job of it until he got greedy and started selling drugs out of the office. Been charged with possession with intent to distribute. Fucker had a couple kilos worth of cocaine waiting to be doled out. Tough as the drug laws are, he'll be going away for a long time."

Well, shit. "What are you going to do?"

His chest rumbles at my back as he growls in frustration. "Let him use our attorneys. Pretty much the only way we might have a chance of him keeping his mouth shut."

Which means if he doesn't, his fate will likely be very different. I turn around and place my hands on his chest, needing some space. I can't stumble around in the dark anymore. I've already done two jobs for his organization. With Isaiah in hiding, the chances of me taking another life are pretty high. I need to know what Nick does with the people who betray him. "What happens if he doesn't? What if they offer him a deal? If he was stupid enough or desperate enough to run drugs while engaging in other barely legal activities, his loyalty might snap."

He dips his head, his gaze locked on mine. "I think you can guess what happens." His voice is quiet, the words final and brutal, the last swing of the gavel. "The organization demands loyalty. Learning the scope of who we are and what we do is only given once trust is earned. You break that trust, you pay. Whatever that price might be. It's always high, and it's never what you expect. Right now, he's probably thinking if he talks, we'll come for him. We might. It might be his brother. It might be his wife."

My stomach clenches in a violent, shuddering knot, my mouth dry as I stare at him. No. No *way*. Innocent people. He uses them like…like… tools. "His *wife*? You go after women? Do you murder children too?" *Say no. Please say no.*

In the low light, the shadows on his face take his blank expression and twist it into something sinister. "We do what needs to be done, Cassidy. Sometimes that means using whatever leverage we've got. Sometimes that's women and children, though those are last resort measures."

I back away, out of his arms, skin prickling as the truth hits home. I knew Nick was as deadly as me. Without seeing it in action, I guess I didn't really believe it.

I sure as fuck do now.

Chapter 2

I am the hypocrite I accused Nick of being. My own words come back to haunt me, a reminder I convinced him we're not so different.

Yet I can't move past my initial horror.

Women. He'll take women as collateral. As revenge. As payment. It doesn't matter if they're clean of any wrongdoing of their own. If the punishment fits the crime, he'll send them to the guillotine.

Am I a hypocrite? I've never killed someone to punish someone else.

Or maybe I have.

The plane ride to LA is painful. He's brutally polite, the distance between us mere inches and as wide as the Grand Canyon. Each brush of his arm against mine makes me squirm, the two of us crammed together in our coach class seats. My fingers twitch with the need to lace our fingers together, tight enough they'll never break apart.

At one point, I fall asleep, waking to find myself curled up against him. His heart's a steady *thump* under my ear, lulling me back under.

If the plane ride is painful, the drive from the airport to Nick's house in Santa Monica is torture. It's mid-afternoon. Too soon to go to bed, and we're both too tired to do much of anything. Nick weaves in and out of traffic, his eyes on the road, the muscle in his jaw jumping like crazy. It's the only indication he's pissed.

Well, good for him, because so am I.

I'm angry at him, but mostly, I'm angry with myself. I let myself be seduced, swayed, blinded by my own loneliness. I *knew* this about him. I knew his brutality could outstrip mine, and I convinced myself it didn't matter because he was the first person to come along in forever that I didn't have to lie to.

I kill people for money. I don't ask if they're guilty. I don't even ask what sins they've committed. Because of the measures I've put in place to ensure I don't know any more than necessary, I could have easily killed someone for revenge, killed to send a message. I was right, all those weeks ago—his hands are just as bloody as mine.

I feel sick.

"You alert enough to go to the grocery store?"

I startle at the question, the first thing Nick's said since we left Bangkok. "I think so. Why?"

He slides a glance at me. "I need to run through my security feeds, check in with Constantine and my father, then I need to crash. There's no food in the house, though. If you feel up to it, you can take the car and go to the store. Otherwise, order what you think we'll need and have it delivered."

The store. The beach. I could go to the beach for a little while, kick some sand around, berate myself some more. It'd give us some time apart, and if I dawdle long enough, he might be asleep by the time I get home, and I'd have more time to work through my tangled mess of thoughts. Plus, he needs sleep. He looks awful, his hair rumpled, faint lines bracketing his mouth, his eyes bloodshot.

He flinches as I trace the line of his jaw with my fingertips, but I don't pull away. It's like having to learn him all over again, this hard and soft man, figure out where he puts that ruthless part of him so I know not to poke it with a stick. Some of the tension leaves him as I rub my fingers along his skin.

"Almost home," he murmurs.

Home. I drop my hand. I'd forgotten I'm basically homeless, and his comment brings it screaming to the forefront. As long as I'm with him, I have a place to stay, but it's not the same as *home.*

I wonder if he understands the difference.

We ease into the driveway and climb out of the car, the cooler Santa Monica air freezing compared to the tropical heat of Thailand. It perks me up a bit, stripping away the top coat of travel fatigue, and I grab my bags and follow him through the front door.

Inside, I hesitate in the hallway leading to the bedrooms. There's a guest room at the end of the hall. Will Nick want to share a bed with me? Better question, do I still want to share a bed with *him*? Our last night in Phuket wasn't exactly blissful, the tension between us so intense he actually got up at one point and left.

I found him sitting on the front steps, forearms braced on his knees. We watched the sky lighten with the coming day, the water in front of us populating with early fishing boats, then packed up the rest of our stuff and headed for the airport.

If I use that as my indicator of what I should do, it pretty much screams *nope nope nope.*

Casting a longing glance at Nick's king-size bed as I pass the master bedroom, I carry my bags into the guest room and dump them on the floor. I skip unpacking and dig around until I find clean clothes and my shower gear.

Fifteen minutes later I'm clean, dressed, and ready to drive to the grocery store. I pause at the doorway to Nick's room as I make my way down the hall. There's no sign of him there or in the bathroom, so I keep looking.

He's in a small room off the living room, a place I haven't been before. It's crammed with tech gear, much like the second bedroom at his condo in Manhattan Beach, monitors taking up most of the available surfaces, cables and wires snaking along baseboards and across the floor. Black and white pictures are frozen on most of the monitors, and he's fast forwarding through something on the monitor directly in front of him.

"Hey." He spins his chair toward me, and I manage a half smile. "I think I'll take you up on your offer of the car. Where are your keys?"

He fishes them out of his pocket and tosses them to me. "You need cash?"

I shake my head. "I'm good. Want anything special?"

"An IV drip of coffee."

"Can't help you there." I look past him to the picture frozen on the screen. "Are you looking for anything particular?"

He turns back to the monitor and restarts the image. "Routine check. Usual prowlers. Neighbor's cat's been using one of the back flower beds as a litter box again. Need to move the cameras around this weekend and do a software upgrade."

"Sounds exciting." The keys dig into my palm, the metal teeth cutting into the soft flesh. I hate this distance between us. I hate it even more knowing I'm the one who caused it.

Worst of all, I hate that I'm trying to justify what he's done so I don't push him away.

We'll never get anywhere if we don't talk, and it's my responsibility to open those lines. "Nick?"

"Yeah?"

I rest a hand on his shoulder, inching around until my butt runs into the edge of the desk. The warm, silky weight of his hair on my fingers doesn't distract me from noticing he's gone stiff with tension. I'm not running, though. I broke this; I'm going to fix it, dammit, one baby step at a time.

The words won't come. I'm not ready to apologize. I don't know I have anything to apologize *for*. But I don't want to just walk out of here without doing *something*.

I bend down and press my mouth to his, and after a paralyzing second he responds, lips moving in those minute adjustments we learned all those weeks ago, a fraction here, a smidge there, and then he parts his lips and his tongue slips out, a delicate probe requesting entry. The next thing I know I'm on his lap, the keys are on the floor, and my fingers are tangled in his hair.

When I kissed him, I didn't mean for it to end up like this, all heat and need and fierceness. I wanted to reopen the circuits, not fry them completely.

The brush of his fingers along my spine makes me whimper and squirm, and I tear my mouth away, gasping. "Crap. Sorry. I didn't mean for that to happen."

He slips his hand under my shirt, stroking up my back to rest between my shoulder blades. "Glad it did." His eyes have lost their glaze of fatigue, replaced by a healthy serving of lust. Nice to know some things haven't changed.

I slide my hands from his hair down to his face, cupping it. "I'm sorry about the other night and how I reacted."

He arches a brow. "You *are* the one who convinced me we weren't all that different."

"I know," I whisper. "I want to tell you it shouldn't be any different when I'm provided with evidence of that, but *thinking* you're just as ruthless as I am and *knowing* it are two separate things."

"I wasn't lying. Women and children are an absolute last resort. If a wife or son is used to set an example, the entire organization knows damn well the offense was serious." He glides his hand down and stops just above my butt. "You're not as ruthless as you think you are. You compartmentalize everything, you shut off when you have to, and you're not afraid to get your hands bloody if that's what's necessary. But you want out of the game. I don't. This is my life, Cass. This is what I do. And I don't have any plans to change that."

Hearing it tears into a little fantasy I didn't know I had. He'd dismantle the organization or turn it over to Constantine, and he'd be content to expand his tech empire. The pieces of it start to flutter away, the whole of the picture growing more tattered by the minute.

The words tumble out before I have a chance to stop them. "Would you use me? If I stand by my decision to stop, would you try to sweet talk me into taking on one more job?"

The stiffness returns, his body granite. "If I did?"

More pieces float off, and a fierce ache develops low in my throat, my nose tingling. "I'd leave because it would be pretty fucking clear you didn't respect me enough."

He drops his hands to my hips, all the warmth in his face gone. In its place is the mask of the cool, hard man who runs the city's largest crime family. "Respect's a two-way street." He nudges me from his lap. "Have enough for me to support your choice."

Shame burns in my chest. I should have kept my mouth shut, gone to the store, and put this conversation off until tomorrow when we were both rested and capable of carrying on intelligent conversation.

Not once has he indicated he thinks I should stay in the game. All he asked was I hold it together and live with my guilt until this is over.

I swallow against the ache, fisting my hands hard enough my nails dig into my palms. "I do."

I scoop up the keys and hurry from the room, eager to get away from Nick and the falling line of dominos. The rapidly fading light has turned the sky purple, and I stare at it, blinking to keep the tears from forming. Repairing the damage I've caused will be harder than I thought.

Headlights flash when I punch the button to unlock Nick's car. I climb in and adjust the seat, breathing through the momentary surge of panic. I've never driven anything this nice. With my luck today, I'll probably end up scratching it.

Annoyed, I huff out a breath and start the car. Nick's obviously not worried about damage if he's letting me drive it, so I shouldn't, either.

At the end of the block, I glance to my right where the beach is. It would be deserted, most likely, this late and this cold.

I'm also too fucking tired to stay up much longer. I might have scored some sleep on the plane, but it'll only keep me awake for a couple of hours at the most.

The store's crowded with after-work shoppers, and I have to dodge more than one small child as I make my way up and down the aisles, filling the cart. The trip takes less than an hour, and all too soon I'm pulling into the driveway, full dark only minutes away. The light in the living room is off, the front of the house barely illuminated by the light over the front door.

It's quiet when I enter. Nick's not in his office. I tiptoe down the hall and inch open the door to his bedroom. He's sprawled on his stomach, face smashed into his pillow, broad shoulders bared because the sheets have migrated halfway down his back. Need for him rises, warm and sweet, and I shove it aside. Tomorrow. We'll straighten it out tomorrow. We've gone through too much to let miscommunications push us apart. I slip inside his room and pull the blankets up, then head for the kitchen to deal with the groceries.

The dark's soothing. These shadows are friendly, and they wrap around me as I move through the kitchen, guided by the dim light over the stove. He left one of the dining room windows open to chase out the stale air, and I make a mental note to close it before I go to bed.

The night's so quiet the crack of a foot stepping on a downed branch is like a clap of thunder, jump-inducing. Without thinking, I free one of the knives from the block on the counter, testing its weight. Slightly better than my own kitchen knife. It'll have to do.

Aside from the sliding doors in the dining room, there's a second door off the kitchen that opens onto the backyard. The kitchen island's perpendicular to the door, providing me with the only hiding spot in the room. I don't want to wake Nick until I have to, so I crouch behind the kitchen island, ears straining to hear what's going on outside. The doorknob rattles slightly, metal clinking off metal, and I roll my eyes.

Someone's picking the lock. Stupid human, breaking into the house of a *mafiaso*.

As long as I stay where I am, I won't be seen once the idiot enters the kitchen, and I might stand a chance of catching him off-guard. If I'm really lucky, he'll give up and leave us alone, and I won't have to wake Nick at all.

I don't get lucky. The knob rattles again as it twists, the door opening with a slight *click*. I breathe out, breathe in, lock everything inside, and shift my grip on the knife, letting the cold emptiness take over.

Soft footfalls come closer to my hiding spot, and I focus on the patch of floor where he'll pass by. His approach drags on for a century, each beat of my heart loud enough I swear he has to hear it. My legs are going numb. When his foot comes into view, I press back against the island, muscles tensed to spring.

It takes me all of two seconds to register that this man is not here on a social call. The silencer he's screwing on to the barrel of his gun is a pretty big fucking clue. He passes, and I jump up, launch myself at his back, and sling an arm across his chest. The blade slices through the skin of his throat in a rough *tug tug tug*, like the teeth of a serrated knife. Hot blood drips onto my hand, and he flails around, dropping the gun to the floor.

I let go and sidestep him, scooping up the gun as I do. He goes to his knees, hatred gleaming in his eyes before they glaze over and he lands face first on the tile.

I place the knife and the gun on the counter and step around the island to wash my hands. There's some blood on the cuffs of my hoodie, which sucks because it's my favorite sweatshirt, perfectly broken in, and unless I can get the blood out, I'll have to burn it. And blood *never* comes out.

Nick's still sound asleep in the same position he was in when I checked on him the first time. Waking him is going to suck, hardcore. At least I won't have to do it with bloody hands.

I shake him until he pries open an eye. "What?" he mumbles.

"How do you get blood stains out of ceramic tile?"

Chapter 3

Nick takes in the pool of blood on his kitchen floor and scrubs a hand over his face, pulling his jaw down in the process. "Shit. Didn't think about setting the alarm."

"You were dead to the world when I came in. You probably fell asleep as soon as your head was on the pillow." He'd pulled on a pair of sweats after I woke him, but not before I got a good look at his naked ass. It was enough to temporarily jostle me from my numbed state.

Seeing the dead body lying on his kitchen floor pushes the images of naked Nick into the recesses of my brain where they belong.

I crouch next to the body, nose twitching at the sickeningly sweet tang of blood. "I'm not much use at this part. I always leave the bodies to be found. Of course, in a perfect world, he wouldn't have gotten into the house in the first place."

Nick shoots me a look. "Why *did* you let him in?"

"There was no *letting*. He picked the lock. He'd probably have shot me on sight if I'd made my presence known, and I'm not exactly excited about the prospect of adding to my collection of scars. Waiting to see what he'd do seemed like the best option." I stand and poke the body with my toe. "What do we do?"

He stares at the dead man on the floor for a while longer, then turns around and pads out of the kitchen. The blood's stopped spreading, but it really will be a bitch to get out of the tile if it's there much longer. Of course, Nick can afford to have the floors redone if he wants.

Maybe he should replace the locks while he's at it.

Thirty minutes later, there's a crew of four men in the kitchen, all bearing black duffle bags. They greet Nick with silent nods and don surgical scrubs, down to pairs of papery-cloth booties over their shoes. One of them pulls a hacksaw from his bag, another a pair of scissors. They flip him onto his back, the tarp crinkling under his weight.

His eyes are open. Sightless, blank, dark. Hard to believe he'd glared at me only moments ago. The wound isn't the neatest one I've ever made, either, the edges ragged and gaping. The guy with the scissors begins cutting away his clothing, baring his skin to the harsh kitchen light. In the short time between when he bled out and now, he's gone waxy.

I imagine most women, no, most *people*, would have left by the point they've reached now, hacksaw poised above the ankle. I've never had any real desire to find out how you'd take a body apart for easy transport, yet I can't stop watching. Is it necessary to cut off the feet? What about the hands? If the torso's big, like his, do you split it in half, just under the ribs?

Nick wraps an arm around my shoulders and steers me from the room. "You don't need to watch."

I nod. He's right. Those are pictures I don't need running through my brain. "What happens next?"

He stops at the door to the guest room. "You change your clothes. I'll need your pants and sweatshirt. They'll take care of disposal when they leave."

"Can I borrow your keys again?" I unzip the hoodie and hand it over.

"No beach tonight, Cass. I don't want you leaving the house alone."

I pause in the act of unbuttoning my pants. "Did I or did I not just take down the intruder by myself?"

"Not the point. We've already underestimated Isaiah. Assuming he doesn't have a back-up plan would be foolish. You're not leaving the house, and neither am I. Pants. Now." He crooks his hand in that same *c'mon* gesture I've seen a hundred times before in the movies, his gaze never leaving mine.

I toe off my shoes and strip off my jeans, leaving me in a T-shirt and panties. Unfortunately, Nick's point is valid. Anyone who has the forethought to plan something like this, knowing we'd be vulnerable from fatigue, won't leave anything to chance.

He gives me one last long look, then turns on his heel and strides down the hall to the kitchen.

Despite having already taken a shower, I head for the bathroom anyway, hoping to salvage at least part of the ritual. I pile my hair on top of my head, flip on the tap, and step under the spray, shutting my eyes as the hot water hits my skin.

It's not the same. I keep running different scenarios to find a better way I could have achieved the same results. I can't turn off Cass the Assassin. She's in full control, and after several minutes of standing there, hot water streaming down my body, I resign myself to dealing with it tomorrow.

This time around, the water makes me sleepy, the warmth seeping into my bones and softening them. I soap up, scrubbing beneath my fingernails, just in case, and rinse away the film of death coating me.

Curiosity takes me from the bathroom to the kitchen instead of the guest room, where I'm sure Nick prefers I'd stay. Dark red blood pools on the tarp. The body is missing its arms up to the elbows and legs up to the knees. Two men are working on opposite ends with hacksaws while the other two hold a murmured conversation, cradling bottles of water.

Seeing them engaging in such normal activity is more disturbing than the dead body missing limbs.

Nick's not with them, but I don't go hunting for him. Not this time. I do my best imitation of a good girl and head for the guest room. I shut the door, climb into bed, and close my eyes. Every cell in my body is crying for sleep.

Unfortunately, my brain has other plans. It's the shower all over again. I had enough time; I could have woken Nick. I could have surprised the intruder and caught him outside the door.

I could have come home ten minutes later, and Nick could have been the dead guy, not the other way around.

Frustrated, I thump my pillow and flop over on my back, annoyance rising as my pajamas bunch and twist. I sit up, yank the tank top over my head, then boost my hips and rip the shorts off as well. I adjust the covers and stare at the ceiling, willing sleep to come.

It doesn't. I shut my eyes, open them, squeeze them tighter, and still, it's elusive. I'm so tired I want to cry. I'm tired and my head hurts and yet I'm wound tighter than a jack in the box. The ocean is blocks away. If Isaiah had any other plans, he'd have put them on hold when he saw Nick's crew arrive to deal with the body. I could sneak out the window. I can practically hear the waves crashing on the sand.

If this is what dependency is like, I can see why so many addicts fall off the wagon.

I roll over again, the blankets sliding down to my waist, and I leave them there. The cool air feels good on my overheated skin. Maybe I should read for a while. That might tire me out, help disconnect my brain.

The door opens as I'm reaching for the lamp on the bedside table, and Nick steps inside. "You still awake?"

"Can't sleep," I admit, tugging the sheet up to cover my breasts. He's seen it all, but he doesn't need to see it tonight.

He closes the door behind him, and I stiffen, muscles locking as he walks around to the other side of the bed and stretches out on top of the blankets. He doesn't say anything, just lies there, hands behind his head.

Finally I break the silence. "Did they leave?"

"Yeah. House is locked up, alarm's on. Anything else happens tonight, we'll know." He shifts onto his side, lifts a finger, and traces the faint line on my neck, his gaze following his finger.

The air's so heavy I'm surprised we're not suffocating. Regret, desire, and frustration tumbles together, becoming a potent stew of emotions. He hooks a finger on the top of the blankets and eases them down, knuckle brushing my sternum. Once the blankets are around my waist, he feathers his fingers over my belly, following the puckers of the scar there. Given the nature of the wound, the surgeons weren't able to minimize it as much as they had with the one on my neck and the one on my arm.

I'm uncomfortable, bared to him like this, practically naked while he's still mostly dressed and distant, so distant. Like our first kiss, his touch fractures the cold emptiness, allowing the warmth to flow into the cracks, washing over the harsh reality of the evening. He traces a single finger along the line of my hip, his expression obscured by the shadows.

I miss him. Miss him so much it hurts, and he's right here for the taking, if only I have the courage to ask him to stay. "Either get in or leave."

He withdraws his hand and sits up. Grabbing his shirt between his shoulder blades, he draws it over his head, then boosts his hips up and pulls the sweats down, leaving him naked. A rush of heat sweeps up my face. I forgot he wasn't wearing any underwear. I should have told him to just leave.

He works his way under the covers, his hand finding my hip once more. Then he does the strangest thing. He scoots down, wraps his arms around my waist, and rests his head on my chest. A move I'm familiar with because I've done it often enough myself, but the positions are reversed, and it feels weird.

I hesitate before threading my fingers through his hair, propping my leg up on his hip. He's hard, his dick pushing against my thigh, but he doesn't make a move. The longer we lie there, not talking, not sleeping, his warm breath on my skin, the more I relax.

I swallow and force the words out. "I'm sorry about earlier. I know better, given how you reacted when I told you what I do. I know you'd never ask me to take on a job for you." It's the reason I trusted him so quickly, the reason I went to him after Josef tried to slit my throat, the reason I stayed when I had no need to.

"Apology accepted," he mumbles. The quiet stretches out, the house settling around us, seconds slipping into minutes, but we're still not sleeping. I'm waiting for something, brain too awake and active to flip to sleep mode. I just don't know what it is.

"I missed you. In Thailand. Every time the phone rang, I'd get my hopes up that it was you on the other end, and it never was. It was stupid. You had shit to deal with, and I would have been pissed as hell if you'd gotten hurt because you were worrying about me, but I wanted you there. At the very least, I wanted to talk to you. Know that you were okay, that there weren't bullets whizzing past your head." I tighten my grip on his hair, digging my fingers into his scalp, then stroke away the small hurt.

Until the words rushed out, I didn't know they were there. They're all true, though. I clamp my mouth shut to keep the words inside, the ones that have no place here. Doubts I never got a chance to voice but won't go away, whiny, needy ones better suited to a middle school girl, stupidly grateful ones that he's here and unharmed and, for some reason, he wants *me*.

"Would it make you feel better if you beat on me?"

I laugh. "I doubt it. I wasn't coming up with creative ways to kill you while I was there. I was just…"

"Worried." He tips his head back far enough I can see the answering shadow on his face. "Worried your recovery wasn't going well or Isaiah would find you anyway. I didn't want to take that chance, Cass. I figured you sneaking out in the middle of the night, not telling anyone where you were going, was the best way to distract Isaiah. He'd concentrate his efforts on me, and you'd come back after things had calmed down. Problem is, you're here now, and I'm still fucking worried. If he saw you, he'd have shot you, silencer in place or not."

The muscles of his arms harden as he holds me tighter. His words sneak in and poke holes in my doubts. Panic whips through me. For the last four and a half years, since the start of my senior year of high school, I've put off serious relationships. It was one more person to lie to, one more person to hide things from, and I couldn't do it. There's no reason to lie anymore, not to Nick, and the prospect of drowning him in all my pent-up emotions is kind of scary.

I cast about for something to say, something snarky, something to break apart the tension, to lift the heaviness draped over us both. But nothing comes, and my breath stutters out as he places a soft kiss on my collarbone, nuzzling my throat.

"Will you go for a run with me in the morning?" I blurt.

He draws back and frowns. "You sure you're up to it?"

No. "I need to start somewhere. I'll probably make it to the end of the block and collapse. I want to find a dojo or something too."

"What discipline?"

I suck my top lip into my mouth, then release it. "Not sure. I've tried a bunch over the years. I like Wushu best. It's the most effective for someone without a lot of brute strength. Always wanted to try Krav Maga. A lot of the maneuvers are similar to ones taught in self-defense classes, and God knows I've taken plenty of those. Turner will have a good idea of where to go."

"You want to see your dad." It's a statement, not a question, flat, with a hint of disbelief.

"Crazy, right? But he's the one who trained me. He knows what I can handle, what will challenge me." Apparently I'm still capable of lying even when I don't need to; I want a relationship with my dad. One that doesn't involve me killing people for money because it's what he does. This is the only way I can think that will keep us in touch.

Nick huffs out a breath and shuts his eyes. "Tomorrow?"

"Or the next day. No rush."

"Fine. Can we sleep now?"

I brush a stray lock of hair from his forehead. "I was exhausted before and I couldn't sleep."

He presses on my hip. "Roll over for me?" I do, not stopping until I'm on my side, facing away from him. He snugs himself up against me, bodies aligned, my head tucked under his chin and his arm draped over my stomach. It's a perfect cocoon of safety. "Nick."

"Cass."

I want to squirm. "I don't need to be protected."

"Fuck yes, you do. Go to sleep."

Chapter 4

I'm dying. Forget lights at the end of tunnels and floating above yourself. Death is a jog through Nick's Santa Monica neighborhood. My lungs are on fire and my throat's closed off and the muscles in my legs have disappeared. "Stop," I gasp.

The ass just chuckles, turns around, and starts jogging backward. "Barely gone half a mile, Cass. C'mon," he coaxes, "there's an ice cream cone in it for you."

"I hate you."

"Nah. You love me."

He realizes it the instant I do, the L-word, the one neither of us has said. Because it's not true, not yet. It's not part of the plan.

"Ice cream. You make it two more blocks, and there's ice cream." He faces forward again and shortens his stride to keep pace, his expression neutral.

"It's nine in the morning. Too early for ice cream." Also too cold for ice cream. "Brownie," I spit out between labored breaths. "I want a brownie. With the ice cream."

His lips spread in a grin. "Brownie with the ice cream is two extra blocks."

"Fuckin' A." Seven lousy blocks, and I'm panting and heaving like an asthmatic at a marathon. I was laid up for less than two months. I could not have gotten this out of shape in that short amount of time. I suck in air, clench my fists, and push on.

Four blocks later, I'm forced to a walk. My face burns with the heat of exertion and embarrassment. Before I ended up in the hospital, I could do three miles without problems, and if I really wanted to push myself, I'd shoot for five.

I groan, bracing my hands on my lower back. "Pathetic."

Nick hasn't even broken a sweat. "Do I have to remind you, you died? Twice? You're allowed to be out of shape."

"Thanks for the reminder." Or is he reminding himself? I squint against the morning sun. "Are you okay?"

We walk another block, the pace brisk enough to keep my muscles warm and loose, slow enough the burning in my lungs has eased.

"No. Yes. Last night could have gone wrong a hundred different ways, Cass. I slipped. Compromising my own safety is one thing. Compromising yours is another."

"Hey." I place my hand on his arm, stopping him. "You're forgetting that none of those wrong things happened. He didn't even see me coming." I might have given up the shadow game, but it's nice knowing I haven't lost my touch. "I'll get stronger. There's plenty of time before next term starts, so I'll be able to focus on building my strength." The current term would be ending in another week or so. The pang of longing, knowing Denise is getting ready for finals, is unwelcome. I mean, *finals*. Who'd have thought I'd be jealous of people taking exams?

"I don't think you should go back next term. Too dangerous." He starts walking back to the house.

We already had this discussion. "I'm going back to school, Nick. There's a whole month between now and the start of the next semester. Anything could happen." Which reminds me I need to stop by the registrar's office and check on how to return after a leave of absence.

"We had this discussion before someone broke into my house with the intent of killing one or both of us. Likely both of us."

"Nick." I step in front of him, forcing him to stop again. "I'm not made of glass. He didn't kill me. He tried, damn hard, and if he tries again, I'll be ready for him. Can't you trust me to take care of myself?"

"Maybe you should move back out to the condo. No one knows where it is except Con. You'd be safe there."

I stifle my huff of frustration. "Sure. If it'll make you feel better, we can move back there."

He frowns. "No, just you. It'll look suspicious if I fall off the radar again."

"And it won't look suspicious if I disappear so quickly after I returned? Everyone thinks I'm your girlfriend, buddy. Or were you planning to feed them some break-up story?"

His expression turns sheepish. "Hadn't thought of that. Might be a good idea, though."

From the look on his face, I know he's seriously considering it. I don't want to be his dirty little secret. "No." I walk past him and then kick up my pace to a jog, lungs screaming in protest.

The ten blocks to the house pass in a one-sided argument. I let Nick run his mouth as I concentrate on my breathing, on the ache in my lungs, the tension in my shoulders. I'm wobbly and sweating insanely as I slow to a walk about a block from his house, listening with half an ear to yet another reason why it's best for me if his family, his business, and the organization at large thinks we're no longer together and I move back into the condo at Manhattan Beach.

"No," I say again, standing in the kitchen, water glass in hand. "No, because we're safer together. You can't chain me to the condo. You leave me there, I'll just walk out. And I'll keep on walking.

"You're the one who insisted I come home. I could have stayed in Thailand." I probably would have gone nuts from being so isolated, but that's another story. "You convinced me to come home, that I'd be safe here, and that I'd be with *you*. I want what you promised me. You can't deliver, that's fine. But the only way you're getting rid of me is if you actually dump me." I drain the glass, ignoring the cracks snaking their way through my heart. We're doomed to misunderstandings and best-for-yous, those painful words and gestures that always do more harm than good. I've let him make too many decisions about our relationship. If he makes this one, it'll be the last time he does.

I brush past him and head for the bathroom and the shower. Stripping aside my running gear, I flip on the tap and wait for the water to heat. He'll do it. If his vigil in my hospital room is any indication, he'll break up with me for real to keep me out of harm's way. Though I'm not sure there's going to be any breaking up involved. We haven't gone on a date. The only couple-like thing we've done is sleep together.

Is this the world of dating post college? The ambiguity sucks ass.

The door opens, but I ignore it, reaching for the shampoo, steeling myself for the blow that's about to fall. "Go on," I say. "Get it over with."

There's a faint rustling on the other side of the shower curtain, and it twitches and pulls away from the wall, far enough to reveal a naked Nick. He steps into the shower and takes the shampoo bottle from me, motioning for me to turn around. When I don't, he nudges me until I'm facing away from him.

Seconds later, his hands are in my hair, soaping it up. "I'm a little fucking paranoid. Cut me some slack, okay? It's a lose-lose situation, love. You stay with me, you're a target. I let you go, you're still a target.

I tell people we're no longer together, you're still a fucking target. I can't get the bulls-eye off your back." He combs his fingers through my hair, rinsing the soap from it, then glides his hands down, along my shoulders, skimming the curves of my breasts, trailing along my sides to my hips. He pulls me snug against him, his arms crossing my belly and holding me in place. "Hard to get to know you better if you're gone."

"You're still stuck on that? I thought you knew me pretty well by now." We've spent quite a bit of time talking, about everything and nothing. It's added to the fast forward feeling of our relationship. "Black and white, Nick. Am I staying or going?" I tip my head back onto his shoulder, the shower spray hitting my neck.

He presses a kiss to my jaw. "Staying. Who else is going to keep me guessing?"

"Isaiah," I say dryly. Nick's fingers caress the scar on my stomach, distracting me. It's this constant reminder that life is more fragile than we think, and he can't stop touching it. I want more from him than his concern, more than his care. I miss the lust in his eyes and the giddy anticipation that any second, he'd give in to his frustrations and just... attack. That he'd push me against the wall, or onto the couch, and show me in no uncertain terms that he can't get enough of me.

I miss his mouth on mine, on my skin, his tongue driving me nuts, his fingers finding new ways to string me out and leave me hovering on the edge, ready to beg. I've been so focused on staying alive that I've forgotten how to *feel* alive. I want Nick to show me. And I want him to show me now.

"I think you need to be re-educated," I say, covering the hand on my stomach. I've done this with him. We've been here before. He'll like it. Older men like this sort of thing. Right? This taking charge of my own pleasure, demanding it from him?

"How so?"

I guide his hand down, stroke it along the crease in my hip, following the joint out and back again, slipping his fingers along my inner thigh. Arousal heats my blood, and I twist my head to the side, seeking his mouth. "I'm not going to break," I whisper, the words ragged.

I suck the droplets off his jaw, running my tongue along the cords of his neck, bumping my hips forward, against his hand. I take his free hand and use it to cup my breast. "This is what you do with a naked body in the shower."

"Cass—"

"No. Re-education, remember?" I squeeze his hand around my breast. "This is what we do in the shower." The few times we showered together always ended this way, unable to keep our hands to the task of getting clean.

His fingers dance around, sidestepping the most important parts, and I squirm in his hold, scraping my teeth over the skin of his jaw. "Touch me. Just fucking touch me." I drop my hand from my chest, reach behind me, and wrap my fingers around his cock.

Hard. Hard as rebar, making the man a liar. He needs this as badly as I do. This is what we *are*, what we are to each other. This is the part we've always understood, even when we fought it.

"Stop, Cass," he hisses and removes his hand from my breast to pull my hand from his dick. "This is about you. Only you."

And he thrusts his fingers into me.

I cry out, the sensation zigging and zagging through my blood. I cant my hips forward, seeking more. Seeking friction. His hand returns to my breast and plucks at the nipple, tugging, rolling it between his fingers, pinching it hard enough I cry out again.

It feels *amazing*. This is my reward for all those nights when I sprawled across the bed, wishing he was with me. The sharp, bright pain, the buzzing heat surging through my veins, his hard body holding me up while he destroys me with strokes and glides and the barest hint of his fingertips on my skin. He surrounds me and keeps me safe even as he pushes me for more.

He rubs his thumb around my clit in tight, slippery circles, pushing down every so often, the surge of pleasure rising higher every time. When he crooks his fingers inside me and withdraws, I moan, just like he knew I would.

"Did you think I didn't miss this?" he murmurs. "A couple weeks, Cassidy, of you in my bed, as hungry as I am. I fucking love how responsive you are. You seduced me."

There was no seduction. Only greed. The desire to take as much as I could from him because that was all I could handle. It was never about feelings and always about lust.

He twists his fingers as they plunge, and I whimper. "I've been patient," he continues. "I'll wait as long as you need. But fuck, I need you." Another press of his thumb, and he wiggles it from side to side. The pressure's building, and he fucks his fingers into me, fast, shallow thrusts. "You're getting hotter. Slicker. You'll do anything I ask, won't you? Strip in the middle of my office and spread your legs."

I would.

"Let me lick you unconscious."

He'd almost succeeded one time.

"Will you let me in you bare?"

No condom? I've never, *ever*, gone that far before. Never wanted to. Never wanted to feel the heat of him, every ridge rubbing unemcumbered against my swollen tissues, never—

The orgasm breaks over me like a tidal wave, swamping me, smashing into millions of pieces, the aftershocks drawn out as his hand continues to move. My legs are noodles, each breath laden with damp and the scent of sex.

He kisses the side of my neck, the underside of my jaw, the corner of my mouth, bringing me down to earth. "Better?" he murmurs.

"Uh-huh." I let him take most of my weight, willing my heart to slow down and the strength to return to my legs. First orgasm in over a month. I guess I needed that.

The hard length of him presses into my ass. I turn around and shift to the side, kissing his chest, his throat, the strong line of his collarbone. I scratch my nail lightly along the underside of his shaft and slick my thumb over the head. He groans and bucks his hips, his fingers digging into my shoulder.

Turnabout's fair play. I'm not sure I can find the words to send him over the edge like he did with me, but I'm going to try. I stroke him slowly, firmly, chasing drops of water across his chest with my tongue. "You're right," I say, and it doesn't take much to make my voice husky and low. "Whatever you want me to do, I'll do it. Get on my knees. Let you take me against the wall." Strangely, that's one we haven't tried.

I bring my palm over the top of the crown, squeeze gently, and slide down again as I stretch up to trace the shell of his ear with my tongue. I suck his earlobe into my mouth, thinking of all the sweet and dirty things we haven't done. His cock throbs in my hand, growing harder. "Is that what you want?" I whisper. "To slide into me, feel me around you? All slick and hot and tight, knowing you made me that way?"

The words have the desired effect, and he sags at the knees, my name echoing off the tile as his release spills over my fingers.

In the ensuing quiet, the impact crashes down on me. What the hell did I say? What did I *do*? It's a dangerous game, this sex roulette. I don't know the rules, and I'm afraid I just made a move I can't back up.

The water's growing cool, so we finish our shower quickly, not speaking. He turns off the tap and reaches around the shower curtain to snag towels. He hands one to me. I dry off and twist the towel around my hair, avoiding his gaze.

I get away with it until he hitches his towel around his waist. He traps me against the sink, eyes intent on mine. "What the fuck was that?" he says quietly.

He's asked me that before, the night I met his family for the first time. A tipping point when we finally figured out we both want this, whatever *it* is, for however long it lasts.

Following through on those dirty words implies a whole new level of trust. "I don't know."

He narrows his eyes. "I think you do." He kisses me, hard and quick, leaving behind a burning imprint of his lips on mine. "Not yet. We need to talk about it when we're not right in the middle of it."

He's right. Of course, he's right. It'll give me time to figure out if it's what I want. If I'm willing to take that step. It's an important step. A huge one. It pushes us forward, faster, and opens me up to heartbreak. I don't know that my heart can handle it.

Chapter 5

Turner's indifference is an anvil on my shoulders, pushing me farther and farther into the ground. His attention is focused on his monitor, finger clicking the mouse every so often.

I entertained some fantasies about how this reunion would go, having not seen each other in weeks. They all involved hugs and a genuine smile from my dad, and sometimes he looked at me like he used to, like I was his little princess caught escaping from the tower. Come *on*. I died. That should be all anyone needs to shed their masks and reveal their true feelings. Isn't that what Nick and I were doing?

But no, Turner took my request to resume martial arts training like I asked him if it was going to rain tomorrow. The warmth I harbored over a happy, or happyish, reunion freezes slowly, chilling me to the bone. He clicks through link after link, sometimes pausing to read a description. He hasn't spoken a word beyond asking what I was considering. Wushu, I told him, same as before.

"Have you considered more of a challenge?"

The flat note in his voice seals the ice into my skin. There's no father and daughter here. We're just Cass and Turner, mentor and mentee. The only thing that might bring a gleam of joy to his eye is me telling him I've changed my mind; I'll continue in the family trade.

How is it this man has no problem showing how devoted he is to my mother and can't bring himself to even give me a pat on the shoulder? It's pathetic that I'll settle for a "there, there," but damn.

"Krav Maga," I say, and my voice is just as flat as his.

I should ask my mother some time what she does to make my father respond, to give her more than this robot sitting on the other side of the desk. Because the only affection I receive from him is when I'm standing in range of my mother, where the warmth he shows her has no choice but to spill over onto me.

He flicks his gaze from the monitor to me and back again. "There's a gym that offers it out near Nick's house. I'll check them out."

"No." I've had enough of pretending I'm okay with this. "I'm a big girl. I can do it myself."

He sits back and places his hands on the armrests of his chair. "There's no need to be dramatic, Cassidy."

I arch a brow. Seriously? It was one line. "You want dramatic? I can do dramatic. How about the part where I died twice and was forced to recuperate in a foreign country, all alone, because we couldn't be certain I wouldn't get nailed again while I was laid up? How about the part where I'm your fucking daughter, and you can't even be bothered to say, 'Hey, I'm glad you're back'? Are you even glad I'm *alive*?"

His gaze is passive. Blank. He's not even impatiently waiting for me to finish. I swallow against the lump in my throat. "Is it too much to ask for a hug? Oh, someone broke into the house the other night. Guy didn't even see me coming. Nice and clean, though he bled all over Nick's kitchen floor. That should make you proud. I get it. I'm a disappointment to you. At some point, it would be nice if you could get over it and be my father again, but I'm not holding out hope."

The ice cracks and shifts, and I let the hurt trickle through. "I needed you, Dad," I whisper. "I needed my *dad*, not an assassin. I needed reassurances that everything was going to be okay, and you know where I got them? From Nick. I wanted them from you."

I stand and move around the chair to the door. "I'm done trying, Turner. You know where to find me."

Walking out of my dad's office this time is harder than the last. I ignore the greetings and waves as I head down the hall to the entrance. Sunlight blinds me as I step out into the parking lot and walk over to the car. Constantine's leaning against the driver's side door. His presence is Nick's concession to my request I handle this on my own. I had no idea if this meeting with Turner would end badly, but if it did, I didn't want Nick to see me. I don't particularly relish the idea of dealing with Constantine right now, either, but you pick your battles.

I pull out my sunglasses and slip them on, then nod to Constantine. "Ready when you are."

He unlocks the car. I slide into the passenger seat and snap on my seat belt. The hurt and anger shaking my insides is so intense the rest of me should be shaking, but my hands are steady.

"Everything all right?" He pulls out of the lot, merging smoothly into traffic.

"Fine."

The streets fly by, scrubby palm trees breaking up the monotony of the sidewalks. "Did he have any good suggestions?"

"Yup."

"You going to answer all of my questions with a single word?"

"Probably."

He shuts up after that, and we make the drive out to Santa Monica in silence, allowing me to box up my rage and shut it in a closet.

The streets become more familiar, and I realize we're close to Nick's. "Can we make a detour by the grocery store, please?" I feel like brownies. Lots and lots of brownies.

If I can't cry, can't scream and kick things, I'll eat chocolate until I'm sick.

* * * *

The air stinks of chocolate. Chocolate, chocolate, and more chocolate. I'm nauseous with it, and yet I can't stop myself from pinching off another piece of the brownie on my plate. Cartoon mice are running around on Nick's flat screen and singing about making a dress for Cinderelly, and I'm on brownie number six. Or seven. Either one of the two, on top of the four or five chocolate chip cookies I ate.

Eating sugar until I puked seemed like a better idea than drinking until I puked. At least my mind would still be clear. The flaw in this plan is I decided to go ahead and add some rum to the mix. Now I'm seriously considering expelling all this excess from my stomach. It's a roiling, tumultuous mess, jumping at the sound of the front door opening. Saliva pools in my mouth, and panic rises along with bile. I don't want him to see me like this. Weak and sullen and wondering what else has to happen before my father will finally be the dad I want.

Nick's footsteps are unnaturally loud on the hardwood floor before stopping next to the couch. One brow lifts in question. "Did the Keebler elves move in while I was gone?"

I wish he'd stayed gone for a few more minutes.

Swallowing convulsively, I stand up and hand Nick the plate with the brownie on it, then hurry down the hall and lock myself in the bathroom.

My stomach spasms and clenches, my eyes watering in protest as I hunch over the toilet.

When my stomach's empty, I slump against the side of the tub and tip my head back. Throwing knives at trees probably would have been a better idea. Or talking Nick into hard, bruising sex. I never want to see another brownie. My stomach rumbles in agreement.

"Cass. Open the door."

Groaning, I stagger to my feet, unlock the door, and brace my hands on the bathroom counter. "I'm okay," I rasp.

"Since when does eating half a pan of brownies and then bending over the toilet equal okay?" Nick guides me over to the toilet and puts the lid down. I collapse, not convinced I won't have to scramble up in another minute or so.

Less than a minute. I slide off the toilet onto my knees and push up the lid. My face burns with embarrassment as I retch, Nick's fingers tangled in my hair as he holds it back.

He hands me a damp washcloth when I sit on my heels. I wipe off my face, clammy and shivering with sweat. I feel disgusting, inside and out, and if I thought I could stand long enough to take a shower, I'd strip and hop in.

"Thanks," I murmur when he helps me up. I grab the water glass, fill it, and rinse my mouth, careful not to swallow. I'm pretty sure a single drop would cause my stomach to revolt again. "It wasn't just brownies. You forgot the rum."

"Wondered about the bottle of Kraken on the counter."

"Yeah, well, drinking on an empty stomach didn't seem like such a smart idea, and I was already making cookies. It just sort of"—I wave a hand around—"spiraled from there."

He smooths my hair away from my face. "What did your dad have to say?"

The last of the nausea balls in the pit of my stomach and settles like a rock, one with jagged edges. I manage a shrug. "About the same as my visits with Turner usually go. There's a place nearby that offers Krav Maga. He recommended a Wushu dojo out here as well if I wanted to continue the discipline."

He studies me for a long moment, his gaze probing, and I give him a bland stare back. "I'm fine. Really. Just didn't want to stop eating the brownies." If I could go back to the couch, all will be right in my world.

"Bullshit. But I'm not going to make you tell me what's wrong."

That's a relief.

"At least not until you're feeling better."

I catch myself before I press my lips together in anger. I should have done something healthy. Gone for a run. Baked all that shit and then passed it out to homeless people. Thrown knives at tree trunks. But nooo, I had to give in to my inner child and sulk, and Nick caught me at it.

I'm only twenty-one. I'm allowed to have the occasional juvenile tantrum. That doesn't stop me from being absolutely and completely mortified that my older and much more sophisticated and mature boyfriend caught me at a weak moment.

He helps me out to the living room and then disappears, returning minutes later with a heavy mug, steam wafting out of it. "What's that?" I ask warily.

"Mint tea. My mother always gave us mint tea when we were sick. It's supposed to calm upset stomachs." He sits next to me, the warmth of his body more soothing than any magic drink.

I take the mug from him and hold it, using the unspoken excuse that the liquid is too hot to swallow. Cinderella's in the garden in her ruined dress, sobbing for all she's worth, when Nick shoots a pointed look at the mug. Fighting a grimace, I take a sip of tea.

By the time the glass slipper's on Cinderella's foot, the mug is empty and I only feel like death, not death warmed over. My head's propped on Nick's shoulder, and I could fall asleep, just like this, warm and cared for, the offending cocoa scent having faded to the pleasant smell of sugared air.

Then his phone rings and ruins everything.

He untangles us and boosts a hip off the couch, pulling his phone from his pocket. "Kosta." Dropping an absent kiss on my forehead, he gets to his feet and wanders over to the dining room. I'm determined not to eavesdrop. He'll tell me if it's something important, something I need to know. I pull up the queue and scroll through the movies. I settle on an old James Bond movie, one with Sean Connery. My mom loves these movies. She's seen every single one of them multiple times. The summer I was fifteen, she sat me down, and we watched them together. It was another thing between us, something Turner didn't intrude on. Girl time, she'd tell him, and go back to her bowl of popcorn.

And he'd always smile and kiss her cheek, leaving the two of us to our movie and me wanting to run after him and beg him to stay.

The opening credits are starting as Nick hangs up and stalks over. I hit pause. "Bad shit?"

"Bad shit," he confirms, face grim. "Two dead. Lucas took a bullet to the leg, and Nikos managed to catch one of the fuckers."

Nikos? So there are some Greek-named associates in Nick's merry band of men. Besides Constantine, of course.

Nick shoves his phone into his pocket and kisses me again, a slow, tender gesture at odds with the fury vibrating off him. "I've got some interrogating to do. There's more tea in the cupboard to the right of the stove if you want it."

I should stay home. This isn't my fight, and I feel like ass, but... I'm not the little mistress, content to putter around the house, wringing my hands while I wait for my man to return. Isaiah came after *me*. He may have shifted his focus to Nick and taking him down, but he won't for long, and the sooner he's neutralized, the sooner my life, and Nick's, will return to its regularly scheduled programming.

And this is a chance I didn't know I'd get. I might be able to get some answers to questions no one's been able to answer. Questions about Marc.

I push to my feet. "I'm coming with you." My stomach offers up a rumble of protest, and I rub a fist over it.

"No, you're staying here. Where it's safe and there's a toilet nearby."

"Very funny." I glare at him. "Look, like it or not, I'm a part of this. Isaiah's not splitting his resources, trying to track us separately, not yet, but while he's probably okay with having someone else finish you off, he wants me for himself. He's made it personal." I gamble and play my trump card. "How do you know he's not waiting for you to leave? He's already shown he's not afraid to send someone to strike where it hurts the most."

Nick clenches his jaw to the point stress lines dig themselves into the skin around his mouth. I pull out my hammer and drive the final nail home. "Do you want to hear me say it? All that chocolate was a mistake. I did a stupid thing today and made myself vulnerable. I'll be safer with you. Besides, I might be able to help. New eyes, new ears, new brain sometimes equals new ideas."

His eyes darken, hands twitching and flexing at his sides. Tension mounts and stretches taut as a high wire as we continue to stare at each other. We need this show of force, and if he thinks about it long enough, he'll realize I'm right.

We are in this together, and this is our first chance to show everyone we mean it.

His acquiescence flashes over his face before he speaks. "Go. Get in the car."

Chapter 6

All those interrogation scenes where the captive's bound to a chair, sometimes drenched in water, sometimes sitting in his own filth, are lies.

The man sits in a metal folding chair, his arms cuffed behind him and his ankle cuffed to the chair leg. No one has a gun trained on him, and he's not trembling in terror. His hair's a mess, and his clothes are rumpled. There's a bruise forming on his jaw, another around his right eye, and blood's drying under his nose. He's also the first person I've seen who isn't around Nick's age. Based on the faint lines around his eyes and the silver threading his dark hair, I put him in his forties.

Constantine's leaning against the opposite wall, carrying on a conversation with one of the other men, someone I haven't met before. With his messy blond hair and golden skin, he looks like he ought to be on the beach, not in this florescent-lit room. Constantine's gaze slips from Nick to me, brows drawing together in a frown.

The room itself is pretty bare. Aside from the chair the captive's in, the only other furniture is a card table near the door littered with weapons: a couple of guns, multiple knives, plus what looks like a pair of brass knuckles. The building is empty. Convenient. No one will be able to hear him scream.

Constantine breaks away and comes over, an easy smile on his face and violence in his eyes. "You've got to be fucking kidding me."

Kidding about what? I glance between Nick and Constantine, Nick's shoulders a rock-hard line. "She's in this just as much as I am. She stays," Nick says, his voice low.

"I get that she's more than a piece of ass to you, bro." His smile hardens. "Just don't think she has to see this."

I stiffen. "Why don't you worry about whether this guy will tell you anything useful instead of worrying about me? Or were you saving the beating until Nick got here?" I brush past him and take his spot on the wall, shoving my hands into my pockets. Surfer Dude shifts on his feet, and I push my lips up into a smile. "Hey." This close, I see the fine lines around his eyes, putting his age closer to the guy in the chair than Nick and Constantine. Good. I was starting to wonder if everyone in the organization was some young hotshot.

"Hi." He draws the word out, uncertainty dragging it down.

I nod at the guy in the chair. "He works for Isaiah?"

"Loyal to him, yeah," Surfer Dude says.

I glance over my shoulder. "Does Isaiah hold the same position as you within the family?" I ask Nick.

He shakes his head, his expression resigned. "Similar position. He has men who report to him, but he doesn't have the leeway Con or I do. It's a fairly recent decision by my father."

"How recent is recent?"

"Last two years."

One of the pieces slides into place. That explains where Isaiah's men came from and why they listen to him at all. Satisfied for now, I refocus on Surfer Dude. I point to the man in the chair. "You're going to cause him pain, right? Broken bones, bruises, probably some bleeding?"

He shoots a glance over my shoulder. "Likely."

Since we've established this isn't the movies, I doubt the guy handcuffed to the chair is going to say anything of worth. "What happens if he rolls over? Gives up Isaiah's current safe house? What will you do with him?"

Nick answers. "You already know the answer to that, Cass."

Surfer Dude's eyes widen slightly. I turn to Nick. "Do you kill all of them? Or just the ones who really deserve it?"

Nick shuts his eyes and mumbles something under his breath. "If they all ended up dead, no one would have any motivation to talk, would they?" His eyes snap open, as cold and blank as I was earlier today. "Let's get this over with."

"Wait." I walk over to the table, conscious of everyone's gaze on me. Picking one of the guns at random, I check the safety and close my hand around the butt, the grip too large to be comfortable. That's okay, though. I have no intention of shooting anyone.

Nick and Constantine have matching impatient expressions when I make my way back to them. "Mind if I ask him a few questions?"

"Cass," Nick says.

I didn't know it was possible to fit both a warning and uncertainty into the same syllable. I lift a brow. "If I wanted to kill him, I'd slit his throat. I'm better with a knife, remember?" Swallowing my resurging nausea, I face the guy in the chair. "What's your name?" There. Best way to ensure I won't kill him. Give him a name.

"Demitrios." Constantine answers for him.

"Demetrios." I shift my grip on the gun. "Did you know Marc?" Behind me, Nick sucks in a breath. God, I hope he doesn't interrupt me.

Demetrios clearly isn't expecting the question because he frowns. "Yeah."

"Well? Did you know him well?"

He flicks his gaze over my shoulder. "He was my cousin."

Is everyone related in the Kosta organization? Surfer Dude probably isn't. I give myself a mental shake. "The months before he was killed. Had he changed?" I ask. Demetrios gives me a blank stare. "Gotten quieter? Harder to get a hold of? Looked like he lost weight or hadn't been sleeping?" He should have had circles under his eyes, hollows under his cheekbones, and a scraggly beard on his jaw. His shoulders should have been perpetually slumped and his mouth downturned.

Marc hadn't looked like that at all. He held his head up, gone about his business, smiled when he had to. He'd shown the world a picture of a man content with his life, fully capable of handling the stresses of the path he chose. Maybe it was my own guilt wanting to see the sadness weighing him down. But if I didn't ask, I'd never know.

An unnatural hush falls over the room, as if everyone's holding a collective breath. Had one man's death had that much of an impact? Did I have to worry about that many more people wanting my head on a pike? Demetrios lowers his gaze to his knees, a line appearing between his brows. "He'd been talking about getting out." His voice is quiet and rusty. "Didn't do it a lot, usually just an offhand comment. Last month or so, he didn't smile as much, kept to himself more than usual. Said he wasn't sleeping well. Figured it had something to do with a deal Isaiah was working that he'd been brought in on. It fell through after Marc died."

"Nautilus?" I ask, and he nods. The scrap of information might point toward Isaiah's motives for wanting Nick out of the picture, but it's not the confirmation I'm looking for. Proof of Marc's suicidal thoughts are my absolution.

Demetrios lifts his head. "Why?"

"Because I'm the one who killed him. Someone took out a hit on him." The peace in his eyes just before the light went out of them is imprinted on my memory. His absolute surrender, waiting on his knees.

This will never stop hurting.

I embrace it, let the guilt wash through me one last time. "Not someone," I say quietly. "Marc. I think Marc took out a hit on his own head because he wanted it to be over."

Grief floods Demetrios's eyes, coats his features in a thick film. He blinks a few times, staring hard at a spot over my shoulder. "Not surprised to hear that," he says, voice tight and rough. Controlled. "I thought maybe something was up, but he didn't want to talk, and I didn't push it. I assumed it would pass."

"So did I."

I glance at Constantine, leaning against the wall. He scuffs a hand along his jaw. "Shit, I bet a lot of us did. Dom?"

Nick shakes his head. I give my full attention to the man chained to the chair. "You're not going to tell us where Isaiah's hiding, are you?"

His lip curls in a halfhearted smirk. "No." He jerks his head in the direction of the men behind me. "They know it too. I'm their fucking punching bag."

"Not tonight." I flip the gun around so my hand's around the barrel. He's my messenger, however reluctant he might be, and I'll use him.

The metal bites into my palm as I shift my grip. I can't hit hard enough with my fists, and using my feet seems ridiculous when I can just clobber the guy. "They're going to dump you someplace Isaiah will find you easily, and you're going to tell him that he's going to have to be smarter than sending someone to break into Nick's house to get the jump on me again." I lean in until I'm nose to nose with Demetrios. "He should have made sure I was dead before he walked away," I murmur, ignoring Nick's growl. I draw back, rolling my shoulders, letting the anger overtake the guilt. Isaiah. "Sorry, this is going to hurt. A lot."

And I smash the butt of the gun into the side of his head.

* * * *

"Remind me not to piss you off." Constantine watches as Surfer Dude—I never did learn his name—and Nick pick up Demetrios and haul him toward the door. One set of handcuffs dangle from the chair leg. The other pair are firmly around his wrists.

"Why?" I have a temper, sure. Nick and I have already had our share of disagreements. I've never participated in any sort of interrogation, though that wouldn't be obvious to someone like Constantine. "The only people I want to smack on a regular basis are Nick and my father."

He snorts. "Right." He cups my elbow and guides me toward the door, and we follow the others out into the hall. "So your father's an autocratic asshole?"

I slow, putting some distance between us and Nick. He doesn't need to overhear my insecurities. "I wouldn't say that. He's an ass a lot of the time, and heavy handed, but if he was really an autocratic asshole, he wouldn't bend to anyone's whim, and he almost always bends to my mother's." Except on one very important thing.

If she'd left him, taken me with her, I wouldn't be here. I wouldn't have to lie to my best friend and random strangers all the time. Sometimes I wonder just how hard my mother tried to get me away from Turner, or if her newfound happiness that everyone was getting along was more important.

Constantine tightens his hold on my elbow, and I move closer to him, wishing Nick were next to me. He would slide an arm around my waist and press a kiss to the top of my head in that sweet, casual display of affection I've quickly come to crave. Instead, I get Constantine's arm around my shoulders and his fingers playing with my ponytail. "I still don't think you should have been here," he murmurs.

"I get that. Nick's right, though. I'm in this too."

"And you're trying to get *out*. Dom's said a couple of times you were giving up the game. You should," he adds. "If that's what you want, don't let anyone talk you out of it, especially not Dom.

"Do you know what you're getting into? Think about it. Think about who Dom is, what he does. He keeps his women separate from the family. They don't know what goes down. Him letting you in this deep, and this is deeper than his sisters go, is a big fucking deal." He shoots me a glance. "You might get out, but you stay with Dom, you'll always be straddling the fence."

Nick and Surfer Dude are at the end of the hall, waiting for the elevator, and Constantine points to the door leading to the service stairs. Nick's lips flatten into a thin line, and he nods. "Stairs are safer than the elevator. Easier to avert an ambush," Constantine says.

"We have to worry about that?" It makes sense; the building we're in houses one of Nick's companies. Most of the upper floors of the building are unoccupied, including the floor we're on. "Why is Nick taking the elevator?"

"Ever dragged an unconscious man down seven flights of stairs? Makes a lot of noise. Carrying him will tire Dom out and weaken him in a fight. Isaiah could find us if he wanted to. He's going to want to get Demetrios back, dead or alive, and dead gives him an excuse to come out swinging."

"Which means…" Nick's anticipating an ambush in the parking garage. By taking the stairs, I'll have a better chance of remaining out of the line of fire. Unease prickles the skin on my neck. I want to run after Nick, beg him not to take the elevator. I change the subject instead. "After Josef, who would you send to get rid of someone in the organization?"

"Not Xavier. The guy you jumped in the kitchen," he explains. "He's like a billy club." He pushes open the door to the stairwell. "If I wanted it done fast and quiet, if I wanted to prove a point, I'd hire your dad. And we have before. Dom's used him a few times."

I wish I hadn't asked.

The stairwell is dimly lit and cavernous, our footsteps thunderous against the cinderblock walls. "Was he used while I was gone?"

Constantine pauses on a landing and looks up at me, perched a few steps above him. "Yeah." He waits until I've descended the last couple steps to stand in front of him. "And we'll use him again. He's pretty fucking brilliant. In, out, like a shadow." There's a reason he's called The Ghost. Turner *is* brilliant. I just wish he'd be a brilliant *father*. Constantine shrugs. "Frankly, we probably would have used you a time or two if Dom didn't know who you were by now."

I'll never get out. Not completely. Not if I keep trying to have a relationship with my dad. Add in my desire to be with Nick, I'll be surrounded by blood and shadows for however long we last.

I just have to decide if that's something I can live with. Or, better question, if Nick is someone I can live without.

Since I would rather put off that debate for as long as possible, I nod, and we continue down the stairs in silence. After we pass the landing for the third floor, Constantine changes his gait, limbs stiff to silence his heavy footfalls, and I do the same without being asked. Panic flares in my belly as his earlier words race through my brain. An ambush. Nick and Surfer Dude had no choice but to take the elevator. Demetrios was a dead weight between them, his booted feet dragging down the hall. The elevator opens with a clear view of the garage. They'll be sitting ducks.

We hear the fight before we see it, and the panic spreads into a full-on flame. On the landing above the entrance to the garage, Constantine bends over and removes a gun from an ankle holster, then hands it to me. It's more compact than the ones that littered the table and fits better in my palm. I give him a half smile, automatically check the safety, and race the rest of the way down the stairs, uncaring if they hear me coming.

When Constantine pushes his way in front of me and eases open the door, I slip behind him. We step out into the darkened garage, weapons at the ready, gunfire ricocheting between the support pillars.

The fight's centered in the wide lane between parking spaces. Four men have taken refuge behind cars. A fifth man is on the ground, bleeding from a wound to the stomach, and I can't stop the sympathetic wince. Two of them have their backs to us, occasionally popping up to squeeze off a shot. At the next barrage of gunfire, Constantine darts forward and grasps one of their heads, giving it a vicious twist. It snaps like a dry branch, and the man slumps to the ground. His partner doesn't recover quick enough. He raises his gun to fire. I line up my shot and send the bullet through his temple.

Brain matter splatters on the car. I hurry forward, blind to everything except the two remaining men. I crouch behind the car and peer around the bumper at the elevator. Surfer Dude is down, though it's unclear if he is severely injured or just playing possum. Demetrios lies in a slowly expanding pool of blood, his eyes already blank and lifeless. From my spot, I can't see Nick at all, but I hear a gun, firing bullet after bullet.

One of the two men pops up, and I fire, my shot skimming the top of his head. He returns fire, and I'm forced to pull back as I wait for the shots to stop coming.

The quiet that comes next is eerie. No one moves. No one breathes. Constantine points to the recesses of the garage, away from the fight, and makes a circle, indicating he's going to swing wide and try and come up behind them. I nod, and as he creeps off, I fire over the top of the car to cover the noise.

I peek around the end. No sign of Nick or the two gunmen. I withdraw and make my way back to the body. Easing his gun from his grip, I switch it out for mine. It's not a comfortable fit, too bulky and awkward, but I've already emptied my magazine, and Constantine didn't give me a spare. I readjust and edge around the body, then poke my head over the top of the car.

Still no one. I pull the trigger twice, firing blindly into the space I think the assailants are and wait for the fighting to resume.

One head comes up quick, and he's picked off by Constantine, his shout of pain echoing off the cement. The other remains absent. I really don't want to crawl around trying to find this guy.

I don't have to. Another shot rings out, answered by an all clear from Nick. Constantine heads for Surfer Dude and Demetrios, and I stand slowly, sure there are stray bullets waiting to find me.

But there are none. Just Nick standing in the middle of the chaos, smears of blood painting his jeans, and a gun in his hand. His face remains a mask as I emerge from my hiding spot. He jerks his head toward the bodies. "Gonna be here a while."

I figured as much.

Chapter 7

I head for the beach as soon as we get home. The dark is soothing, the crash of waves more so. Push pull, push pull, over and over again, taking more of the sand with it each time, bringing a little of it back. I dig my hands into the fine grains and fist them.

Since I hooked up with Nick, I've killed more people than I have in the last three years put together. Constantine's warning reverberates in my skull. A jacket drops over my shoulders, and Nick sits, forearms on his knees. The breeze off the water musses his hair, a lock falling over his forehead. I brush my hand off on my jeans and push it back.

"I see why you come here. It's peaceful." He stares out at the black waves crashing onto the sand, lights from the Santa Monica pier gleaming off the obsidian surface.

Peaceful is only a part of it. "I like that it's so constant. The change. It's different every day, but it's the same, you know? Like the waves are shattering and coming back together." It sounds lame spoken out loud. When I shrug to cover the heat of embarrassment racing over my face, the jacket falls on the sand at my back. "It's a sort of meditation. Out with cold, calm Cass. In with student Cass, the Cass who gets to feel."

He picks up the jacket and wraps it around my shoulders once again. His fingertips ghost down my back as he drops his hand, and the loss is so acute I inch over and lean against him, abandoning my solitude.

The pressure of his arm around my waist, his hand flexing on my hip, is more comforting than I'd like, but I want to wallow in it. I crook an elbow around his leg and shift so I'm flush against his side. "It's not always going to be like this," I say quietly.

"No."

"It's always going to be there, though. The possibility. The need to carry a weapon, the need to defend myself. I will never be totally and completely out of danger. Leaving that life behind isn't an option. Not if I stay with you."

Sometimes a lack of words is reassuring. Not in this case. Nick's mouth stays closed for far too long. "Constantine's been talking, hasn't he?"

"Yeah."

He grunts and holds me tighter. "He likes you. Respects you. He's also right. If you want out, you'll never be completely out of it with me. You'll have the freedom to turn down jobs, and maybe eventually people will stop contacting you with offers. There's always a risk, though, that someone will try to use you to get to me."

If Constantine is to be believed, none of his past girlfriends were close enough to be threats. *Why* is on the tip of my tongue. Why am I the special one? Why am I the one who's worth it? I swallow the words. I'll ask him. Someday. Possibly. Possibly not. I might not have to. This could all be over tomorrow if Nick decides I'm in too deep and it's a risk he's unwilling to take.

I can't lose him. I've just gotten him back, and as rocky as it's been, I can't walk away. He's the one person I don't have to lie to, and I will not give him up without a fight.

Does he know? Does he know what he's done? Embracing this, *us*, allowing me to see that dark, twisted side of him? Allowing me to show him mine? He has to. He's not stupid. He has to know the significance.

"What happened with your father, Cass?"

Let's introduce a topic I really don't want to talk about. And let's do it in the bluntest manner possible. "Nothing out of the ordinary. He made some suggestions. I told him I'd check them out. Then I left."

"I call bullshit." His voice is mild, but the underlying steel is unmistakable. "I've talked to him a few times. I've seen the two of you together once. Forget that I don't have the IQ of an astrophysicist, it doesn't take a genius to see you don't get along."

Oh, if only it were that easy. "We get along just fine. All I have to do is go along with his wishes, and we're good." I try to squirm away. Nick responds by pulling me onto his lap, imprisoning me there.

"Please let me go." This is supposed to be my time. I'm done sharing. I need to find Good Cass again and make sure she's firmly in place.

Backlit by the glow of lights from the street, his face is barely visible. I don't need to see his eyes to know he's glaring at me. "Bull. Shit. You don't make yourself sick on rum and chocolate if you get along *just fine*."

He moves a hand from my hip to my face. He strokes my jaw in a sweet, tender gesture that threatens to break me in two. "There's no point in talking to him if all he does is upset you."

I bite the inside of my cheek to keep from wailing. He's right. There's no getting through Turner's hard head. I'm a failure to him, and it's time I work on accepting that.

I press my forehead to his, willing the hurt away. "Can we go back to watching old Disney cartoons now? That's about all I can handle at the moment."

"And eat brownies?"

I shudder. "No. No brownies. No sugar. In fact, I think we should throw out all the sugar in the house and dump the rum down the sink."

He stands with me in his arms, the display of strength sparking desire low in my belly. "I'm keeping the rum and the cookies. Constantine will happily take the brownies off your hands."

He starts walking up the beach toward the sidewalk, and I wriggle. "You can put me down. I'm not injured this time." He releases my legs, and they flow down his body, his hands skimming to my lower back, dipping to palm my ass. "I'll wrap the brownies and take them to him tomorrow," I say.

His hands flex, and I catch a wince on his face before it blanks again.

"What?" Even as I ask the question, my stomach sinks. I'm not going to get my alone time with Nick anytime soon.

"Con's on his way over. He was going to follow us home, but I told him you needed an hour. He thinks he's uncovered some more information about where Isaiah's hiding, and we need to jump on it tonight if we can."

Oh. I should have figured as much. Disappointment replaces my short-lived contentment, and I force a smile. "That's fine. As long as you guys don't mind my cartoon watching."

He adjusts the jacket over my shoulders and tips my chin up, covering my mouth with his. The kiss is tender and threaded with heat. It says *not tonight, Cass, but soon*, and I remember what he'd said yesterday in the shower, how he imagined being bare inside me, and that we'd talk about it later.

It's later.

It's also another topic I don't want to talk about, although I figure if we talk about *that*, we aren't talking about Turner, and I'd rather face a firing squad than discuss my daddy issues. I flick my tongue over his lips and slip it inside his mouth, drawing the heat out to wrap around myself.

On a growl, he breaks the kiss, scraping his teeth over my lower lip. "Don't tempt me," he murmurs.

"You can have more of that once Constantine leaves." I step back and link my hand with his, and we wander up the sidewalk. "So. Um. About yesterday." His hand tenses in mine, and I squeeze gently. "In the shower. You were serious, weren't you? About wanting me like...that?"

"I am."

Simple as that. Two words. Two words that, if I push him, will change everything for me. "I'm clean," he says. "It's not something I do with every woman I sleep with, and it's not something we have to do." There's a trace of longing and lust in his voice. It zips through me, fanning the flames of my own desire. He strokes his thumb over my knuckle. "I'd be lying if I told you I don't think about it. How good you'd feel."

Wings flutter in my stomach, bats or butterflies or hummingbirds. He wants this. Wants *me*, all of me. "I was tested in the hospital. I'm on birth control." Thank God for my insistence on an IUD. The doctor hadn't wanted to put one in, and I'd badgered her until she relented. I didn't want to have to rely on little pills and needing to take them at the same time every day to have maximum protection. I blow out a breath. "I've never done this before."

I have never wanted someone as badly as him. I want this connection, this show of trust and commitment.

If I take that step, I can't go back.

We walk in silence the rest of the way home, but he stops me at the end of the driveway. "You tell me when, or you tell me no. It's your decision." A brief kiss, and he leads me past Constantine's car into the house.

I don't think no is an option. If I want Nick around for the long term, if I want to take that chance of laying my shriveled heart on the line, I can't say no. If we stand any chance of working past the age difference, I have to say yes. Because *yes* means I trust him. *Yes* means I can handle whatever the consequences are. *Yes* means I'm mature enough, sure enough of myself, that I can do this and come out on the other side mostly intact.

Constantine hugs me hello, and I leave the two of them talking in the entryway and head for the kitchen. It's a disaster zone. Flour and sugar dust the countertops. Cookie sheets sit abandoned next to the stove. The cap's off the rum, the lowball glass next to it empty. The half-eaten pan of brownies are on the island, along with the dirty mixing bowls and measuring cups. Half of a stick of butter sits unwrapped, softened to the point it's starting to melt.

At least I remembered to put away the milk and eggs.

I pull out a plate and transfer the brownies, holding my breath the entire time. Setting them out of sight, I hunt through the cupboards for a cookie jar.

"Help you find something, Cass?" Nick rests a hand on my back, and I twist around.

"You don't happen to have a cookie jar, do you?"

He grins. "Never needed one. No one's baked for me since my mom when I was a kid."

So Cecelie never baked him anything? Interesting. I shield the tiny kernel of smug triumph and retrieve another plate. "You need a cookie jar. Cookies belong in jars, not on plates."

Constantine snags a cookie from the wax paper I'd laid them on to cool. "Cookies belong in my mouth. Not in jars."

I point at the offending brownies. "Take those. Please." Even the sight of them has my stomach clenching.

"Fuck yeah!" He scoops up the plate and cradles it to his chest, the amount of excitement in his eyes bordering on ridiculous. A giggle escapes, and I turn back to the cookies and the plate, grinning when he moans.

"Con, do you want to be alone with the brownies?" Nick picks up another cookie and bites off half.

"Shut up," he mumbles.

Nick piles dirty bowls and trays next to the sink. I nudge him out of the way when he turns on the water. "Nope. My mess. I clean it up. You have shit to talk about. Go. Take the brownies with you."

He cups the back of my head and nibbles a line up to my ear. "We'll stay out of the living room." Leaving me free to watch dancing mice and singing fairies and talking dogs, if I should so choose. Leaving me to remain ignorant of what the next steps are to tracking Isaiah.

Giving me an out.

It would be easy to allow Nick to take over. It would keep me out of harm's way, which would make him happy. But that's sending him to fight my battles for me, and I'm perfectly capable of protecting myself.

I plunge my hands into the soapy water and scrub the first cookie sheet. One by one, the dirty dishes become clean, the water swirling along with my thoughts. I set the last bowl on the counter and dig out some clean dish towels. After wiping down the counter, I unfold the towels and place everything that wouldn't fit in the drying rack on the towels, then wipe off the kitchen island. I cap the Kraken and stick it in a lower cabinet.

I wander out into the living room a few minutes later, another mug of mint tea in my hands. My chest squeezes and relaxes, unhappy with my options. I have to back my words with actions. I have to back *Nick's* words with actions. I'm in this. I can't bury my head in animated, Technicolor sand and let others decide what should happen next.

They'll be in his study.

I pause outside the door, my legs shaking as my hand rests on the knob. Through the door, I hear their voices, too low to make out the words.

Their jaws snap shut when I enter. I lower myself to the floor, careful not to spill the hot liquid. "So. Isaiah."

Nick's lips twitch once, twice, before settling back into a neutral line. "Isaiah." He points to a monitor with a satellite map. "Last we heard, he's holed up somewhere around here."

I can't see the map from where I'm sitting. Clutching my mug like a lifeline, I get to my feet and pick my way across the floor. Major arterials are written in tiny letters, the only indicators of what neighborhood it might be. I reach over and enlarge it once, and smaller streets pop up.

It's my old neighborhood. It's the neighborhood Denise is still in with Charlie. Unprotected. Dread ices my skin, and I swallow tea to melt it away. Denise will be safe. I'll make sure of it.

I draw in a breath. "Gentlemen, I think I can be of use."

Chapter 8

Denise is already seated when I walk into El Dorado the next day. I duck behind a giant leafy palm tree for a moment and take a mental inventory of all the lies I'll have to tell her to get through this meal. There are a lot of them, and the possibility is huge I'll get tangled up and back myself into a corner.

I let out a breath. As long as I don't tiptoe anywhere near the truth, I should be okay. I slip out from behind the palm tree and wave at Denise to get her attention.

"Cass!" She jumps up from her seat, jolting the table in the process. Water spills onto the surface, but she ignores it as she throws her arms around me and hugs me like we've been apart for years.

I should talk. I hugged her back just as hard.

We finally pull apart, her face flushed, eyes bright. Her gaze lands on the faint scar on my throat. I stifle a groan. Nick's preoccupation with my various hurts already drives me nuts. "Don't. Don't say it. I get enough of it from Nick."

Her lower lip pokes out. "Shut up. My bestest friend in the whole wide world almost dies and then escapes to Thailand for a month. I am allowed to freak out."

She has a point.

We slide into opposite sides of the booth, and she picks up her napkin and begins mopping up the water. "I didn't get a lot out of anyone while you were in the hospital, and then *you* didn't say much of anything either while you were gone." She gives me an accusing look. "What the hell are you into, Cass? Does it have to do with Nick?"

Showtime. I hold up my hands in surrender. "Nothing. I swear. Nick owns a couple of businesses. He's not, like, some nefarious criminal or anything." The lie trips easily off my tongue. I just hope the next one goes as smoothly. "What happened was an accident. I tried to fight back, the guy didn't like it, and he caught me in the stomach. I got really lucky it was the garage for Nick's office and he found me in time."

Neese worries her lower lip, biting it repeatedly.

"Stop it," I scold. "You're going to make yourself bleed. I'm alive. Nick found me, he's being incredibly overprotective, and I'm not going to be dying any time soon."

A server appears at the end of the table, and we both order without thinking—enchiladas with mole sauce. I opt for water while she orders a Negro Modelo to go with her food, and we dig into the basket of chips between us, Denise wrinkling her nose as she accidentally lays her arm on the wet table.

"So." I lick salt from my lips. "What's it like living with Charlie? Does he pick up his clothes? Put his dishes in the sink?"

She grins. "You know, I think he's so amazed by the fact I actually agreed to move in with him that he's on his best behavior. I came home from class the other day and found him vacuuming. *Vacuuming.*" She snags a chip from the basket. "I mean, for realz, yo. And yeah, he puts his dishes in the sink. Sometimes he even rinses them first.

"It's nice, you know? Waking up next to him every morning, knowing I don't have to run home first because I forgot something, getting to come home to him every night. We'll probably have a fight soon and ruin everything, but I'm just going to enjoy it while it lasts."

Envy swells, and I push it back. She and Charlie have worked up to this. They've been together for almost two years, and they are absolutely gone over each other. I'll get there with someone eventually. Then I'll be the one amazed by the vacuuming and the dishes in the sink.

Denise leans forward, an eager gleam in her eyes. "So? What's it like?"

"What's what like?" I'm pretty sure I know what she's asking about, but I'm going to make her say it anyway. Out loud. Because I'm mean like that.

"Nick! Come on. Details. Because hi, yes please, and thank you."

"Mmm." I crunch down on a chip. "Well, he certainly knows what he's doing." Times about a million. My experience is miniscule compared to what the man knows.

Although…

Denise and Charlie are my barometer of what a committed relationship should be like. It's safe to assume they've done the sorts of things you only do once you've been with someone long enough to trust that no matter the outcome, you'll deal with the fallout together. All I have to do is pony up and ask.

"I *did* want to ask you something." A blush works its way over my cheeks to my ears, the tips heating. "Have you and Charlie ever, um…" Crap. I can't do this.

"Ever what?"

Dammit. I need to ask this. I need to talk to someone who's been here before, and Denise *knows* me. She'll get it. "Have you ever done it without a condom?" I ask in a rush.

From the red spreading over her face, I assume the answer is yes. She tries to play it off with a shrug. "Yeah. For a while now. One night the condom broke, and we just never went back." She reaches for her beer and chugs it down. "Why? Are you—" Her eyes widen a fraction. "Damn, girl. I knew this was serious business, but this is *serious*."

I wave off her comment. "Not really. I like him a lot, and he feels the same way. There haven't been any declarations of love and devotion or anything like that." His attentiveness and concern for my safety have seen to that.

Though he did point out it wasn't something he did with every woman he dated. And his L-word slip the other day when we were out running hadn't gone unnoticed.

"It just came up the other day. We waited until we'd calmed down to actually talk about it, but nothing's been decided. He says it's my choice." I pick up a chip and start breaking it into tiny pieces on the table. "I sort of feel like I don't have one," I admit. "He's older. He's done this before. I want to prove to him that I trust him and that I'm… I dunno, mature enough for him. It's not the only way to do it, but it's one way."

Denise thunks her beer bottle on the table. "You always have a choice. Always. And if you think he's pushing you into making one you don't want, that's not a choice at all, and you can walk away. You *should* walk away."

This time I do wave off her comment. "I know. It's on the table. He's said I can say no if I want to, and I may just do that." I leave out the part where I'm afraid if I do, he'll get tired of me that much faster and I'll be on my own.

I didn't imagine the violence of his orgasm the other morning. Didn't imagine the heat in his voice when he murmured in my ear.

And if he had any idea what was going through my head, he'd take the choice right out of my hands and insist on condoms every time. Nick would never pressure me into anything unless my life is in danger.

"I'm a little surprised," she announces and takes a sip of beer.

I frown. "Why?"

She looks up as our plates are set in front of us, and she goes about cutting up her enchilada. "You haven't dated anyone long-term since high school." She would notice; we've known each other too long for her not to. "Never figured you'd end up with someone so much older. And from your mom's firm, no less."

That's right. We told her Nick works with my mom. I don't know how to back out of the lie gracefully, to tell her that no, Nick's family controls a large portion of LA's criminal underworld.

I am *never* telling her that.

"Wait." She pauses with a forkful of enchilada halfway to her mouth, eyes narrowing. "Nick owns several businesses? And he works for your mom's firm?"

Busted.

I stare at my plate, searching for answers in the mole sauce. "Nick owns businesses. Tech companies, mostly. He doesn't work at Mom's law firm." I swallow hard, wondering how much further I'll have to dig before I hit bottom. "I didn't want to tell you how we met because it was so dangerous, and you'd worry even more than you already were."

Her fork clatters on the plate. I glance up. Her arms are crossed over her chest, her expression stony. "How did you meet?"

Half-truth time. "I don't know if it made the news or what, but there was a shooting at a Mexican restaurant, over near USC? We got caught in the crossfire. We ended up in the alley behind the restaurant together and just kept running. He was afraid someone would come after me, so he convinced me to stay with him for a few days."

Her face darkens. "And the wound to your stomach isn't a result of this first shooting?"

Do. Not. Squirm. I shake my head. "No. It was a random mugging. The guy didn't believe me when I told him I didn't have anything on me and wouldn't settle for taking my phone."

"Well, that's true." She uncrosses her arms and picks up her fork, her forehead scrunched in a frown. "Cass, is that the whole truth? What about the scar on your throat? You told me someone tried to slit it."

I had. "That's true too."

"So two random violent incidents happen to have you as the victim?" She studies my face for a long minute, and as the seconds slip past, the closer I get to breaking down and telling her the truth. "I'm sorry," she says at last. Her face is blank, tone carefully neutral. I've seen her do this once before after a fight with Charlie. She's shutting me out. "I need to get home. Got a final tomorrow."

It takes everything I have not to beg her to finish her meal. "Sure. Hey, did I tell you I'll be back on campus next semester?"

Her smile doesn't reach her eyes. "That's great."

We call for the check and take-out containers, then pack up our dinners in silence. I don't know why lying to Denise sucks so much now. I've been doing it for years. Making excuses when I come home late, or not at all, or when the job closes in and distances me from everything. She'd never understand that switch inside me, the one I can flick so easily.

Walking with her back to Charlie's is awkward. I can't find the words to make everything okay between us. This time, when she smiles, it's sad. "Sorry. I guess… You've probably kept things from me before, but this was a big one, Cass. Huge. When it involves your life and a man who's connected to you being in danger, I don't know what to think."

"I get it." If I had as little information as she does, I'd probably feel the same way. "Nick really wanted to come with me tonight." It's not quite a lie. The only reason he gave in to my request that he stay home is because I sicced Lia on him. He's entertaining his youngest sister at the moment. "But I wanted to see you alone, not with my own personal bodyguard looming over my shoulder, you know?"

She twists the bag handle around her fingers. "I want to be happy for you, Cass. I just…" She bites her lip and winces. "Ouch," she mutters. "Since you've started seeing him, you've been seriously wounded. That's a really big black mark in my book."

The urge to defend Nick and tell her the truth is so strong I almost blurt it out. I drop my gaze to the sidewalk. "I'm sorry," I whisper.

There's nothing left to say after that. Bags swinging, we exchange hugs, and I head for Nick's car parked under a streetlight a few hundred feet away. I put the take-out bag on the passenger seat and drive off, hunting for a new parking spot.

Wallowing in my grief will have to wait. I've got a recon mission to execute.

I find a place a few blocks over, not quite under a streetlight. If Isaiah's hiding out here in my old neighborhood, it shouldn't be difficult to find evidence of it.

Up one block, down another, cutting through alleys, I scan the streets as I walk, looking for a clue. A Greek-looking guy disappearing into a building would be a big honking one, but that's too much to ask for.

I end up in front of my old building and finger the keys in my pocket. I still have them. Our lease isn't up until the end of January, and Denise and I were supposed to talk about cleaning the place over dinner, now that the police were done with it.

Since I'm here, I might as well pick up more clothes. I let myself into the building and take the elevator rather than the stairs. The tape across the door is gone, but the place is still disheveled from the fight with Josef. A large section of carpet is missing next to my bed, cut away by scene techs most likely. My textbooks and laptop are, surprisingly, where I left them on my desk. I pull a bag from the top shelf of my closet and fill it with more clothes, then tuck the books and laptop on top.

The strongbox at the back of my closet is undisturbed. Extra cash, a blank passport, and the 9mm Glock my dad bought me for my eighteenth birthday along with spare clips stare back at me. This shouldn't be here, either. I thought techs were thorough. They should have taken this with them.

I shut the box and stuff it into the bag. My breath huffs out when I lift it. It's heavier than I thought it would be. I make a sweep through the living room and open the front door, stiffening when I hear voices coming from the stairwell. They're low and decidedly masculine, and the back of my neck prickles, my stomach tightening.

Follow your gut, Cass.

My gut says to set the bag on the floor and wait and see who these men are. Shutting the door so it's only open a crack, I keep my gaze trained on the door to the stairwell, willing it to open.

Isaiah steps out, a scowl on his face, the other man looking just as friendly. I ease the door shut, holding my breath as I wait for them to leave the hallway. Sweat beads at the nape of my neck, a drop slipping down my spine.

As quietly as I can, I open my bag, unlock the strongbox, and pull out the 9mm, automatically checking the magazine. I zip up the bag and count to a hundred. Then I do it again. On the third count, I open the door, slip into the hallway, and lock the door, wincing as the tumblers click home.

I shoulder the bag and dart for the stairwell. I open the door with an agonizing slowness to minimize noise. The descent is just as agonizingly slow, and instead of exiting through the lobby, I continue down to the parking garage.

The shadowed space sets my teeth on edge, but it's the best way out of here. Careful to keep my footsteps from ringing too loudly, I make my way to the exit. The door sticks as I push it open a crack and give the surrounding area a quick scan.

Using alleys and quieter streets, I weave my way back to the car, taking my first full breath when I pop the trunk to toss my bag inside. No one saw me, and I've found the one piece of information that will end this stupid little war faster than you can say "meep-meep!"

Lia's car is gone from the driveway when I pull in. I put my leftovers in the fridge and drop my bag in Nick's room, idly thinking maybe I ought to go get the rest of my stuff out of the guest room.

He's in the small room off the living room, as I suspected he would be, and from the way his hair is mussed, he's been here longer than I thought. "When did Lia leave?"

"A while ago." The words are short and clipped. Pissed off about something.

"Oh? I thought she was going to stay for dinner."

The muscle jumps in his jaw, and I rub my fingers over it. He leans into my touch. "That was before she told me she was dating one of her instructors."

Cheering would not be the smart thing to do, but God, I want to. I'll have to call her later and get the details. "And you're not happy because he's older?"

"Then she called me a hypocrite."

I tuck my tongue firmly in my cheek. "Well, she kind of has a point."

He wraps an arm around my waist and tumbles me onto his lap. "We're not talking about us. We're talking about Lia, and she should be with someone closer to her own age."

I nod solemnly, agreeing with Lia's hypocrite assessment. "Would you like a distraction?"

He nuzzles my cheek, then kisses his way to my ear. His tongue trailing along the rim sends a ripple of pleasure down my spine. "What did you have in mind?"

Not this, but I could totally get on board with it if it weren't for the vital information burning a hole in my brain. "Isaiah's staying in my old building. Same floor."

He stills. "You're certain?"

"Saw him coming out of the stairwell myself with some guy I didn't recognize."

"Were you inside? Never mind. Not important right now. On your floor? Did you get a unit number?"

"No," I admit. "I figured getting out of there intact was more important. There are ten units per floor, and we know one of them is mine, so that leaves us with nine. Less than, actually. The stairs are kind of in the middle, with four units on my side, six on the other. He turned away from me, so that means it's not one of the remaining three. So, really, only six."

He tucks my hair behind my ear and releases me, then nudges me toward the door when I stand. "I'm calling Con," he says. "Go get some caffeine. It could be a long night."

Chapter 9

I turn off the TV and slouch down on the couch, scowling at my feet. Nick and Constantine left almost an hour ago, and I'm still pissed.

The negotiations didn't go well. He met every one of my arguments with a flat *no*. I finally planted myself in front of him and pointed at my chest. "Hello? I lived there. I know the building. I know the frickin' neighborhood. I should come with you," I said.

He remained in *mafiaso* mode, his face a cool, blank mask, eyes flat. "You're staying here. I'm not taking a chance the minute Isaiah sees you, he'll open fire."

I continued to argue, and he grew colder and more distant until I forced myself into the same space. They left, and I wandered out to the back deck and sat, staring into the dark for a while, packing my anger into a little box before going into the house and finding something to read.

I couldn't concentrate, though. I skimmed pages, closed the book, picked it up, and tried again. I checked my phone every thirty seconds and shoved it into my pocket so I wouldn't text Nick and distract him. I picked up the remote and flipped channels, hoping something would catch my attention.

Nothing did.

I want to be there. I want to stare Isaiah down, see him on his knees.

At the same time, I understand Nick's fear. With me there, his attention would be on any possible danger to me, and that's not right.

Constantine and Nick took my apartment keys and drove over with the sole intent of figuring out which unit Isaiah was hiding out in. *Then* they'd decide on an action plan. I warned them the building is full of students, and they couldn't just go busting down doors.

Turns out Nick's *no, really?* face is the same as his *I give a shit* face. If I wasn't so mad at him, I'd have giggled.

As terrible as the plan is, it's still action. I think I've earned the right to be where the action is.

"But noooo, I'm stuck *here*, wringing my hands, waiting for the men folk to come home after taming the big, bad wolf," I mutter.

He's definitely not getting laid tonight.

My phone buzzes, rattling across the coffee table, and I scoop it up. Lia's name flashes across the screen. I thumb the lock off. "Hey."

"Is he there?" she asks immediately.

"Nick? No. He and Constantine are off doing manly man things."

"Oh, good. Sounds like you're pissed at him, too, so I can vent without feeling guilty."

I laugh and get comfortable on the couch, the cushions shifting under my ass. "Okay, first, why the hell didn't you tell me? And second, your brother *is* a hypocrite, and I will tell him as much the next time I see him."

She groans. "I know, right? Noah's not even that much older. He's only twenty-six. Or twenty-five. One of the two." A car rolls down the street, bass thumping, and I glance out the front window as it passes. The driver neglected to turn his headlights on. Smart move, buddy. Real smart.

"Still. I'm pouting because you told Nick first when you knew he'd freak out."

She growls. "I *didn't* know. I thought after I moved out of Mom and Dad's he'd gotten it through his head I'm a big girl now and I don't need him helicoptering me."

A sudden image of Nick worrying over his baby sister living it up flashes through my mind. I grin. "You should have seen his reaction when I told him you were out getting into trouble. He got all sexy and broody, and I just wanted to cuddle him." Crap, had I said that out loud?

"*Cass*," she whines. "You're supposed to be on my side. I don't need to hear about how sexy my brother is, thanks. And I was planning to tell you, but Nick started interrogating me about what I was up to and how I was handling being on my own. And now I know why," she says darkly.

The bass-thumping car passes by again, and I get up to move to the bedroom. I need to unpack anyway. "Good. He needs to focus on someone other than me for a while."

"Well, dying is a great way to ensure he won't stop worrying about you any time soon."

The thought turns my stomach to acid. We have to move past this, the protector and the protected, because if we don't, it's all I'll ever be to him. "Hey, I was thinking of taking up Krav Maga. Wanna join me?"

"Ugh. No thanks. Too violent."

Something hits the front window with a *thud*, followed by another, then another, a succession of them until there's a high-pitched creaky, cracking sound. I drop to my knees and crawl forward to investigate, vaguely aware of Lia's voice in my ear. "Sorry, what was that?"

More cracking, and a *whoomph*.

"I was asking if you want to go out clubbing or something soon."

"Sure." Another *whoomph*, accompanied by flames crawling over the rug. "Hey, Lia, I have to go. I think the house is on fire." I disconnect on her squawk and hurry to the end of the hall and study the flames, sliding into that cold, empty place in my head where the jobs live. The living room is on fire. Not completely on fire. Just partially, confined to the front under the windows, though it looks like it might have reached the couch. It's far enough away I'm safe where I am in the hallway with plenty of other escape routes at my back.

I pull out my phone to dial 911 and make it to the bedroom in time to see another bottle smash through the French doors. Nick must have not felt it necessary to use the bullet-resistant glass throughout the house. The bottle bursts into flames. Fire spreads rapidly over the rug to tug at the bed linens. My bag sits next to the door. I grab it and run down the hall to the guest room as the dispatcher picks up. "911, what is your emergency?"

There had better not be another bottle coming through the guest room window. "Someone's set my house on fire."

"Okay. Ma'am, are you all right? Are you able to get out?"

Not if I have to stay on the phone. There are two windows in the guest room, one facing the street, one on the side of the house. Both are about waist level. The one facing the street is spiderwebbed with cracks, radiating out from a small hole roughly in the middle. I have maybe two seconds before a bottle comes crashing through that window. It also means there's someone watching the front of the house. My only option is to backtrack and hope whoever's out there hasn't thrown bottles through the dining room windows too. "Maybe."

A bottle smashes through the window, flame eating the rag hanging from the end. The bottle lands in the middle of the bed, and the fire catches on the blankets, eating up the fabric, little by little. I hang up and shove the phone into my back pocket.

I'm a statue. I'm stone, immobile, witness to the flames consuming the bed. The fire's bright and mesmerizing, the heat drifting closer. A few steps, and I could touch it. I might be able to squeeze along the wall to the side window.

They've got the house surrounded. The bottles came in through the front and the back, and if I manage to get out through the side, I'll still have to pass them. I'm a sitting duck.

Panic threatens, tickling my throat, threatening to close it over. I shut my eyes, lock it down. I can panic later when I'm outside, where there's no fire waiting to swallow me whole. Where I can breathe without inhaling smoke. Where I only have to worry about dying by a knife or bullet wound.

The bed is a fluid mass of red and gold, the heat and smoke stinging. After dropping to the floor, I unzip the bag and pull out the Glock. If I make it out of this house alive, I'm not going to be unarmed.

Giving up the exit from the guest room as a lost cause, I crawl along the hall before pausing at the door to the master bedroom. Lost cause number two. Fire's starting to work its way up the far walls. I crawl to the hallway entrance, phone buzzing against my ass.

The living room is a death trap. Sparks fly and pop as the TV explodes, and I throw myself flat on the ground and cover my head. Lifting it when the sounds die away, I scan the room. The couches are toast, the curtains shreds. The hardwood floor groans, sending up more sparks as a portion collapses.

But the way to the kitchen is still clear.

I could be trapped in the backyard. Someone could be waiting in the kitchen to finish me off. I have to get out of the house, though. Leaving through the kitchen is a chance I'll have to take.

Pulling my shirt up over my nose and mouth, I get to my feet and run for the kitchen, eyes blurring from tears. Another flaming bottle crashes through the dining room window as I fumble with the lock on the kitchen door. My fingers slip on the smooth metal. Eyes burning from the smoke, I squint and force myself to slow down.

The lock disengages as tears begin tracking down my cheeks. Shifting so my back is flat against the door, I open it and peer around into the darkness of the backyard. Through the smoky haze, I can't see anything.

Another portion of the living room floor collapses, startling me into action. I run into the backyard and yank my shirt down, drawing in a lungful of air.

Click.

React. I'm so tired of just reacting, and yet when it comes down to it, that's what I do. I react. I fire the Glock in the direction of the sound, dropping to the dirt the moment the bullet leaves the barrel, rolling away from the house. I pop up, blinking furiously, tears still streaming from my eyes.

The smoke…

There's more of it. The master bedroom is fully engaged, fire clawing its way through the walls to the bathroom. Beyond the bathroom is a huge linen closet full of fuel. If it catches, it won't be long before the gas line ruptures.

Something about the fire, the pure gold and red, is beautiful even as it destroys. It's hypnotizing, and it takes more effort than I'd think to tear my gaze away. I can't afford distractions now, not when there's someone or multiple someones hanging around, waiting for me to appear.

Nick will be so pissed if I end up with another scar.

A bullet whizzes past, and I drop to a crouch and spin around. That *click* must have been a bullet being chambered. I scan the rear of the yard, the smoke not helping as I struggle to make out the shape of a man coming toward me.

I don't bother aiming. Either the bullet hits him or it doesn't. The point is to distract him so I *can* aim properly and hit him. If I'm lucky, he won't return fire. If someone sees fit to grant me a miracle, he'll leave me alone.

It's too dark to see where the bullet lands. All I know is he's still coming toward me, didn't flinch a bit, so he wasn't hit. I step back, one step, two steps, retreating as he approaches. The light from the fire plays over his face, blurring his features.

Stop moving, Cass. Stop running away.

I don't want another body on my conscience. Raising the gun, I fire again, dead center of his chest. He jerks to a halt.

Watching him crumble is surreal. First his knees buckle, his legs bending in half until he hits the ground. His torso goes all mushy, folding like his knees did. When he falls forward, he twists and lands on his shoulder.

Over the roar of the fire, wood creaks as it crumbles inside, furniture busting through the hardwood floors. Sirens screech to a stop in front of the house, and the man remains on the ground.

Fuck. There are sirens out front, a man's been shot, and I'm holding the gun.

Throwing it away isn't an option. I flick the safety on and scan the back of the house. The fire's likely close to the kitchen now. If the line blows, the lawn could catch next. The lot is fenced, the space between houses mere feet. To get around to the front of the house, I'll have to climb the fence to the neighbor's yard.

I tuck the gun in the back of my waistband, hissing as the warm metal makes contact with my skin. The fence is solid wood. I run straight at it and jump, splinters digging into my toes as I scramble for the top. The rough edges scrape my palms. I wince as I haul myself over the top and land on gravel. I choke back my yelp of pain. Gravel? Seriously? Yards should have grass, not gravel.

Feet smarting, I walk as quickly as I can to the front. Firefighters uncoil hoses and adjust helmets, fanning out along the sidewalk, staying away from the flames. "Hey!" Picking up the pace to a jog, I try to get the attention of the nearest firefighter.

"Miss, please stay back." He tries to point me off to the other side of the street.

I stop out of touching range. "It's my boyfriend's house. The stove's a gas range."

His eyes widen, and he spins around, shouting instructions at the other men. "Other side of the street, miss." He turns to me. "Now."

I back away, waiting until he's focused on the house before doing as he asks and walking across the street, safely out of range of any explosions. My phone vibrates for probably the hundredth time since I hung up with Lia. I pull it out. "Hello?"

"Is the house really on fire?" Lia asks.

"The house is really on fire, and I shot a guy in the backyard. He may still be alive, but if the gas line ruptures, he'll probably die."

"Got it." It's her turn to hang up on me.

As I stare at the house, the gas line explodes. Shouts ring out, feet pound over the pavement, and the hoses crank on, water steaming and arching, the drops sparkling in the firelight.

They don't make a lot of progress. The fire's a monster, a living, breathing creature, gleefully smashing and choking everything in its path. People come out of their homes, huddle in pairs and small groups on the sidewalk, pointing at what used to be Nick's house.

A car races up the street, tires squealing when it stops in front of the house next door. Two men get out and run toward the fire trucks. More shouting ensues, the words unintelligible. One of them backs off and strides across the street. "Cassidy!"

Nick. Oh, God, *Nick*.

He's looking at the wrong part of the sidewalk. "Nick!"

"Cass?" He finally spots me and strides over. He crushes me to his chest in a hug. "Fuck," he whispers. "You okay?"

I take one of his hands and guide it to my lower back. "We need to do something about this first."

Nodding once, he releases me enough to lead me to his car. He opens the passenger door and I sit, pulling the gun from my waistband and sticking it under the seat.

He crouches in front of me and grasps my hands. "Body in the backyard," I say. "He was waiting when I ran out of the kitchen. I fired three times. Hit him once in the chest. I don't know where the other two bullets ended up. They were mostly a distraction."

"We'll worry about it later." He tugs me to my feet and cups my face, rubbing his thumbs over my cheekbones. "I'm going to kill the bastard. Slowly. Then I'm going to do it all over again."

I press a kiss to the heel of his palm. "I was the one in the line of fire, so I think I should get to do the killing."

"Shut up, Cass."

Chapter 10

The fire's still burning as we get ready to leave. The fire marshal has a bunch of questions about how it started, so I tell him everything I think I can, leaving out the man I shot in the chest. Nick stays pressed to my side the entire time. Great. If he was worried before, he'll never let me out of his sight now.

Apparently satisfied with my answers, the marshal sends me to a waiting ambulance to get checked for injuries. I point a finger at Nick. "Don't even think about picking me up." My bare feet are cold more than anything else right now, and I can walk perfectly fine. He helps me into the back of the ambulance and hovers while he watches the paramedic pull the slivers from my skin.

The medic looks up. "You've got a couple of shallow scrapes. Do you have any shoes?" I lift a brow, and she shakes her head. "Right. No shoes. I wouldn't recommend walking around barefoot. They may not be deep, but they're still susceptible to infection." She scoots away, giving us room to maneuver ourselves out of the ambulance.

Nick grins and slides an arm under my knees, his other arm around my shoulders, forcing me to hang on or flop around like a damsel in distress. He crouches down and jumps from the back of the ambulance, and I tighten my grip on his neck. Satisfied I'm not going to fall out of his arms, he nods to the paramedics and walks away. "Con offered to put us up for a few days. He stopped by Lia's to pick up a couple things for you to wear until you can go shopping to replace everything."

I figured we'd be going to the condo in Manhattan Beach. "So we're staying with Constantine?"

He waits until we're in the car to answer. "If you'd rather relocate to the condo, we can. Keep in mind we'd be disappearing and reappearing a few times a day, and that increases the risk someone will find the place."

"And staying with your cousin doesn't increase the risk to his life?" I point out.

"He lives in a condo. On the twelfth floor. Hard to throw a firebomb through the window that high up." He puts the car in gear and pulls away from the curb.

The drive is short, about thirty minutes. Constantine's home is in a newer building. Fifteen stories tall, the exterior is similar to the other new construction around it, sleek and light-colored, with few flourishes and very little character.

We take the elevator to the twelfth floor, and Constantine has the door open before we reach it. "Fuckin' sucks, bro." He drags a hand through his hair, the already messy locks becoming even more disordered. Then he grabs me in a fierce hug. "Glad you got out all right," he murmurs into my ear. At Nick's warning growl, he releases me, and Nick immediately snakes an arm around my waist. "Come on. Guest room's all set up for you."

He leads us down a short hall. He opens the second door on the left and waves us inside. The room's bigger than the one in the condo, dominated by a king-size bed and a large, blocky black dresser situated under the room's single window. The walls are bare and painted a pale gray, set off by carpeting in a deeper shade of the same color. "Bathroom's through there," he says, pointing to a door in the far corner of the room. "Lia wasn't sure what would fit. Said if you wanted something different to stop by." He gestures to a plastic bag at the end of the bed.

He claps Nick on the back. "Let me know if you need anything else." He shuts the door, leaving the two of us alone.

I hold up my hands to ward off his approach. "I need a shower." Smoke's sunk into my hair, permeated my clothes, and those clothes are dirty from having to roll around in the yard to get away from the man outside the house.

Stripping to the skin, I walk into the bathroom and turn on the shower, climbing in once it's heated. The warm water soothes away some of the stiffness in my shoulders, my feet tender and tingling from so much contact with cement.

I reach for the shampoo as the bathroom door opens. "How'd it go with Isaiah?" I ask.

"'Bout as well as we figured. The floor was quiet the whole time. Based on your information and the layout, I'd guess he's holed up in one of the two end units. He'd want to be close to an escape route." There's another staircase at the end of the hall.

"Any thoughts on how you'll get to him?" It was one of the things we'd argued about. Storming the battlements won't work in a building full of students. Waiting in the hallway won't work, either, for a variety of reasons. When they left, they were still discussing ways to get to him.

Nick pushes aside the curtain and steps into the tub. "Tomorrow. We'll talk about it tomorrow."

I know that look. That's the look he gets when he's about to pounce. That's the look he had when he stormed my office several weeks ago, shoved my skirt up to my waist, and ripped away my panties, shouldering my knees apart so he could lick me into a pile of goo.

Reaching up, I lace my fingers through his hair and yank his head down, launching the first strike. Mouths clashing in a flurry of slickness and need, the kiss is all about greed, and there's nothing gentle or sweet about it. The month-long recovery, Nick's hesitation to touch me again, the anxiety and anger over being targeted once more all falls away as our lips slide and rub, tongues stroking and thrusting.

He glides a hand down and palms my breast, squeezing a bit too hard to be pleasurable. My nipple catches between his thumb and forefinger, and the pinch of pain makes me gasp. He rolls it between his fingers, tugging, tightening, and then he's kissing his way down my neck, scraping his teeth on my collarbone before making his way to my nipple.

The bite isn't gentle. The sting zips right to my clit, the little bundle of nerves aching to be touched. I circle my hips, seeking friction and not finding it. Dammit. I run my hands over any part of him I can reach, trailing my fingers over his back, digging them into his hips when his mouth gets particularly enthusiastic. My whimpers bounce off the tile, drowned by the water raining down on us.

Wrapping my hand around his cock, I twist on the upstroke, jolting when he shoves his fingers inside me, thumb pressing on my clit. "*Fuck.* Are you ready, Cass? Is this what you want?" He thrusts his fingers into me, and I rock on him, my strokes faltering as I focus on the mounting pleasure.

Yes. All of this. "Nick. Don't make me wait." Tonight of all nights, I need this. We both do.

He swears and tears his hand away. "Now. Against the wall. *Now*."

I turn away and brace my forearms on the wall of the tub, rising up on my toes and tilting my ass, inviting him in.

The blunt head of his cock presses into me, and he stops. "Shit. No condom."

Over the fall of water, his ragged breathing fills my head, blocking out everything else. Including reason. *Make this move. It's time.* "Do it," I whisper.

He doesn't need any further prompting. He plunges forward in a brutal stroke, groaning. "Fuck. Fuck fuck fuck *fuck.*"

"Nick. *Move.*"

He withdraws, then pushes back in, each stroke as hard and steady as the last. He hasn't stopped swearing. The temperature in the shower rises with every snap of his hips against mine, the running water no longer loud enough to cover the sounds we make. It's fast and vicious. A taking. A *branding.*

He'll mark me, this first time, skin on skin.

He pinches my clit, the sting rocketing through me and twisting everything tighter. "More." I shove my hips back at him.

"Jesus. Hot. So fucking hot." He slides an arm under my breasts and yanks me up, and I twist my head to the side as his mouth comes down. Licking inside my mouth, he pinches my clit a second time, and the jolt's stronger. He groans. "You like that? Come for me."

He rubs tight, slick circles, then pinches me a third time. I'm not quite there. Orgasm's so close, I want to claw toward the bright, shiny climax. My breath catches in my throat as he grows impossibly harder inside me. I've never been able to feel that before. Before I find release, Nick curses and thrusts one last time, holding on to my hips in a grip hard enough I'll likely have bruises.

Panting, bracing my arms on the wall, I rest my forehead on the slick tile as my ability to think clearly returns at a snail's pace. I just let Nick fuck me. Without a condom.

My stomach is a block of ice.

He gentles his hold and rubs my hips to ease some of the pain from his grip. "You're fuckin' perfect." He drops an absent kiss on my shoulder, and then another firmer one on my jaw. I straighten and brush my lips over his, willing my legs to hold me up a while longer.

"Mmm. You know, I did come in here to get clean." I stretch past him for the shampoo, giving him a lazy smile, hoping like hell the confusion and panic inside isn't showing on my face.

He takes my mouth again, slower this time, the sweetness of it weakening my knees. "I'll get out of your way."

I manage to wait until he's shut the door behind him before I lose control of my legs. The hard porcelain of the tub under my ass barely registers. Nick's been demanding before. He's taken me hard, but it's never been anything like what just happened. The slickness between my legs is a reminder that it's not all water. What we did very much left a mark on me.

Will he notice?

* * * *

Constantine's living room is kind of boring. Of course, that could be because I'm sitting here in the dark. I like the dark. I'm used to the dark. It does a good job of hiding things I don't want to see.

Unable to sleep, I stole Nick's shirt and wandered out here, making myself comfortable on the couch facing the windows. Constantine doesn't have anything on his balcony other than a couple of chairs. It needs plants. A grill. I thought all men had grills. It's part of the man code. Thou shalt have a grill.

"Can't sleep?" Nick walks into the living room clad in his boxers, scrubbing a hand over his jaw.

"Yeah." As he sits down, I pull my legs toward me and wrap my arm around my knees. "Lot of stuff happened in a short period of time." My stomach hasn't thawed. If anything, it's grown heavier, the ice threatening to spread through my limbs.

I could have died in that house. I could have been sitting on the couch when the bottle was thrown. I could have been shot. Instead, I'm alive and fretting over something as silly as a lack of condoms.

He stretches out a hand to me, and I crawl over to rest my head on his shoulder. "Where'd you get the gun?" he asks.

"Eighteenth birthday present from my dad."

"Figured as much. Want to tell me why I had to hear about the fire from my sister?"

I trace circles on his bare stomach with the tip of my finger. "Didn't occur to me to call you." I'd been more concerned with getting out of the house alive and then getting away. I hadn't thought to call *anyone*. "I was on the phone with her when the first bottle was thrown. She called me back several times before I answered." I lift my head. "And I didn't want to distract you. I had no way of knowing what was going on, where you were, if you were busy trying to stay alive yourself."

He strokes his hand down my side and walks his fingers under the hem of his shirt to tickle my hip. I squirm. "Stop it."

"Nope." Leaning in, he nips my earlobe. "Don't think I didn't notice," he murmurs.

I stiffen. "Notice what?"

"Now you've distracted me because I sure as hell noticed *that*." His fingers aren't gentle as he grips my chin with his fingers, his face almost completely obscured by the dark. "What happened?"

"Nothing."

He tilts my head up. "No bullshit. Something happened."

I pull free of his hold as I stand and wander to the window. "It's…what we did in the shower," I admit. "I got caught up in the moment. I was ready. Then I wasn't. Not afterward." A shiver tiptoes up my spine, and I cup my elbows, wishing the dark would hide me now.

I've never felt more naked.

When he doesn't respond, I glance over my shoulder. His expression is shuttered, and my heart sinks. "Never mind. It's not important." Truth—there are much more important things to talk about than our sex life. My mouth curves into a smile I don't feel. "I'm going back to bed."

The hallway is too long and not long enough. Every nerve ending is on alert, waiting for Nick to react, anxiety growing with every step. Blowing out a long breath when I reach the guest room, I ease the door shut behind me and climb into bed, facing away from the door.

I should have said something. Told him no, dropped to my knees and sucked him off, *something* that would have averted this stupid mess. I lie there, fatigue finally settling into my body, and I welcome it.

But I can't fall asleep. Willing it to come doesn't work. Tensing and relaxing my muscles doesn't work. I've resorted to counting sheep when the door opens. Nick slides into bed, staying on his side, leaving me curled in a ball.

I've already dug this hole. I might as well see how much deeper I can make it. "Sex hasn't meant much to me the last few years. It's fun, it's a great stress reliever, but it's not something I think of as bringing me closer emotionally to my partner." He shifts on the bed, and I plunge on. "It's a trust issue for me. I figured when it happened, it would be with someone I love."

Love, romantic love, isn't something I'm familiar with. What I'm starting to feel for Nick has me questioning whether I've really been in love before or if I just convinced myself of it.

Any love-like feelings die a hasty death when the mattress starts shaking. I roll over. He's laughing. He's got his fist jammed in his mouth, body jerking like crazy as he *laughs*.

Something breaks inside me. A mistake, taking that step before I was certain. "Knew I should have kept my mouth shut," I mutter. I slide off the bed and grab my pillow, then yank the comforter from the bed. I bundle everything in my arms and hobble toward the door, my progress impeded by the comforter twining itself around my legs.

"Cass, hold on."

"No, thanks, that's quite all right." I would rather go back to his burnt-out house than share a bed with him right now. I fumble a hand free and reach for the handle.

Arms like titanium bands wrap around my waist. "I said hold on," he whispers, warm breath tickling my ear.

Then he picks me up and tosses me on the bed.

Chapter 11

I'm going to kill him. With my bare hands.

He halts my attack by grasping my waist and pushing me back down, pinning me to the bed. "You must have missed the girl memo where you're supposed to always want to talk about feelings and where your relationship is going and that kind of shit. So yeah, it's funny to me that it obviously embarrasses you when you *do* talk about it." He grins. "Never thought I'd meet a woman so reluctant to talk about how she feels."

Death isn't good enough for him. I'll have to kill him twice.

His grin fades. "You should have said something."

"I got caught up in the moment. Same as you. At least we were smart enough to talk about it beforehand."

"Not smart enough," he growls. "You should have said something *then*. Did you think I wouldn't get it?"

"I did tell you I'd never done it before," I point out.

"What you failed to tell me was that there was a reason for it. Christ, Cass, it's not like I go sticking my dick into every woman I date without protecting myself. There's got to be a certain level of trust first."

Heat flares across my cheeks. "It wasn't just that. It was the whole thing. Nick, I think I have bruises where your hands were. It's always pretty intense, but that... That went beyond intense. I felt *owned*. Like you might as well have just stamped me with a branding iron. And it's kind of scary because I *liked* it."

He braces himself on one forearm and shoves the shirt up to my waist with his free hand, eyes narrowed as he searches for bruises. "Can't see," he mutters. Flicking on the bedside lamp, he hunches over to check the damage. "Shit. I'm sorry."

I glance down. In the dim light, I can barely make out the darkened skin, shaped like fingers, right at the curve of my hip. Nick looks like he's about to crawl off the bed and leave. Calm steals over me, wiping away my fears. It's over and done with, and for the first time since the shower, I feel like he might sort of, kind of, maybe understand where I'm coming from. "Did you not hear the part where I said I liked it?" I ask mildly.

His gaze sweeps up my body, lingering on the soft cotton rucked up around my ribs, my hands clasped over my chest. "It's not a spur of the moment or easy thing for me either, Cass. There's a lot of things about being with you that aren't easy. Don't know what I was expecting, but I sure as fuck didn't expect to fall for someone ten years younger."

There's that damn age difference again. I bring my arms down and try to wriggle away. He closes his hands around my wrists, his hold careful, and he draws them up above my head. Then he stretches out on top of me, hips notched against mine. "But now that I've found you, I'm starting to think maybe I should keep you."

I've lost the ability to breathe. He's telling the truth. It's right there in his eyes, that certainty more frightening than his total ownership in the shower earlier. He releases my hands. "Take off your shirt for me, love."

What is it about his orders that render me helpless to do otherwise? He tells me to do something, and I do it. Probably because my body knows that what's to follow is sure to leave me limp.

Arching my back, I pluck and tug at the shirt, freeing my arms and pulling it over my head. He props himself up on his forearms and lowers his head, sucking my lower lip into his mouth. He slicks his tongue over my top lip and dips it inside, his eyes open and watching me.

I'd never thought kissing with your eyes open could be anything close to a turn-on. Stupid. Pretty much everything Nick does turns me on. His eyes blur as I struggle to keep mine open. My lids drift shut as he doubles his effort, swallowing my gasp when he nudges his hips forward.

He doesn't do anything more than rock his hips into mine and kiss me thoroughly and with painstaking slowness, following every dip and line of my neck with his lips. The thick ridge of his erection is a constant pressure on my clit. With every stunted thrust, every rough slide, I climb higher, hands scrabbling at his back. It's not enough. I'm almost there. I need his hand, his mouth, or his cock.

It breaks over me, the release a low throb that still leaves me empty and aching. His hips stop, and he lowers his head to the crook of my neck. As his breathing slows, he pushes himself up, drops a quick kiss on my mouth, and shifts off.

Oh, no. Nuh-uh. That was *not* it.

I roll on top of him.

"Cass—"

"Your turn. Boxers off." And I grasp the waistband and pull.

His hips come up, and his erection pops free, dark and angry in the lamplight, the tip glistening. Curling my fingers around him, I stroke him, scooting forward to straddle him.

"Condoms are in the bedside table."

I glance up. He wants to backtrack? His expression is strained, jaw taut with lust and determination. "No regrets this time," he says softly.

No. No regrets. I lift my hips and take him in, biting my lower lip to stifle the groan at the back of my throat.

"*Jesus.*" Nick fists his hands in the sheets and arches up, plunging all the way inside in a single thrust. Everything in me shudders and quakes, neurons pinging in rapid fire pulses.

If we'd waited a few minutes more in the shower, we could have had this. It could have been the sweet, intense sex I've dreamed of, one of the few soft fantasies I allowed myself. Nick's gaze burns into me, his hands gentle as he strokes them over my hips. It's like he knows, and he's determined to give it to me now. Intense, close, and as important to him as it is to me.

He sits up and flexes his hips, arms tight and locked around me. He urges me into a shallow rocking motion, the rhythm stunted with our inability to move deeply.

I wouldn't have it any other way.

* * * *

The other side of the bed's empty when I wake the next morning. Locating Nick's shirt, I slip it on and pad into the bathroom.

Wow. I look like I had some epic sex last night. My mouth is swollen, my hair looks like a rat tried to use it for a bed, and my chin and jaw are red and slightly raw. The tips of my ears flush to match my lips, and I yank my fingers through my hair.

Our second time around had lasted longer than the shower. Long enough for us both to fall apart in massive orgasms. Long enough my heart trembled as he lowered me to the bed afterward, brushing my hair from my face.

Maybe I'll keep you.

I fist my hands at my sides, squeezing my eyes shut. The last thing I need is to fall in love and to fall for someone like Nick. Older, unattainable Nick.

Except he's not. He's right there for the taking. Is this an advantage to dating an older guy? He's more secure in his feelings, knows what he wants? If that's the case, sign me up for seconds. And thirds.

I braid my hair away from my face, letting the ends dangle loose, since I don't have a ponytail holder. I gather up my clothes from yesterday and carry them out into the hall. There's probably some panties in the bag of Lia's clothes, but wearing someone else's underwear feels weird.

Constantine's in the kitchen, standing next to the coffee maker. I hold up my bundle. "Mind if I borrow your washing machine?"

He shows me the washer hidden in the long hall closet. Once my clothes are churning away, I head for the kitchen and caffeine. An empty mug sits on the counter, and I pick it up. "This for me?"

"Knock yourself out." He slurps up coffee and leans against the counter, all bare-chested and morning scruffy yumminess. I must have some wicked good karma being surrounded by drool-worthy guys all the time. The corner of his mouth kicks up in a smirk as I pour myself a mug. "Tired of Dom already?"

"No." I lean on the counter myself, crossing my legs at the ankle, and return his smirk. "I'm also not dead. Doesn't mean I can't look."

"Aw, you think I'm pretty?" He ducks his head. I snort, breaking into a full-on laugh when he glances up coyly and bats his lashes.

"Cute," I say, still chuckling. I put the mug on the counter. "Is he around?"

Constantine shakes his head. "Left about an hour ago to inspect his house."

Oh. Right. The reason we're here in the first place. Suddenly conscious I'm wearing basically nothing in front of my boyfriend's extremely hot cousin, I pick up the mug again and clutch it tight, the heat stinging my palms through the ceramic. "Um. Food? Am I allowed to root through your cupboards? Or I could make you breakfast." I swallow coffee to cut off the flood of words. The bitter liquid burns the roof of my mouth.

He waves a hand at the kitchen. "Help yourself."

Why didn't I have the forethought to hang on to my bag when I ran out of the house last night? Then I'd have my own clothes, and I wouldn't have to worry about flashing people. "Be right back."

Ignoring the questioning look on his face, I hurry to the guestroom and dump out the bag of clothes. There are a couple of pairs of panties with the tags still on them. I make a mental note to pay Lia back and paw through the rest of the clothes. It's all skirts and tops, not a single pair of shorts among them.

I step over to the dresser and start opening drawers, fully expecting them to be empty. The bottom one actually contains what look like gym clothes. I pull on a pair of shorts and knot the drawstring waistband to keep them on my hips, then return to the kitchen.

"What happened last night? Dom had to leave before he could fill me in."

I open the fridge. "Molotov cocktails. A couple of them. I was on the phone with Lia when the first one landed in the living room. Someone shot at the living room windows with a high enough caliber gun to break the glass. Did the same with one of the guest room windows. Didn't have to bother with a gun to get it through the master bedroom patio doors or the dining room window."

"So the house was surrounded," he says grimly.

"Bingo." I take out the carton of eggs and go back for the butter. "The dining room was the last hit, which means the kitchen was basically clear, but the living room was pretty much gone by the time I was able to get out. And guess what? There was a guy in the backyard with a gun." I frown. "I wonder if he made it out alive? The gas line blew," I explain. "I shot him in the chest, but I don't think he was dead when he went down. He was awfully close to the house, though."

The man's behavior comes back to me. It was…odd. He shot first, but the bullet went wide enough it was likely a deliberate miss. Maybe Isaiah sent him? If I didn't die in the house, Isaiah may have wanted to kill me himself. "Nick wouldn't tell me what happened with Isaiah."

Constantine huffs out a frustrated sound. "That's because we spent more time arguing over what the hell to do than doing anything. Fuckin' genius, holing up in a building full of students." It's hard to miss the grudging admiration in his voice. "We figure it's one of the two end units, but that high up, and with every other unit occupied, we'll have better luck catching him leaving the building."

I crack eggs over a bowl, duck back into the fridge for milk. "Make sure you monitor the back. Take the stairs all the way down to the parking garage. There's an exit next to the garage door. There's also two side exits. The east one opens onto an alley. The west one opens on a pathway between the two buildings. It's not large enough to be an alley. You can barely fit a person through there." I glance over my shoulder. "Maybe you should write this down."

"Probably," he drawls, "but that'd mean I'd have to go find something to write with and something to write on, and it's more fun watching you cook breakfast while wearing my gym shorts." He motions to the stove. "Go on. I'm hungry."

I flip him the bird and turn back to the eggs. "Anyway. My apartment building's not some impenetrable fortress or anything. There's no balconies, but Nick found a way to get in, *and* he got in and out of the parking garage. With my car, no less."

"My cousin does have some skills," he agrees. "He broke into your apartment?"

"Three days after we met, I tried to sink a knife into his carotid," I confirm. "He snuck into my bedroom at around one in the morning and tried to get me to leave with him."

Constantine swears softly, and I glance over my shoulder. He's staring at his coffee mug intently, like he's wishing a genie would pop out of it and grant him a couple of wishes. "What?" I ask.

He lifts his gaze. "That's not typical for him. Normally he'd wait until you were somewhere public and corner you."

I shrug. "So?"

His eyes narrow. "Remind me again how you two met."

"I tried to kill him. So did someone else. I saved his ass; then he saved mine."

His mouth thins, and he gulps the rest of his coffee. "*That* is typical of him. You were injured somehow, right?"

"Twisted my ankle, then got grazed by a bullet. I tried to get him to leave after he finished the first aid, but he insisted on seeing me back to my car."

The kitchen goes quiet as I continue breakfast preparations and Constantine broods. The toast is done and the eggs are light and fluffy, divided onto plates, by the time he speaks up.

He sticks his fork in the eggs and leaves it there. "Look. I like you. In a lot of ways, you're good for Dom."

"Even with the age difference?" I ask dryly.

He barks out a laugh. "Trust me, the age difference means shit right about now. You've got this blackened, scarred part to you that matches his. He doesn't have to lie about who he is because you already know, and you've proven you can handle it. The shitty thing is it also makes you a huge liability. He's already fucking crazy over your safety."

Cold seeps into my bones. "He's only with me because he thinks I need to be protected?"

"If it was something as easy as that, I wouldn't be so worried. No, it's more. You're more than someone he needs to keep safe, Cass. You actually mean something to him." His eyes lock on mine. "And from what you've told me, I'd say it's been like that since the beginning, whether he wanted to admit it or not."

Chapter 12

Getting out of Constantine's alone is a challenge. He refuses to hand over the keys to his car, and I'm desperate for some time by myself.

"Come on," I whine. "I've already told you where I'll be, and I'll call you once I get there." Since I'm still leery of trying to access any of my bank accounts, my plan is to go see my mother and borrow her credit card, then head to the mall in Century City. It's like high school all over again, right down to bargaining for the car.

"Dom will kick my ass for letting you out of my sight." He crosses his arms over his chest and glares.

"Did he actually ask you to babysit me?"

"No," he mutters.

I smile prettily and hold out my hand, palm up. "Keys, please. I promise I'll return your car in one piece."

He eyes my hand. "Give me ten minutes, and I'll take you. You're missing a license anyway."

I planned to hit up the DMV before my mother's office. The last thing I need is to be pulled over and ticketed for driving without one. Constantine's expression can only be described as mulish, though, so I give up on the direct approach and move on to the sneak attack. "Fine. I'll be over here, waiting patiently." I wander over to the living room couch and flop down. I arch a brow. "Well? Are you showering or not?"

He gives me a skeptical once-over, as if he'll be able to discern my plan by studying my socks. To further the ruse, I pick up the remote, point it at the TV, and flip channels until I settle on some midday newscast. He turns and heads for his bedroom, muttering to himself.

The moment the shower in his bathroom turns on, I race for his bedroom. Idiot has his keys sitting right on top of his dresser. I snatch them up and run for the front door. I pause with my hand on the doorknob to cock an ear toward the bathroom. He's still in there. Good.

My phone rings before I make it three blocks. I fish it out of my pocket and toss it on the passenger seat, grinning. Constantine must be furious right now.

I call him back after I park and start walking toward the DMV. "Let me remind you of a few things. One, I used to kill people for a living. Two, I'll be spending a lot of time at the mall. A *lot*. Most of my clothes were at Nick's. I can't imagine shopping is your idea of a good time. Three, does it really matter if I'm alone or with someone else? Isaiah's determined. He wants me dead. It's not going to matter to him if I'm alone or if I've got twelve bodyguards."

"You stole my car," he growls.

"Borrowed," I correct. "I *borrowed* your car. Oh, and thing four— you're not on bodyguard duty. If Nick threatens to kick your ass, just remind him he didn't tell you to tie me to a chair. I'm at the DMV. I'll text you a picture." I hang up, open the camera app, take a picture of the sign next to the door, and text it to Constantine before walking inside.

The wait is surprisingly short. I spend about twenty minutes squirming around, trying to find a comfortable position in the chair, then my number is called and I'm asked to smile for the camera.

Temporary license safely stowed in my pocket, my phone pings, and I pull it out. *Still at the DMV?*

I text Constantine back. *A miracle happened. I'm done, heading for my mom's. Text you when I'm there, promise.*

My last visit to Mom's office didn't end so well. And our relationship is still strained despite the efforts both of us put into mending it while I was recuperating. But there's a reason I haven't been to see her since I've been back, having instead chosen to call and let her know I'd made it home safely.

Forgiving my mother for not standing up to my father is a work in progress, and some days there's less progress than others.

The drive from the DMV to Mom's takes longer than I'd anticipated because I get lost. Constantine's area of Los Angeles isn't one I'm familiar with, and even with my phone calmly relaying directions in its tinny, mechanical voice, I still manage to get turned around.

The first text comes in over an hour later while I'm circling the block to get back on the street I just left. I ignore it and concentrate on finding my way back to the route my phone insists will take me to my mother's office.

Another text comes in as I zip through a yellow light.

A third while I'm squinting at street signs.

It pings for the fourth time as I'm maneuvering into a parking spot, and I swear it sounds angry. His text reads like it too. *Where the fucking fuck are you, woman?!*

I wait until I'm in front of the building that houses Mom's firm and take a picture of her nameplate on the directory in the lobby. I text the picture to Constantine with an apology for taking so long.

One final text comes in as I'm getting on the elevator. It's a picture of Constantine's middle finger, raised high. I probably should have called him instead of sending that last text.

I call him as I'm stepping out of the elevator. "Sorry," I say quietly. "I got lost trying to get here from the DMV. I don't know your neighborhood."

"He called while I was waiting for you to text me back."

I press a hand to my stomach and slump against the wall. The ninja bats are waking, stretching and fluttering their wings. I just want to get this visit to Mom out of the way so they'll calm down again. "You tell him where I am?" I cast a sidelong glance at the elevator, half expecting Nick to come striding out, all dominating and cool.

"How long will you be at your mother's?"

"Maybe five minutes."

He sighs. "Text me when you get to the mall. If Dom starts bitching, I'll beat on him for a while."

I tell him I will and hang up. The ninja bats kick into high gear as I approach Mom's office. I didn't call ahead of time to let her know I was coming, mostly because if I didn't tell her, I could chicken out. I push open the door and step inside.

The reception desk is empty, and I hurry down the hall. Mom's door is half open, and I knock softly before easing it open.

Her whole face lights up, her eyes fill with tears, and it's hard, so damn hard, not to run bawling into her arms. She does it for me, hurrying around her desk and crushing me in a hug so fierce I'll feel it for days. For a few brief seconds, she's my mom again, the woman who cured all my hurts with a hug and a cookie.

She sniffles, stepping back to give me a critical once over. "You look better." She peers at my neck. "They did good work. How are you feeling? Is Nick treating you well?" Her mouth thins. "Although I can't say I approve of my daughter living with a man ten years her senior."

I fight the urge to roll my eyes. "Nick and Dad both thought I'd be safest with Nick. He put me in the guest room." For one night. "And he's going to help me find a place to live once the man who tried to kill me is out of the picture." Not that I have any intention of asking Nick for help with that.

I'm starting to think I might want to keep him too.

Her mouth relaxes a fraction, and the bats flap harder. "Anyway, um, that's kind of why I'm here." I suck in a breath. "Nick's house burned last night."

She blinks. "Burned?"

"To the ground," I confirm. I'm fairly certain it was unsalvageable. "We're staying with his cousin for now until we can figure out a more permanent solution."

"You'll come home." Her tone brooks no argument. "I don't believe Nick can do a better job of looking out for you than your own father."

The bats stop moving. "No." That came out harsh. "Mom, I can't. I went to see Dad the other day."

She jerks, like I've slapped her. "You saw your father?"

I'm going to hazard a guess and say he didn't tell her.

"I went to ask for his advice on training. I was thinking of taking up Wushu again, maybe Krav Maga." This is Mom. The one person who would likely understand. An ache grows in my throat, and I swallow against it. "I... I thought maybe he'd be different. That he'd act more like a dad. But he still sees me as his legacy, and a failed one at that. Unless he bends, I don't want anything to do with him." As soon as the words leave my mouth, I know they're a lie. I will try until my last breath to have a relationship with my dad that doesn't revolve around the most effective way to inflict poison on someone.

She cups my face, then pulls me into a hug. "He loves you, Cassidy. He does."

If that's the lie she has to tell herself to stay with the man, that's her business.

I stay wrapped in her hug for another minute. "I like being with Nick. After everything I've done, being with someone I don't have to hide that side of me from is kind of awesome." I ease away. "He might be a lot older, but most days, I don't feel like a college student anyway."

Her eyes narrow as her gaze skims over my face. "I'm not going to give you my okay, if that's what you're looking for. I still think you should be with someone closer to your age." She glances at the clock. "I've got an appointment in a few minutes. Would you like to have lunch later this week?"

"Sure." I grin. "Now, can I borrow your credit card?"

* * * *

The mall's not all that crowded. It makes it easier to track the man tracking me. Light brown hair, broad shoulders, though I'm too far away to make out his eye color. I peg him at about six foot. So far he's followed me to American Eagle, Pac Sun, and to the car and back.

He must be supremely bored. *I'm* bored. Replacing your entire wardrobe is probably most girls' idea of a good time. But after an hour of trying on jeans and shoes and shirts, I'm a little sweaty and a lot cranky.

I wiggle my toes in my new Chucks. They're stiff, and my feet are starting to protest, along with my stomach. Shifting my latest shopping bag to my other hand, I trudge off toward the food court.

The food court *is* crowded, mostly with mall employees and high school students skipping class. Another week or so, and the college kids will be getting out for the Christmas holiday. I'll need to go by campus tomorrow and get a new ID, talk to the registrar about signing up for classes for next semester.

Because I *am* going back to school next semester. Even if it means moving out on Nick and into my parent's house for the duration.

The line at the teriyaki place is the shortest. Carrying my tray, trying not to let my soda tip over, I wind my way through the tables, looking for an empty one. Preferably far away from the group of high school girls shrieking with glee. I set the tray on the table, dump my bags on the floor, and settle down to eat.

There's something so deliciously bad about mall teriyaki. I pop another bite of chicken in my mouth when I spot my stalker. He looks pained. As well he should. To maintain distance, he's forced to take a seat near the screaming girls.

I pull out my phone and send a text to Denise, asking if she wants to meet for coffee tomorrow, since I'll be near campus. Then I check my e-mail. Mostly junk. There's an e-mail from the registrar's office, and I skim it. Out of curiosity, I check my other e-mail account. Only a few job requests, easily ignored.

The final e-mail isn't a request.

It's a picture of Denise and Charlie.

Bright light halos their bodies, the two of them close together. She's grinning up at him, and his arms are locked around her waist. It's a fantastic picture, one that clearly shows how in love they are.

A piece of chicken lodges itself in my throat. I reach for my soda and gulp it down, painfully aware of the icy numbness spreading through my limbs. Of the people who know this address, only a few of them would know, or have the means to find out, who Denise is to me.

Forcing my fingers to work, I save the e-mail and sign out, going through my usual precautions to clear my trail. Appetite gone, I dump the rest of my meal in the trash and leave the food court. Everything is normal. Everything is fine. I haven't just had someone threaten to knock the foundation of my world out from under me.

Despite the secrets I've kept from her, Denise is my anchor. She's what has grounded me all these years in the normal life I've tried to have. Now Isaiah's sticking her on the front lines of a war she has no part in.

I still have things to buy. Like running gear and sweaters. And underwear. I wander through the store, find the table with the seven-for-twenty-five deal panties and pick one of each, the small pieces of cotton bunching in my fist as I move from one end of the table to the other. Scenarios run through my mind, ways to get Denise out of harm's way. None of them will work because all of them involve telling her who I am, what I've done, and after the way she looked at me the last time I saw her, I never want to see her look at me that way again.

I take my purchases to the cash register and watch with a grimace as the total climbs. It's only going to go higher as the day wears on.

Nick's waiting outside the store. The faint scent of cinnamon tickles my nose as I walk up to him, and I drop my bags and slide my arms around his waist. "Missed you this morning."

"Didn't want to wake you." Nick's chest rumbles under my cheek, one hand pressed at my lower back, the other sliding into my hair. "Neat trick, stealing Con's car."

I poke him in the side. "I *borrowed* the car. I'm returning it when I'm done." I tip my head back. "Since he told me you didn't ask him to stay with me, I figured it'd be all right. And I needed a few hours alone."

He dips his head, mouth brushing over mine in a barely there kiss. "You done with your alone time?"

The only alone time I had was in the mall, and I spent most of it wishing someone were with me to break up the monotony. "Depends. If I say yes, are you going to drag me home?"

One side of his mouth quirks up. "You forget I lost most of my shit last night too." He releases me and bends down to pick up my bags, then holds out a hand. "Ready?"

I stare at his hand. "Wait. You want to go shopping?" He wants to be seen with me? What's next, we go to a movie? The feel of his hand around mine sends a surge of warmth up my arm.

"I'd rather go to the dentist than be at a mall, but I need clothes." He lifts our joined hands to his lips and kisses the back of my hand. "Judging from the number of bags in Con's trunk, you've probably still got stuff left to buy. Might as well do it together."

"How did you get into his car?" I let him tug me along, and we head for the Gap. The Gap? The man can afford a house in Santa Monica, several cars, a condo in Manhattan Beach, and he shops at the Gap?

"Spare keys. I gave him a ride," he says absently. "How long has Tris been following you?"

I glance over my shoulder. Sure enough, my stalker is lounging on the bench outside the store, fiddling with his phone. "Pretty much since I got here. He's tried to stay in the background. Hasn't done a very good job of it. Lack of people makes it easy to spot him."

He hands over my bags and flips through a rack of shirts. "Strange."

Tris's continued presence reminds me of the e-mail. "I think Isaiah's trying to use Denise to get to me."

"What makes you think that?" We stop in front of a wall of jeans, and he pulls several pairs free.

"Someone sent a picture of Denise and Charlie to me. There was no message or caption or anything, and it was sent to my other e-mail address. Not my regular one."

He drops the pants on a nearby table and holds out his hand. "Show me." I pull up the photo and pass him the phone. He studies it for a long while, ignoring the sales person who comes over and cheerfully asks if we're finding everything okay. "Denise's last name?"

"Lillard."

He digs his own phone out of the back pocket of his jeans and hits speed dial. "Need you to run a check for me. Discreet. You ready?" He gives me my phone back, his eyes on mine. "Denise Lillard." He asks me, "You know where she'd be this time of day?"

Relief rushes through me, and I lean on the table. "Class. She's taking a class on the Israeli-Palestinian conflict, but I don't remember where it meets."

"We can find out." A few more short, sharp commands, and he hangs up. "Bas will find her and report back." He picks up the stack of pants, kisses my cheek, and winds his way through the tables to the fitting rooms.

Shopping with Nick is surprisingly fun. Ogling his ass while he tries on jeans is even more fun. Tris following us is not fun. Nick's shoulders get more and more tense, the line of them so straight it could double as a ruler.

After several more hours, my feet hurt, and we both never want to see the inside of a mall ever again. But the day's not over yet. Rather than go back to Constantine's, Nick drives around for a while, the car quiet. He finds a little Italian restaurant in the middle of some random neighborhood and pulls into the parking lot. "This okay?"

At this point, I'd go anywhere with him if it meant extending regular couple stuff a few more hours.

We're shown to a booth, and I slide in, Nick opting to sit next to me instead of on the other side of the table. He snakes an arm around my waist and I tip my head onto his shoulder, my bones softening as we sit, sealed off from the world.

"I needed this," I admit softly.

"To shop?"

I snort. "No. To do something normal." Normal's been on my mind most of the day. Most of the last few weeks, if I'm honest. "Hard to be normal with everything that's been going on lately."

"Hate to break it to you, Cass, but you'll never be normal."

And there goes my good mood. "Thanks for the reminder."

"If you were normal, would you be here?"

I straighten and pick up a menu. "Here, in an Italian restaurant? Doubtful, though I'm sure I would have eaten in one at some point."

"Stop being a brat." The mild tone is deceptive. He slides a finger under my chin and turns my face toward his. "If you were normal, I wouldn't have met you. So I'm pretty fuckin' glad you're not." His face is inches from mine, the heat of his body cloaking me.

"I tried to kill you." It comes out breathy and feeble, a ghost of a protest, because he's right. If I were normal, I'd never have had a reason to meet Dominic Kosta, businessman *or* crime boss.

"You didn't try very hard," he murmurs, finger stroking the length of my throat.

The words rear up and rush the barrier, breaking through. "I love you."

His hand stills.

This is…not good.

Chapter 13

Why is there never a roll of duct tape handy when you need one? If I had some, I could have slapped it over my mouth, keeping the *I love you* inside where it belongs. My brain must have decided all the sweet lines and tender gestures meant it was safe to tell Nick.

The way he's sitting, frozen, eyes wide and blank, says otherwise.

His mouth opens, and I cover it with my hand. "Wait. The only thing I want to hear coming out of your mouth on this particular topic is that you love me too. If you can't say that, if you don't feel that way, then we're dropping the subject now. Non-negotiable." I don't want to hear a *thank you* or a *I care for you*. The only thing that will make what I said okay is for him to repeat it and mean it.

I lower my hand, and he parts his lips. "Cass."

"Yes?" My heart stutters, turns over, and jumps into triple-time.

The intensity of his gaze and the twitching of his lips make me think he'll say it back. But then he straightens and picks up his menu.

I'm surprised my heart doesn't make a *splat* as it lands on the ground at his feet. I open the menu and stare blindly at the choices. *You asked for this, you idiot.* As much as it hurts, hearing nothing is better than hearing platitudes. Hearing nothing allows the hope to flicker a little longer, that someday he'll tell me the same thing.

I tighten my grip on my menu. Dinner will not be awkward. I can get through dinner, and then I'll find somewhere else to go for the evening. The problem with that is I don't know where I *can* go. Most of my friends are likely studying for finals, and I don't want to deal with Turner just so I can spend some time with Mom. My stomach sinks as I realize Denise hasn't returned my earlier text, and Bas, whoever he is, hasn't called in his report. Our server comes by, and we place our orders.

Once he's gone, I turn to Nick. "Shouldn't Bas have called you by now?"

"Visual confirmation can take longer. If he hasn't called by the time we're done with dinner, I'll call him. May I see the picture again?" I pull it up, and he takes the phone from me. "Any idea when this might have been taken?"

The phone buzzes in his hand, and he passes it back. The text is from Lia, wanting to know if I'm all right. A perfect distraction, one that will keep me from worrying too much about Denise and get me away from Nick for a while. I shoot off a reply, ask if she wants to hang out tonight, and mention I'd love some girl time, since I've spent so much of it lately hanging out with the boys.

It rings a few seconds later. "Oh my God, yes. Please come over. I'm going a little nuts."

I slide a glance at Nick, who's pulled out his own phone. "Give me an hour? Having dinner. I'll be over once I'm done." She promises to text me the door code and her apartment number, and I hang up. "Do you mind dropping me at Lia's when we're done eating?"

He shifts around on the bench until he's facing me. "Avoiding it won't make it go away."

I've never wanted to disappear so badly in my life. I drop my gaze to my lap. "I know. I just wasn't ready to say it. It sort of popped out on its own." My mouth snaps shut hard enough my teeth clack together. Way to go, Cass. Way to take an awkward situation and make it *more* awkward. "I mean it. I do. It's just scary, and there's other shit to worry about and—"

Nick presses a hand over my mouth. "Bas just checked in. Denise is fine."

This time, the relief is so great it's crushing. I ease away. "Okay," I whisper. "Can you help me? I need her protected, and I don't know how to accomplish that without telling her who I am, which I'd really like to avoid. Top scenarios for me are moving Denise and Charlie to a safe house of some sort, telling Denise and Charlie to leave town for a while, or having a few of your guys pull some hidden bodyguard duty." I look down as our server puts plates in front of us. The rich, heavy scent of spiced tomato sauce has my stomach clenching. I pick up my fork and poke at my food.

"There are problems with all three of those," I continue. "The first two involve telling Denise what I've done. The third involves trusting your men, not to mention sparing them in the first place, which I don't even know if you have the capacity to do that."

"You do make it sound like I've got some sort of army at my disposal." I stick my tongue out at him, and he grins. "I can spare a couple of guys. It'd be helpful if Denise and Charlie left town for a little while. I can't do it for long, and having them sit on people that, until now, haven't been connected will look suspicious."

"Then don't," I say immediately. "Charlie's family lives in Colorado. He's probably going home for the holidays anyway. I'll talk to Denise."

"It's not a big deal."

"I'd rather you use them to get Isaiah or his guys to come out and play like big boys." I push the food around on my plate. "Maybe you could have a rumble? You know, with chains and stilettos and everything? You'd have to practice that sideways prowl thing like they do in *West Side Story*, though. I think snapping in time is difficult if you've never done it before."

He lays a hand over mine, quelling my nervous movements. "Cass."

My emotional rollercoaster careens around a corner and drops to the bottom before slamming to a halt. I push away my plate and cover my face with my hands. "One day," I whisper. "One. Fucking. Day. One day where I'm not being followed, my best friend isn't in danger of being killed, and I don't want to sneer at my mother for being so weak." I peek through my fingers at the pasta. "I should get that boxed up. Wasting it would be stupid."

Nick slips an arm around my hips, and I stiffen. "Please don't." My voice cracks, and I swallow a few times, trying to clear the ache in my throat. "I really don't want to be touched right now." I don't have tears. Not for this. All these emotions tumbling around, but no tears.

The frightening one is the sadness. It's an anvil, ready to drop, ready to crush. Once it lands, I can't say I'll have the strength to put myself back together.

If this is what falling in love has gotten me, I'd like a time machine. It's not worth it if everything falls apart around me.

We finish dinner in relative silence. At Nick's pointed glare, I pick at my food, forcing more of it down. It lumps together in my stomach. The server comes by with the check and a to-go box, and I dump the rest of my meal in the box before Nick can pry my lips apart and force-feed me.

The drive to Liana's building is worse. The silence has a sound to it. A long, somber note, like a cathedral bell tolling its final clang. I break it as he pulls to the curb in front of the apartment. "Can I borrow some cash? I'll take a cab home so you don't have to come get me."

He hands it over without speaking, gives me an absent kiss on the cheek, and I climb out of the car and hurry over to the door. I punch in the code and step into the lobby, then locate the stairs.

The stairwell is brightly lit. I stand at the bottom, listening, ready to duck back out at the slightest suspicious noise. Hearing none, I begin the climb to Lia's apartment on the sixth floor.

I'm out of breath, and there's a stitch in my side when I reach her floor. Legs shaky with fatigue, I prop myself up against the wall, waiting for my lungs to stop heaving.

Lia answers the door with a bottle of wine in her hand. She hands it to me. "Here. You need to catch up."

I study the bottle. It's a red, and there's already a good quarter of it gone. I shut the door behind me. "Why am I catching up?"

She snags a half-full wine glass from the coffee table and throws herself onto the couch, her dark hair flying around her face. "Why didn't you tell me?" Her accusatory glare stabs into me, and my blood turns to ice. I've already told her everything, from being hired to kill her brother to her cousin almost killing me. Though it's possible I could have forgotten something. A lot's happened in the last two months.

"Tell you what?"

"That dating an older guy will drive you absolutely fucking insane," she wails.

That's it? I flop onto the other end of the couch. She's got nice furniture. The couch is ridiculously comfortable yet stylish, set off by coordinating end tables and lamps. Must be one of the perks of being a mafia princess. I set the bottle on the table. "Mmm, nope. Pretty sure it won't. Although maybe I'm doing it wrong." Her look of misery is comical enough to make me snort. "Look at you, all swoony and pine-y. What's going on?"

She shrugs. "Twenty's a weird age. You're straddling the line between a teenager and an adult, you know? I can drink and get into places, but I have to make sure I've got my fake ID on me and not my real one, which is a pain in the ass. Better safe than sorry." She blows a strand of hair off her face. "I had a friend get busted for that just a few weeks ago, having both IDs on her at the same time."

"Wait, is Noah giving you crap about your age?"

Her eyes widen. "No! He couldn't care less. It's more..." Her hands flutter in a useless gesture. "He's confident. He knows what he's doing and where he's going. He's got a regular job and doesn't spend his weekends partying and has his own place, doesn't have a roommate." She drops her gaze to her lap. "We haven't had sex yet, and I know he wants to, but I'm, um, not ready."

It feels incredibly wrong to be as happy as I am about Lia's problems, but I can't help it. All my issues fade into the background as I curl my legs under me. "Honestly? I don't think it's necessarily an age thing. My best friend's boyfriend is pretty driven, too, but he's still got a semester to go before graduation. I think it's the person, not their age."

The misery stays firmly in place, though. "Great. But what do I do about the sex?"

Why does everything have to come down to sex? "I don't know. What do you do about the sex? Besides have it?"

She shoots me the bird and reaches for her wineglass, a flush sweeping over her cheeks to her ears.

She's not... "You're not a virgin, are you?"

"Ding ding ding! Give the girl a prize," she says sourly.

There's a bowl of half-eaten popcorn on the table. I lean over and snag it. With the anxiety and sadness dulled, my appetite's back, and I'm starving.

"Are you, like, impatient to just get it over with, or is there a reason you've waited so long?" I scoop out a handful of popcorn.

She holds out a hand, and I pass over the bowl. "Kind of both? Sometimes I wonder why I've held on to it for so long, and then the chance presents itself and I freak out." She dips her hand into the bowl and picks up a few kernels. "Noah knows, and he says he's willing to wait, but I'm still scared he'll get tired of waiting."

Her fear feels familiar, a vague itch I can't scratch because I can't find it. "Sometimes," I say slowly, "the differences aren't there. We're just Nick and Cass. We like each other and have fun together and have some amazing chemistry.

"He asked me to come to a business dinner with him, back before everything went to hell. Sitting at that table with the two men and their wives, I had nothing to contribute to the conversation. I was almost glad when someone started shooting up the restaurant." I motion for the bowl of popcorn. "It sucks, because no matter how secure I feel about us, there's always that fear that it won't be enough." I crunch down on popcorn. "So I'm just going to enjoy it while I can. Of course, I'd enjoy it more if Isaiah would just stop trying to kill me, but whatever."

Lia rolls her eyes. "Oh, right, 'whatever.'" Then she giggles and ducks when I throw popcorn at her.

My phone buzzes, wiggling across the tabletop. Constantine's number flashes on the read-out. I thumb the lock off. "Please tell me nothing's wrong."

"What the fuck happened today?" he growls.

"Um, nothing? I picked up a stalker at the mall, but that's about it. Why?" Lia's eyebrows lift almost to her hairline.

"Because my cousin's hijacked my best bottle of whiskey and refuses to tell me why. Just sits there muttering. Heard your name a few times."

I'm as confused as he is. We weren't fighting when he dropped me off. We weren't talking, either, but that's beside the point. "He's a big boy. You could wait until he's wasted to ask him. He'll probably tell you then." I tip the phone down. "Might need to crash on your couch tonight. Would that be okay?" I ask Lia. Whatever crawled up Nick's ass doesn't sound pleasant, and if Constantine's telling the truth, I'm likely the cause.

"Oh *fuck* no. You are not leaving me alone with Dom. He gets drunk when he's in this kind of mood; he gets fucking morose. *You* can deal with him." He curses, and there's scrabbling in the background. "Come home and wrangle your boyfriend, Cass. I'm not in the mood to deal with him." He hangs up, and I stick my tongue out at the phone.

"Trouble in paradise?"

"Nick's drinking himself drunk, and his cousin's pissed about it." I get to my feet. "Since I'd like to have a place to live for a while longer, I probably should do as he says."

I call a cab, and Lia walks me to the door, uncertainty gleaming in her eyes. I hug her. "Do you trust Noah?"

She nibbles on her thumbnail. "No. Not completely. Not yet." She lowers her hand and sighs. "That's the big thing, isn't it? Trust? I have to trust that he's telling the truth that he'll wait as long as I need?"

"Pretty much," I confirm. "Wow, I feel so old and wise. This is awesome." She pokes me in the side, and I dance away. "It's either that, or trust your instincts, and sometimes that's harder to do than trusting someone else."

She bows from the waist, palms toward me. "O wise one, I heed your counsel." A snicker escapes, and she straightens. "Go on. Give Nicky hell. He probably deserves it."

Somehow I doubt that.

Chapter 14

Nick doesn't even glance over when I walk in the door. He remains sprawled on the couch, staring out the window, glass in hand. I wander to the other end of the couch and plop down. "So. Constantine calls me all growly and says you're being morose."

He mutters and sips his drink, his gaze never leaving the damn window. Scoot closer or stay where I am? There's this tension in the air, like a vibrating guitar string, but instead of trailing off at the end of a long note, it holds a high, thready hum. Giving up, I go in search of Constantine.

I find him in a study much like Nick's, wires and cables everywhere, making the room seem small and cluttered. Three monitors display photos, a spreadsheet, and what looks like some sort of news stream. A lamp in the corner doesn't do much to improve the look of the space. I lean on the doorjamb and tuck my hands into my pockets. "Okay. I'm here. Tell me again what I'm supposed to do?"

He spins his chair around and scowls at me. "He's still out there drinking, isn't he?"

"And not saying anything intelligible," I add.

"Last time he got like this was when Cece gave him an ultimatum. Stop hiding things from her, or she'd leave."

Obviously, he'd let her go. If this is a repeat of that, he didn't handle it well. But I hadn't given him an ultimatum. I just asked him to keep his mouth shut.

"I'll…try talking to him, I guess." I spin around and hurry out to the living room. Nick hasn't moved. Standing in front of him, I lean forward and bring my face close to his, my hands on his thighs for balance. "Constantine's pissed you're drinking all his whiskey."

He snorts.

"Why are you doing this?" I whisper. "Is it because of what I said earlier? When I asked you not to say anything back?" I take the glass from his hand and knock back the rest of the whiskey, hissing at the burn. Then I climb onto his lap and straddle him.

He's wearing a button-up shirt, and I focus on the top button. It's easier than looking at him. "This was never supposed to be about feelings." I maintain my whisper, not because I don't want his cousin to hear, but because I'm afraid if I speak any louder, it'll get more real. "I never thought I'd get that luxury. That I'd meet someone who could know everything. You come along, and it's so tempting to let it all out, dump it all over you. I've got all these feelings bottled up, Nick. I can't turn them loose. We'll both drown.

"I don't think I could handle it if you said something like 'thank you.' Or that you care about me." Fury over the imagined slight rips through me. "I'm just not that into you, baby. Saying you care is the way you soften the blow. If you don't say anything, I can at least pretend you might feel the same way and don't have the balls to tell me."

He snorts again. "How is that better?"

The button's a little chipped. I trace the edges with my finger. "Because everything's better inside my head."

"Your head sounds like a fucked-up place to be."

I meet his gaze. "For someone who's consumed as much liquor as Constantine claims, you're awfully sober."

He drops his head back on the couch. "Con was in a piss-poor mood to begin with. I'm not drunk. Not sober, either."

I don't like this. This not knowing where I'm supposed to be, if he wants me here in the same room as him, or if he wants some space. His head remains tipped back, so I slide backward on his lap, figuring I'll go sort through my new clothes and take off the tags.

He clamps his hands on my hips. "Where are you going?"

"Um, bedroom? There's a mess of bags that need unpacking."

His fingers twitch, and he nudges me forward.

"You don't want to continue drinking yourself into a stupor?"

His head comes up. "Nah. I've got a beautiful woman sitting on my lap. Who needs liquor?" Hands splayed across my back, he presses me against him, lining us up from shoulders to stomachs, hips notched together. My breath hitches, and I hold stiff. I'm afraid to move. Afraid to *blink*.

"Relax," he murmurs. The hand resting on my shoulder blades strokes up under my hair, and he cups the back of my neck.

Cell by cell, I do, fusing myself to him, the faint scent of cinnamon tickling my nose, his heat surrounding me. Plastered to him as I am, I'm expecting my libido to wake up and want to party. It doesn't. It makes a snuffling noise in its sleep and rolls over.

I didn't know this was possible. To want to crawl inside someone, to want to wear their security and affection like a cloak. Despite the erection between my thighs, Nick seems as content as me, sitting in the dark, his hands a heavy, welcome weight on my back. "You think you could stop the world for a while? I'd like to stay here," I murmur.

"Please tell me all your clothes are still on." Constantine stops at the entrance to the hallway, hands shoved in his pockets.

Nick's hands glide down my back as I slide off his lap. The two of us shift in concert, Nick with his back to the corner, his arm tight around my waist, my back to his chest. His free arm comes around, circling me.

I never want to move.

Constantine meanders over and flops into the chair next to the couch. His gaze is critical as he looks past me to Nick. "All right, bro?"

Nick's hold tightens. Constantine glances at me, relief flickering over his face, then gives his attention to Nick. "Cory got back to me. He thinks—"

"That we can talk about this tomorrow? I'm not talking business tonight. Of any kind."

Constantine's eyebrows squish together, his gaze flitting from Nick to me and back again. Nick slips a hand under my shirt and rests it on my stomach, stroking the skin above the waistband of my jeans. It's a standoff, one I don't fully understand, and Constantine glances at me again, one eyebrow raised.

"Thought we'd watch a movie or something." Nick's chest rumbles with his words, the touch of his fingers ticklish. "Cass? Anything in particular you wanted to watch?"

"Something funny," I say, my heart thudding its way up my throat. "Is there popcorn? Constantine interrupted my popcorn eating."

"George gave me a popcorn popper when I bought this place. Never used it. Let me see if I can find it." Constantine gives me one last look and a barely perceptible shake of his head, gets to his feet, and walks out of the room.

I twist around the second he's gone and capture Nick's face in my hands, kissing him hard. "Thank you," I whisper. It's only a few hours, but it's a few more hours where we can continue pretending we're just like any other couple, snuggled together and watching a movie.

He grins, that devastating, sly curve of lips I love to hate. "Who says I did this for you? I needed a break, and I've had enough to drink that making business decisions would be a stupid idea." He captures my mouth before my frown becomes a full-fledged glare. He kisses me until the frown melts and a whimper builds in my throat. "You're welcome," he whispers against my lips.

I untangle myself and go in search of the remote. It's on the bookshelf under the flat screen. Tossing it to Nick, I kick off my shoes and retake my spot, certain I'm purring with contentment I feel so damn good.

The evening is exactly what I'd hoped for. Nick and Constantine trade insults, and both protest my choice of movie when I pull up *Crazy, Stupid Love*. Hey, I said I wanted funny. It's funny. It just happens to be a romantic comedy.

When we make our way to the bedroom, a lingering trickle of anxiety threads through my blood. Last night was a heady rush of sensation and dragging doubts. It had ended well, but that doesn't stop me from wondering what new twists my brain will take.

One look at Nick's face wipes away my nerves. He's exhausted. "Shit. Why didn't you tell me how tired you were?" I reach up and cup his jaw. What time had he gotten up this morning?

He curls his fingers around my wrist. "Don't. I didn't know how much I needed tonight until you were here. I needed this as much as you did, the chance to shut down and do *nothing* for a few hours." He lets go. "Right now, though, I'm fuckin' beat, and I'm going to embarrass myself if I don't lie down in the next ten seconds."

He strips and climbs into bed, groaning softly when his head hits the pillow. His breathing is slow and deep by the time I return from the bathroom, but he seeks me out in his sleep, rousing himself enough to mutter and fumble until he finds me, fits himself to me, his face buried in my hair.

I wake the next morning with my head on his shoulder and his arm heavy around my waist. I don't want to move. If last night was a bubble of average, it's expanded into this morning, and moving will pop it. I can't ignore my bladder, though, and I reluctantly untangle myself and climb out of bed. After a quick visit to the bathroom, I find my new running clothes and slip them on, glancing at Nick as I bend over to tie my shoes.

He looks worn out, even in sleep. Sprawled on his back with two days worth of stubble coating his jaw, I want to crawl back into bed and cuddle him until the line between his brows disappears.

I leave him to sleep alone instead.

Constantine's not up yet, either, so I steal his keys again and work the one for the building off the key chain. I stick it into my pocket as I shut the door behind me. The elevator opens as I walk by, so I get in and punch the button for the lobby.

The lobby's empty as I step out of the elevator, sunlight slanting through the large windows in the front. I push open the door, letting the cool air rush over me. A quick scan of the street turns up nothing unusual, and after I do a few stretches, I pick a direction and start walking.

Before his house was firebombed, we got in a few more runs. I no longer want to die after three blocks, but I'm nowhere near where I was before. Anything over a mile, and my lungs are on fire. Satisfied my muscles won't cramp, I kick into a run and spend the next couple blocks monitoring my breathing.

The neighborhood is boring. It has no charm, no charisma, nothing to distract me while I jog along. It's a bunch of newer construction townhouses interspersed with apartment buildings, and even the storefronts are uninteresting. I pass a handful of people as I puff my way through the streets. They're young couples, moms with strollers, and toddlers desperately trying to get away, and about as captivating as the buildings around them. It's like I've stumbled into a hipster-yuppie enclave.

Tris, however, is not boring. Tris is back, and he's running with a lot more ease than I am. He's been following me since about three blocks from Constantine's building, and I see him behind me every time I pass a window. He's close enough to touch, but far enough away if I stop he won't run into me.

He doesn't speed up, doesn't turn off down some other street, just maintains the distance between us and keeps running. I cross the street, so does he. I stop to re-tie my shoe, he bends over and stretches his hamstrings.

It doesn't make a bit of sense, and it's driving me nuts. Someone told him to follow me. Nick knew who he was, but Tris didn't leave when Nick showed up. So it's highly unlikely Nick has him on babysitting duty. Which leaves Isaiah. Is this his newest plan? To drive me nuts by wondering why I'm being followed?

It's brilliant. It's also working.

Nick's up and in the kitchen staring blankly at the coffee pot when I walk in. I set the key on the counter, grab a glass from the cupboard, and fill it at the sink.

"How long?"

I lick my lips, grateful he's not chastising me for going out by myself. "Almost two miles. After about the fifteenth block, my lungs wanted to collapse." I refill the glass and sip it slowly. "Tris was out there. Following me. Not at some great distance, either. He was maybe a hundred feet behind me the entire time. Never came any closer." I take another sip. "Do you think Isaiah's trying to screw with our heads?"

He frowns into his coffee. "Don't know that Tris following you twice equals a new plan on Isaiah's part, though it's a possibility. He's proven a lot smarter than we've given him credit for." He winces as he swallows. "This coffee tastes like shit."

"Then buy better shit," Constantine says, coming into the kitchen. He pours a mug for himself and takes a careful sip. "Shit. This does taste awful." He puts the mug aside and points at Nick. "You need to talk to Cory this morning. Guy's about to lose it."

The two of them walk out of the room, arguing some point, and I head for the guest room and the shower. If I'm lucky, the registrar's office will still be open, even though the semester ended a few days ago.

I'm halfway through my shower when the bathroom door opens. There's a rustling noise, and then the shower curtain slides back. Nick steps into the tub.

I clutch my loofah to my chest. "Problems?"

He reaches behind me for the soap. "Cory's dead." He runs the bar over his arms, across his chest, and I try not to stare. It's hard, though. He's naked and wet and *right there*. "Found with a bullet in his brain three blocks from his apartment."

He blows out a breath. "Bad enough Isaiah's going after my guys and you. But now he's taking out people who aren't connected to the family?"

That answers one question. Cory's not a member of the Kosta organization. "What did Cory do?"

He swaps out soap for shampoo, and I resume cleaning myself. "He oversaw transitions once a sale was finalized. He's done it plenty of times before. Knew nothing about what else went on, or if he did, he kept his mouth shut."

We dry off and head to the bedroom to get dressed. Nick turns to me. "Come with me today."

I shake my head. "I need to stop by the registrar's office. Besides, you're going to be talking business or strategy or both, right? I won't have much to add to the conversation." This had better not be about keeping me safe, or I might have to hit him.

"Come with me today," he repeats quietly. "I need… I need you to see this. More of this. How everything fits together. I need you to see who I trust so if you ever get stuck and I'm not around, you know who to go to besides Con."

Constantine said something about how I was already in deeper than any of Nick's previous women. I didn't want to read too much into it before. Now? Now I'll take any scrap I can.

I nod. "I need a few more minutes, then we can go."

Chapter 15

Watching Nick work is a lesson in frustration, and judging by the look on his face, I'm not the only one feeling it. He's met with three different men so far this morning, all of whom gave me a brief once-over and dismissed me.

Nick has his head in his hands when someone knocks on the door. "Come in," he growls. The door opens and Surfer Dude walks in. He stops short when he sees me on the couch.

For a moment, I think he's going to do the same thing the other men did—scan and ignore. After darting a look at Nick, he surprises me by coming over. "Peter."

I get up from my seat and shake his hand. "Cass."

Nick arches a brow and motions us both toward him. I follow Peter to the chairs in front of the desk.

"Beta testing's going well," Peter says. "Errors occur about ten percent of the time on Android devices. Cory's assistant forwarded me the data he'd collected, and I think we can locate the problem and duplicate it."

It takes me a few seconds to understand they're talking about work, actual work, and to remember Cory was the man found dead this morning. It also tells me that Peter must be someone Nick relies on quite a bit if he's involved in both sides of the business.

Nick shoves a hand through his hair. "Good. First good news I've heard today." He scratches out a note to himself on a sticky pad. "Timeline for the fix?"

"Day or two, three at the most." Peter shoots me another sidelong glance. "Bas reported in. They were able to locate the apartment Isaiah was using. Gone now, nothing inside to clue us in where he might have moved to."

Nick swears. "Have Bas keep on it. The fucker can't hide forever." I open my mouth to protest and snap it shut with a *click* of my teeth. He levels a blank stare at me. "What?"

I shake my head. "Nothing." If Constantine were here, I'd question Nick in a heartbeat. But as engaging as Peter's been, he's an unknown, and I can't trust him simply because Nick does.

"Cassidy."

I shoot him a look that says *really? You want to do this here?* He motions for me to continue, and I straighten my shoulders. "Why is Isaiah still out there? You've got all these men looking for him, and it seems the only one who's come close to finding him is sitting right next to me." I jerk a thumb at Peter. "And I haven't heard anything about what's going to happen to him once he *is* found."

"The family's gotten too big." Peter shakes his head when Nick turns his scary face on him. "You know it, Dom. You've known for a while."

Nick's mouth firms into a thin line. "Nothing I can do about it."

"You mean Andreas doesn't want to listen."

I've heard that song before. I even know all the words. But I need to be sure. "Does he even *care* that Isaiah's instigating a mutiny?"

"Isaiah's using the structural flaw to his advantage." Peter stretches out his legs like he's preparing to be here for a while. "If Andreas had taken the multiple suggestions to slim down the family, there might not have been so many people willing to listen to Isaiah."

"Anton agrees with him," Nick spits out.

Peter groans, and I frown. "Who's Anton again? And why does his opinion matter more than others?"

"Anton is Con's dad. My uncle. He's Dad's strategy guy." The only outward sign of Nick's displeasure is the tightness in his jaw.

I search for a metaphor that'll make sense to everyone in the room. "So Anton is Tom Hagen." Peter snorts out a laugh, and even Nick cracks a grin. I slot the new information in beside what I already know of Nick's family. "What I'm hearing," I say slowly, "is that I'd be better off not trusting anyone." Nick shuts his eyes briefly as I push to my feet. "I need to get going if I'm going to replace my ID."

He digs into his pocket and holds out his keys. "We'll figure it out, Cass." I nod and turn to the door, stopping when Peter puts a hand on my arm.

"You need something and you can't find Nick, you can come to me." His expression is earnest, and I believe he means it. But I can't just trust someone because they say I can.

"Find out where Isaiah's hiding, and maybe I will." I walk to the door and let myself out.

I take the stairs to the garage. Once I reach the bottom, I scan the dimly lit space before hurrying to Nick's car. He had the foresight to park near the stairs. After the recent gun fight in the other parking garage, I'm surprised he's willing to park in one at all.

The black sedan idling at the curb is far too easy to spot, especially when it pulls into traffic right behind me. Whoever's driving isn't hiding the fact he's tailing me. Blocks pass, and he doesn't bother to let a few cars slip between us. It's probably Tris. Since he hasn't approached me so far, I don't try to lose him.

Traffic sucks. I hit every red light between Nick's office and the UCLA campus, some of them twice because I can't make it through on the first try. The black car passes as I find a parking spot in the surprisingly crowded lot. With classes over for the semester and finals winding down, there shouldn't be so many cars around.

Although, if that means campus will be busier, I'm okay with that.

The shady walkway is empty as I hurry to the registrar's office, and I take a moment to scan the lawn, checking for Tris among the students relaxing on the grass. He's nowhere to be found. I pull out my phone, shoot a text to Nick to let him know I'm on campus and another one to Denise before I can talk myself out of it. Her unresponsiveness makes me anxious. I keep telling myself she's still mad about all the lies I've told, and that's why she hasn't texted back. I feel slightly better after Bas checked on her, but I wish she'd at least respond.

I wasn't sure if the office would actually be open, but it is, and there's no line. I get a new ID printed and move on to one of the older women sitting behind a desk.

She's perfected the look down the nose, peering at me over the tops of half-glasses, the kind used for reading. "You understand that should you withdraw in the middle of the next term, you are running a serious academic risk?"

"I was in the hospital for two weeks and recuperating for a month. I don't anticipate that happening again." Unless, of course, Isaiah steps up his game and manages to catch me unawares, which is always a possibility.

She pushes the necessary forms across the desk and watches as I complete them. I spend the next half hour picking classes for the next semester, annoyed when several I need to complete my degree are full. I manage to find enough credits to give me a full schedule. Nick's definitely not talking me out of returning to class. I'm finishing this degree. He'll just have to deal.

Stepping into the bright sunshine, I debate swinging by the Grateful Bread to pick up more cinnamon rolls when someone calls out my name.

Scott jogs up, a smile on his face, and I stifle a pang of guilt. The boy visited me while I was in the hospital. He'd obviously seen the glowering hulk of a man at my bedside, and yet he stuck around and made me laugh, then called me a few times while I was in Thailand. He deserves the best. Far better than I could give him, at least, regardless of whether Nick was in the picture.

"Hey, you." Will hugging him give him the wrong idea? I hope not. Scott gives excellent hugs. I launch myself at him, and after a long moment, he returns the hug. "What? I'm not good enough to hug anymore?"

He glances around. "No, just not sure your boyfriend would be cool with it."

"If Nick has a problem, he'll have to deal with it. Besides, he's at work." Probably still growling in anger as his men report nothing of use. "Are you free? Do you want to grab some coffee?"

"Depends. I don't have to worry about him swooping in and dragging you off?"

Where the hell did he get these ideas about Nick? "I think we really need some coffee. Come on." Not giving him a chance to escape, I loop my arm through his and steer him down the walkway and off campus to the Grateful Bread. I can get my caffeine fix and cinnamon rolls at the same time.

After we've settled into our chairs outside the bakery, I give him a pointed look. "So. My boyfriend has been intimidating my friends into staying away from me?"

He sips his coffee before answering. "Maybe that's the wrong word. He didn't stop anyone from coming in who wanted to see you, but he didn't look happy about it." After tearing open another packet of sugar, he dumps it into the cup and stirs. "Honestly, Cass? I'm worried about you with him."

I pause mid-bite into my cinnamon roll. "What? Why?" The questions are muffled by the layers of dough, so they come out sounding more like "Wumph? Hwyh?" He grins, and I swallow the bite. "You know, Neese said almost the same thing. He's never hurt me, and what happened a month ago is not his fault." It's not anyone's, really.

A couple of women out for a run pass by our table, their breathless conversation loud enough to be heard halfway down the block. Scott half-turns in his seat to follow their progress. I kick him in the shin, and he turns back to me with a grin. "So, you coming back to class next semester?" he asks.

"Yeah. All registered and everything. You graduate this semester, right?" Scott had taken summer classes the last two summers, setting him free from the school grind a few months earlier.

"Bet your ass I am." His brows draw together, and he drops his gaze to his coffee cup. "Sometimes I wish I hadn't taken those extra classes, though."

Suddenly, he jerks backward, coffee spilling over his hands, and a dark splotch appears and spreads on the right side of his chest, close to his shoulder. His eyes go wide, and some of the color leaves his face.

My brain locks down and clears away the extraneous noise, giving me the speed and room to process what's happening. Blood. It's blood. Someone shot Scott. My chair lands with a clatter of metal on cement as I scramble out of it, pulling Scott to the ground.

No one is screaming. No one is running, crying, or whipping their heads about rapidly, trying to figure out what's going on. No one's doing a damn thing except for Scott. Scott's bleeding. With steady hands, I rip off my sweater and press it to his shoulder. "Scotty?"

He blinks once, twice, slow and dazed. "Cass?"

The shock will help. It'll keep him from registering how badly it hurts, at least for the next minute or so.

"Oh my God!"

Finally, someone's noticed something's wrong. The redhead's standing a few feet away, mouth wide open and her phone in her hand. I jerk my head toward it. "Can you call 911?"

Her head bobs up and down in a puppet-jolt motion, but it takes her a good ten seconds to actually raise the phone and dial. If I wasn't so worried about blood loss, I'd have called myself. It would have gotten done faster.

"Cass?" Scott pats my arm, an absent movement, and he twists his head to the side and bucks, vomiting onto the sidewalk. I glance away, stomach clenching in sympathy. I will *not* be sick. I've seen worse. I've *done* worse. I can handle this.

Worse takes on a whole new meaning when the blood on your hands belongs to someone you know.

I reach under his body and shift him onto his side, probably pressing his face right into the mess he's made, but it's better than potentially choking to death. He coughs wetly a few more times, and then he groans. "Want to sit up? Help should be here soon."

He groans again, and I maneuver him into a sitting position. The redhead seems to have moved past her morbid horror and gone inside the bakery because she returns a minute later with a damp towel. "Here." She tries to hand it to me, and I lift a brow, shooting a pointed glance at my hands, still holding my sweater in place over the wound. She swallows hard and crouches on his other side, gingerly wiping his face clean. "Um. The 911 woman said police are on their way."

A siren wails in the distance the second the words leave her mouth. Scott's a little sweaty and a lot gray. The pain he's in is easy to imagine. I remember the dull, radiating heat of Isaiah's knife wound all too well. The redhead rambles at Scott, patting his hand in an awkward bounce until he finally curls his fingers around it, and she stills.

I study the table. Scott and I were almost directly across from each other, Scott a little closer to the edge of the street. The force of the bullet pushed him away from the table, so it likely came from behind me. Whoever fired was a lousy shot. Another few inches to the left and the bullet would have lodged itself in me, not him.

Or.

Or.

Or maybe I'm not the intended target. Maybe it was Scott all along. I scan the street, looking for Tris. He's nowhere to be seen.

It fits, as much as anything fits with Isaiah's new pattern that isn't a pattern. Following me but making no contact. Threatening me by stalking my best friend and her boyfriend. Now taking potshots at whomever I happen to be with? If I wanted to throw someone off, that's what I'd do.

Apparently knowing me has become a dangerous thing. My chest tightens and my stomach drops as I reach the conclusion I hoped to avoid. I have to tell Denise the truth. It's the only thing that might get her out of this mess unharmed.

An ambulance rolls to a stop at the sidewalk, and paramedics tumble out, one of them hurrying over where we're huddled on the sidewalk while the other moves to the back and opens the doors. I'm nudged out of the way as the first paramedic takes over, and I sit on the ground nearby, anger coming to a slow boil in my blood.

Isaiah is a dead man.

Chapter 16

Hospitals exist in this weird pocket of time, where everything is speeding up and slowing down all at once. The paramedics won't let me ride in the back with Scott, but they allow me to ride up front, and we roll into the loading bay at UCLA Medical Center in a matter of minutes.

After that, everything's at warp speed. Scott's wheeled into a curtained-off area, and a nurse stays with me to find out what happened while people in scrubs crowd around his gurney. She takes the information and points me toward a restroom where I can wash the blood from my hands.

If I were normal, I wouldn't have made it out of the bathroom. I'd be curled in a ball on the floor, whimpering and rocking back and forth, and the guilt that's starting to encroach would have taken over completely. But I'm not normal. I can push that guilt into a corner to deal with later. I can hold myself together until I have time to break down. Nick's right. I'm not normal, I doubt I ever will be, and it's about fucking time I start accepting it.

So I wash my hands, march out of the restroom, and head for the waiting room.

My phone buzzes against my hip, and I pull it out, checking the screen. It's Nick, probably wanting to know why I haven't returned his car. "Hey."

"Cass? Are"—dead air—"done?"

Damn hospitals. "Hold on." I wind through the waiting area and step outside, squinting into the sun. "Sorry, crappy reception. What did you say?"

"Wanted to know if you were still on campus. If you are, I can have Con drop me off, and we can grab something to eat."

I scoot farther from the entrance as another ambulance pulls up. "Constantine should drop you on campus so you can pick up your car.

I'm at the hospital right now, and I don't have any way of getting back to the car other than walking."

He's quiet for so long I pull the phone away from my ear to check to see if we're still connected. "Nick?"

"You can't say something like that and just leave me hanging."

I wince. "Sorry. I'm fine. Scott was shot. I came with him. I should get back inside. They'll probably be taking him up to surgery soon." Since I'm not family, I doubt the staff will tell me much, but I need to be there for Scott.

The redhead from earlier wanders into view, and I wave her down. "I need to go," I tell Nick.

"Text me the location of the car." He doesn't *sound* pissed. He doesn't sound happy, either.

We hang up as the girl stops in front of me, shifting her weight onto her back foot. "Hi?" Her fingers curl tight around the strap of her messenger bag. "Um. I'm Tori. Victoria. Tori. Call me Tori." A blush sweeps over her cheeks.

I manage a smile because she looks like she needs it. "Cass. Are you here for Scott?"

She nods. "Is that his name? I thought..." She looks at the door. "I thought I'd see how he was doing."

"I think they're going to be taking him up to surgery soon, if they haven't done so already." She pales, but before she can stumble away and babble an excuse, I grab her hand. "Come on. I was about to go inside."

Scott's being wheeled out to the elevators when we return, and his bleary gaze drifts past me to Tori. He perks up, and his mouth curves in a grin before the door closes, leaving the two of us standing in a fluorescent-lit hallway.

I gesture to the call buttons. "Do you want to come up and wait with me?" She slides a glance at the waiting area, her body tensed to leave. Crap. I should have just let her go. She doesn't owe Scott, or me, anything. "Or if you need to go, I understand."

Waiting for her answer is strangely agonizing. Scott's in surgery. He'll be there for a while. Me sitting around waiting for him to come *out* of surgery isn't going to change the outcome. But my calm is eroding the longer I stand here. I need to be up there. He took that bullet because he was with me. If he hadn't been, he'd still be whole. My guilt's reached a whole new level in the space of an hour.

"Yeah," she says softly. "I'll come with you."

I punch the button, and we stare at the doors like doing so will magically make them open. I'm grateful to Tori for distracting Scott and being concerned enough about his wellbeing to follow up. But I don't know what to do with her. I don't know how to act or what to say. I can't say with absolute certainty that bullet was intended for Scott. I can't say it wasn't, either.

We don't speak as we step inside or while we ride to the surgery floor. I cast about for something to say. If I'm talking, I'm not trapped in my own head, waiting for the guilt to crush me.

"Thanks for your help earlier," I say.

The elevator doors open, and we make our way to the waiting area. The space isn't the most welcoming with the standard doctor's office decor and brilliant, blinding overhead lights. Our shoes squeak on the linoleum. Tori chooses a chair with a view of the long hallway to the restricted double doors. "You're welcome. Um. Do you think he'll be okay?"

"It was his right shoulder, and he was conscious the whole time. There'll be blood loss and risk of infection, definitely some rehab to regain full use, but he'll be fine." Probably. Turner's training didn't just focus on the best places on the body to ensure a mortal wound.

Tori stares at me. "How do you know?"

It's on the tip of my tongue to lie and say "pre-med," but I can't. "The heart's on the other side of the chest, and there's no major arteries in that spot, either. The worst thing that could happen is he'll lose some functionality in his arm."

She's still wide-eyed, and I shift in my seat. "What's your major?"

A long moment passes before she answers. "Accounting." She drops her gaze to her hands and picks at one of her fingernails. "Are you and Scott, like, together or anything?"

I shake my head. "No. We're just friends." Speaking of friends, Denise will be furious if I don't tell her what's happened. "Do you mind if I leave you here for a minute? I need to call someone."

She flaps her hand. "Sure."

I hightail it out of the waiting area for the stairs. The cinderblock walls throw sounds back at me, my footsteps loud as I pace the small landing while I wait for Denise to pick up.

The call goes to voicemail, and a niggle of irritation sneaks through. "Neese, it's me. Scott's at UCLA in surgery. He was shot, but I think he'll be fine. I know you're probably still mad at me for lying, but if you could—" My breath catches, and I suck in air. "I'd really like it if you could be here. At least for Scott." I hang up before I start bawling and tuck the phone back in my pocket.

I hate this unease, this not knowing what's going on inside Denise's head. I used to know what she was thinking before she said it, and I never had to wonder if she'd return my call. Since that night at El Dorado, though, she hasn't responded to any of my communication attempts.

Without her, I'm afraid I'll lose my grasp on Cass the College Student and remain Cass the Assassin.

I'm afraid I'll end up like my father, unwilling to show affection or emotion.

Tori's in the same place I left her in, her hands clasped in her lap. She looks up when I plop down on the short couch next to her chair. "How are you so calm? I don't know him, and I'm a mess."

At first glance, she looks fine. A second pass proves otherwise. Her mouth is tight, and her hands are knotted so hard together the knuckles are white. "I guess I'm used to this sort of thing," I say slowly.

She peers at me. "Used to it? This happens a lot?"

"No. Not to my friends. This is a first. I just… Violence isn't anything new in my life." If that line gets back to Scott or Denise, I'll have a hell of a lot of explaining to do.

Aside from not being sure how she'll react, I haven't told Denise for legal reasons. If she knowingly withholds information about a crime, regardless of evidence, she could end up in trouble. She might be a stranger, but Tori deserves the same courtesy.

Rubber squeaks across the floor, and a tall, dark-haired man comes into view. I'm not surprised to see it's Nick. What is surprising is the look on his face. It's completely devoid of anger and the frantic concern I've become accustomed to since I almost bled out on the floor of the parking garage. There's concern, yes, but it's almost nonexistent in comparison.

"Still in surgery?" he asks when he sits beside me.

"Just went in. It'll probably be a while, but I couldn't get much information on his condition before he went in. He was conscious. That's about it."

He regards me steadily, then leans forward and presses a kiss to my forehead. "Let me see if I can get anything out of them." He gets to his feet and walks over to the nurse's station.

"Holy shit, is that Dominic Kosta?" Tori hisses. I whip my head toward her, and she's gaping after him. "You know Dominic Kosta? You're *dating* Dominic Kosta?"

Her reaction is strange. "Um, yeah. Why?" Most people seem to ignore Nick, as much as it's possible to ignore someone who has enough presence for ten people. Nick's not someone you disregard.

"You mean aside from he's got the fastest growing technology conglomeration in the city, he's also one of the hottest men in a city full of them." She stares after him with something like hero worship on her face. "And you're dating him. Wow."

Learning more about Nick's business, his legal business, has moved to the top of my list of things to learn about Nick. If he's as important as Tori seems to think he is, being with him will put me in the spotlight in more ways than one.

He comes back and takes a seat next to me, wrapping an arm around my shoulders and cuddling me into his side. I immediately stop shivering, something I didn't know I was doing until tension rushes from my body, replaced by warmth. "What happened to the sweater you were wearing earlier?" he asks.

"I had to use it on Scott's shoulder."

He lets go and leans forward, holding out a hand to Tori. "Dominic Kosta."

"T-T-Tori. Um. Tori Sutherland." Her mouth hangs open a little, but then snaps shut with a *click*, her cheeks turning red.

"Nice to meet you, Tori." He gives her that slick, devastating smile, the one that used to make my knees disappear until he started smiling at me with a warmth that crept into the cracks in my soul. His arm goes back around my shoulders, and I stifle a sigh, tipping my head onto his shoulder. One finger at a time, I'm losing my grasp on the hard, impenetrable ice I needed to get through the shooting. It's something that only used to happen at the ocean, the gradual slip and slide of the pieces of me reordering themselves.

It happens more and more with Nick around when there's no ocean in sight.

"Cass?" Denise walks up, clutching Charlie's hand, and the ice breaks completely. I jump up and throw my arms around her, so relieved she came I'll probably start wailing in a second.

She digs her fingers into my back, holding on as tight as I am. Eventually we draw apart, and she does a double-take at Nick seated on the couch. "Hi, Nick," she says, caution dripping from the words.

"Denise. Good to see you." Again he holds out his hand, this time to Charlie. "Dominic Kosta."

Charlie glances at his girlfriend before taking Nick's hand. "Charlie Parker."

Nick's mouth quirks up. "Like the trumpet player?"

Charlie scowls. "Yes."

Denise and I share a giggle, and she sits next to him. "Charlie's a recovering jazz musician. Seems living up to the Birdman was too much for him." She bats her lashes at him, and Charlie turns his scowl on her.

I take my seat next to Nick and gesture to Tori. "Tori, this is Denise and Charlie. Denise is my roommate and another friend of Scott's." Nick stiffens at the word *roommate*, so I pick up his free hand and thread my fingers through his. They exchange greetings, and Nick relaxes once more.

He rubs his thumb along the back of my hand. "They'll only release information on Scott's condition to family, so other than what Cass knows, we'll have to wait for Scott to get out of surgery."

I figured as much. I fill Nick, Denise, and Charlie in on what'd I'd seen of Scott's wound, and we settle in to wait. At one point, Nick and I switch places so he can quiz Tori on her courses. Beyond her awe, the girl is ecstatic. I'd be jealous if I wasn't glad it gave me the chance to talk to Denise and Charlie about their Christmas break plans.

"So you're going to Colorado for the break?" Please, please go to Colorado for the break. Please get out of the city and away from the men with knives and guns and other implements of death.

She nods, a hint of sadness in her eyes. "I'm going to miss Christmas with my family, but I want this." Charlie kisses her temple, and she smiles. "And we'll have to get used to it, anyway, being away from family."

I frown. "Why?"

She pulls on her lower lip. "Charlie's applied for a graduate program at Cambridge. If he gets in, I'm going with him."

Change is inevitable. That doesn't make it any less stunning. Denise is leaving me to deal with life after college alone? I was prepared for her to move in with Charlie, but part of that preparation was knowing she'd still be in the same city. Cambridge is not the same city.

But she'll be safer thousands of miles away.

"You should come visit. We'll hit the pubs and ride the Tube and see plays and the Tower of London and Shakespeare's house and the Globe...." Denise's gaze drops to her lap. "We're ready for this, Cass," she says quietly. And when she looks up, I understand she's not just talking about her and Charlie making a move that's tantamount to marriage.

It's time we went our separate ways too.

The knife doesn't hurt as much as I'd thought it would. Maybe it's all the years I've spent keeping part of the truth from her, or maybe it's the past month or so that has given us the space we need to grow, and grow up. She'll always be my bestest, closest friend, but already I'm making room for others. Lia. Constantine.

Nick. Nick who can hear everything I have to say, if only I have the courage to say it.

The doctor pushes through the double doors, and we straighten as one. Nick's arm drops over my shoulders once more, and Tori inches to the edge of her seat.

"Are any of you family?" the doctor asks. He swipes the cap from his head and runs his fingers through his hair.

Nick stands and approaches the doctor, the two of them stepping off to the side, while the four of us stare at them. How's he going to pull this one off? Nick can be charming, extremely so, when he wants to be. But this guy's a surgeon. He's immune to charm. Plus, he's male, and likely straight.

After some headshakes and rapid gestures, they come back and Nick sits, taking my hand in his. "We have to wait for Scott to wake up. He can't tell us anything."

I turn to the surgeon. "But he came through the surgery okay?"

The doctor nods. "Once he's out of recovery, you'll be able to see him."

He leaves, and I lean in and kiss Nick on the cheek. "Thanks for trying."

He trails his fingers over my cheekbone. "We can stick around until you can see him, but we need to talk," he says, a hard, greedy edge in his voice.

And every nerve ending in my body sits up and takes notice.

Chapter 17

Nick doesn't say much after we leave the hospital. Aside from telling me where he's parked and a few questions to ascertain I'm okay, he's silent. He still doesn't seem angry or overly concerned and protective, though.

His lack of response should have been my first clue something's up.

He drives back to Constantine's. Before he unlocks the front door, he turns to me. "Pack a bag," he says quietly. The low, dark tone glides through me, the three words setting me on edge.

Pack a bag. A few of the least sexy words in existence, and Nick manages to make them sound like a threat and a promise.

I nod and head straight to the guest room. How long will this captivity last? We need some alone time. Whenever we manage to steal some, it gets interrupted. He has to be taking me to the condo. I hope so. I seriously hope so. Because if he's dragging me off somewhere just to yell at me, I'm going to be disappointed I didn't go in armed.

I throw a couple changes of clothes in a bag and grab my toiletries from the bathroom. Nick's gone silent again as he moves around the room, tossing clothes in a bag, ducking into the bathroom to retrieve his toothbrush.

The ride is torture. His words hang between us, sucking all the air from the car. And damn him, he's back to the serpentine maneuvers, trying to avoid a tail. Which confirms what I guessed: we're going to Manhattan Beach, and Nick wants me alone.

Over an hour later, he's growling and his hands are clenched tight on the steering wheel as he pulls into the underground garage. "Upstairs," he spits out. Like I'm going to argue.

The instant the door shuts behind us my back is against it, his hands at my hips to hold me in place. The heat of his mouth on mine is a shock, one I thought I was prepared for. I'm not. Seconds in, and I know whatever leash he's on has snapped.

This is who he was all those days and nights he spent at my side while I was tied to a hospital bed. This is who he was when he lay next to me in Thailand, when I ached for his touch and knew I couldn't handle it.

I'm not sure I can handle it now.

His mouth punishes mine and rewards it, feeding me molten kisses. The fire sparks and spreads, and I need his hands everywhere. I need *him* everywhere. His mouth on my skin, his hands on my ass, his cock buried inside me.

He growls again, and I shift against him, straining for more.

Then he backs away. And stares. His gaze is a vicious, black thing, the lines of his face tight with hunger. His hands clench into fists.

"Nick?" What's going on? He looks like he wants to devour me, and holding himself back is torture.

"Bedroom. Strip."

From the way he trapped me there as we walked into the condo, I imagined ripping clothes and clawing hands, teeth, and nails, and Nick taking me against the door. There's still violence in his eyes. But it's not on his face or vibrating through his body. He's thrown up a wall, and while it's barely holding everything back, it's there where it wasn't before.

Trepidation slinks in as I make my way to the bedroom and toe off my shoes. I keep my clothes on, though. Nick stops just inside the doorway. I go to him and run my hands up his chest to his neck.

I was wrong. So very, very wrong. He's rigid with anger. He's just doing a damn good job of making me think he's okay. "You're scaring me." It's only a half-truth. I don't know that I could ever be scared of Nick, but his behavior is...concerning.

His mouth curves into a smile that doesn't reach his eyes. "Liar." He reaches up and clasps my wrist, bringing it to his mouth before he takes my hand and leads me to the bed. "You can't seem to stay out of the line of fire, can you?"

"It's a gift," I quip. He sits on the edge of the bed, and I straddle his lap, looping my arms around his neck. "Are you okay?"

He studies my face for a moment, his fingers worming their way under my shirt. "I need you. More than I realized. And it kills me I can't keep you safe, that I can't get rid of the source of the problem."

I have no words. None. He's taken them all. I don't want to be needed. *Need* is such a heavy burden.

He tips his forehead to mine. "I need you tonight, Cass."

I can't deny him this. Whatever feelings he's got for me, it's rooted in sex. It's how we tell each other the things we don't have words for. And if this is how he'll know that everything's going to be okay, this is how we'll do it. "Whatever you want."

He grins, the spark of it warming his face. "Careful there, love. I could take unfair advantage of you."

I press my mouth to his. "You won't."

He slicks his tongue over my lower lip. "A challenge. Perfect." His hands leave my hips, and he threads his fingers through my hair. "I mean it, though. I need you. And I'll take everything you've got tonight."

My answer's lost to his mouth, his careful, seeking mouth, a total one-eighty from the kisses he demanded earlier. There's sweetness and uncertainty and affection and lust, tangling together and tangling me up so I can't breathe. His tongue rubs along mine, and he strokes his hands through my hair and down my back to pull at the hem of my shirt. "Clothes off," he says quietly.

I inch my shirt up and over my head, and he unclasps my bra before drawing it aside. He steadies me as I slide off his lap, unbutton my jeans, and push them down my legs. Then I'm left in nothing but my panties, my healed scars on display.

The way he looks at me makes me forget about them for the moment. Everything I want to hear from him is right there on his face, and I don't need the words. "Turn around," he says hoarsely, getting to his feet.

I shake my head. "I need to see you." I slip my hands under his shirt, and he pulls it off. His skin's so warm, so familiar now. His abs ripple under my fingertips as they glide down to the waistband of his jeans. A tug, a flip, and the fly's undone. I curl my fingers into the stiff fabric and push them over his hips. He steps out of his pants, leaving him in his boxers.

Stretching up on my tiptoes, I kiss him, swaying as he grasps my hips. He shifts to splay his hands over my back, the tips of his fingers flexing and digging into my flesh. "Turn around, Cass. Please."

He nudges me away from him, ignoring my confusion. It disappears when he sweeps my hair over my shoulder and runs his hands over my skin, dropping kisses along the curve of my neck. They move with *purpose*. He's searching for something, but not finding it, and with every new inch he touches, his relief grows, turning those touches to caresses.

He strokes his hands around and up, cupping my breasts, rolling my nipples into tight, aching points. I pull free and spin around. "I'm okay," I whisper. I'm not hurt. I'm not bleeding.

We crawl onto the bed and reach for each other, mouths coming together like two parts of a whole. He scrapes his teeth over my lower lip, nips into it. Braced above me, hips notched against mine, he breaks me down, his mouth crumbling the last of my shoddy defenses.

I love you. I can't tear my mouth away long enough to breathe, let alone say it. It doesn't matter. My ability to think clearly is fading as the air grows heavy and the heat rises. I rub my lips over his stubble-roughened jaw, groaning when he rocks into me. Over and over, the hard ridge of his cock presses into my clit. Constant shocks of pleasure radiate outward.

I have to touch him. I need to put my mouth on him, know he's falling apart because of *me*.

I push at his shoulders, bowing up when the movement presses my clit harder against his cock. I'm throbbing now. Where release wasn't necessary before, now I can't stop until I've reached it. I buck under him, and he grabs my hips, rocking faster, faster, faster still, and then I fall apart on a moan.

He nuzzles my throat, holding my limp body close. "Again," he murmurs.

He's kissing his way down my body while my brain's trying to re-engage. He finds every hidden spot and works it over so I'm squirming and writhing. Curling his fingers around the sides of my panties, he pulls them off, trailing kisses down my legs. This isn't how this goes. It's my turn. "Nick—"

"Shhh." He licks me, one broad, flat stroke of his tongue, and we both groan. "*Jesus*, Cass." He traces the folds with the tip of his tongue, dipping inside and flicking over my clit. When my hips jerk and squirm of their own accord, he flattens his forearm across my hips and holds me down, plunging his fingers into me.

Then he sucks. Hard.

There's no pattern or rhythm to it as he makes love to me with his mouth. His kisses are as thorough and hot as they are on my lips, and when he twists his fingers and scissors them apart, my hips shoot off the bed, heedless of the hold he has.

I lace my fingers through his hair and pull. "Up here. Inside me. I need you inside me, Nick." The next time I come, I want him to feel it. I want it to push him over the edge.

He sheds his boxers and crawls up my body. With one hard thrust, he pushes into me. "I love you," I whisper, the words catching on the jagged edges in my throat. He's surrounding me again, the thick, hard length of him perfect inside me, holding me tight and pushing the air from my lungs. It's okay. I don't need the words. I need this more, this ability to reassure him I'm whole, I'm alive, and I'm here with him, always.

"Tell me again."

"I love you."

"Again." He punctuates the word with a roll of his hips, and we go back and forth, sweat beading and slipping, the space between us so slim you can't fit a sheet of paper there. Every undulation brings us closer to the breaking point, his thrusts shallow, his hips circling in that way he knows drives me insane.

"*Cassidy.*" Another hip roll. "Do you know what you do to me?" He takes my mouth, a sweet, sweet kiss that adds to the roaring inferno inside.

Just when I think I can't handle anymore, that something has to give, it does, splintering into a thousand tiny shards. Over the roaring in my ears, Nick groans, low and long, his body rigid with pleasure.

He's shaking when it's over, his breath coming in harsh pants. He kisses my forehead and shifts off me. I manage to push myself up and head for the bathroom. I return a minute later and stretch out beside him.

He plays with the ends of my hair as I trace hearts all over his chest. "I'm never going to get used to it." Despite how quiet they are, his words echo in the space between us. "Once Isaiah's no longer a threat, there'll be a new one. Either to you, or me, or both of us. It may not be right away. It may be years from now."

Of all the things we could talk about after sex, he picks the topic guaranteed to kill the mood. My post-orgasm glow is basically gone. I lift my head. "You suck at pillow talk, Dominic."

One dark brow rises. "Dominic?"

I'm pissed. His full name felt appropriate. I sit up. "There's no food here, I'm guessing. What are we doing about dinner?"

Nick's got me pinned to the mattress in a heartbeat. "You could destroy me," he says softly, his tone at odds with the intensity in his eyes. "If something happens to you, if Isaiah or someone else tries and succeeds in killing you, fuck, even hurting you, I will be *done*." He presses his thumb to my lower lip. "I love you."

My heart stops. *I love you.* The words echo in my head. He loves me. Nick loves me. He *loves* me. Despite everything that's happened, the age gap, the violence, my increasing doubts, he loves me. What's here is staggering and beyond anything I've felt before. "What?"

His lips find mine. "I love you," he murmurs against them.

"Again."

He smiles. "I love you."

The kisses ignite, and by the time we manage to leave the bedroom, my legs don't work properly anymore. I curl up on the couch and try not to fall asleep while Nick orders Chinese.

"How long are we staying here?" I ask when he joins me on the couch, picking me up and moving me into his preferred position, my back to his front.

"A day at least."

I twist around to stare at him. Staying here is like taking ten steps back. It's a retreat, and it leaves Constantine vulnerable. "Are you going to work tomorrow?"

"No. We're getting you outfitted for weapons."

Plural. "I've already got a gun."

"And you need a new blade. Two, preferably." He rubs his thumb over my lower lip. "I'd lock you in here if I thought you'd stay." He laughs at my scowl. "And that's why I won't."

"Bossy and overbearing aren't attractive on you."

"Yet you love me anyway."

I do. I sniff and turn around, tipping my head back to rest on his shoulder. If we're picking out knives, I should think about stocking up on the rest of my supplies. Hit up the shooting range. "I'll need to get in touch with some of my contacts. I should check out that Krav Maga place Turner found.

"I wonder...." Maybe we're going about this all wrong. "Why are we always reacting? What are we doing wrong that's got Isaiah strutting around like he can defeat whole armies?"

Nick places a hand on mine and laces our fingers together. "Not whole armies, maybe, but he's got us on the defensive for the most part. Peter's right. The family's gotten too big, and Isaiah's using it to his advantage. Picture it like…a failing company. There aren't enough upper-level managers. Isaiah did what he was supposed to do, and the lack of oversight and his new position of power enabled him to whisper a few words in some well-placed ears."

"So we need to lure him out." I dig my teeth into my bottom lip. "He shot Scott. Because of me."

"That was my thinking, yes."

I squirm around to face him. "Scott wouldn't have been shot if he wasn't my friend."

Nick raises a brow. "He could have been shot walking down the street even if he wasn't your friend. It's LA. Crime happens."

Immature as it is, I can't stop myself from sticking my tongue out at him. "Yeah, but this happened because he had the bad fortune of knowing me. What if this is part of the plan? Distract me, make me think any one of my friends could be the real target, and we waste so much energy protecting the wrong people we're too late to save whoever he's really after?" We need to hit back, we need to hit him hard, and there's no room for error.

Our evening of us, and only us, in our hidey-hole, disappears. "We can't keep sitting around. We need a plan."

He sighs. "Yeah."

Chapter 18

The house reminds me of Nick's. It's a normal house with multiple bedrooms in Glendale. There's a tricycle in the driveway, and the neighbors have a swing set. The street's quiet in the mid-morning sun.

Nick stops at the end of the front walk and studies the house. "It's a house."

I roll my eyes. I was against him coming with me for this part, unsure how the doctor would react. "Very astute of you. Will you go back to the car?" We parked several streets away.

He doesn't bother responding, just continues his perusal. "You sure this is the place?" he asks.

"Very. Your house didn't look like it belonged to a member of LA's criminal underworld, did it?" He snorts and steps forward. I stop him with a hand on his arm. "Don't say anything. I mean it," I add at his raised eyebrow. "He doesn't know my real name. It gives him a measure of security, knowing he can tell the authorities he doesn't know who I am and he's actually telling the truth. So keep your mouth shut, and we'll be in and out soon enough."

He thins his mouth to a firm slash and slips his hands into his pockets, nodding for me to precede him.

Doctor Joe is a veterinarian, one of a couple Turner rotates between. When Turner first brought me to him, I'd just completed my first job. It was the one and only time I'd been to his house. The few exchanges we had after took place at a trendy cafe on Colorado Boulevard in Pasadena.

So when I texted him to ask for supplies, I was surprised when he told me to come to his house. Either he no longer cares if he's caught or he's getting sloppy.

I knock, and half a minute later the door swings open. Doctor Joe gives me a nod in greeting, then freezes when his gaze slides to Nick. "Can I help you?" His tone is polite, but every muscle in his body is tense.

Great. I *knew* I should have snuck out to handle this. "Do you want him to wait in the car?"

Doctor Joe gives Nick one last, long look and shakes his head. "No. Come in."

He leads us into the living room. Toys are strewn around one corner, and the shades are drawn. The vials sit on a scarred coffee table next to broken crayons and a couple of Legos.

Dealing with outside parties requires trust. It doesn't matter that no names are exchanged, no pertinent details passed on about lives or loves or why the hell a twenty-one-year-old woman needs multiple vials of potassium chloride. I have to trust that the person selling me the goods isn't about to rat me out, and he has to trust that I'm not setting him up or sending him up the river. It's a mutually distrustful trusting relationship.

Still…

"I'm surprised you asked me to come here," I say. The change in protocol is surprising, though not unexpected, I guess. He's a vet. He doesn't think like I do. He may very well just have been at home and decided to get it over with.

He shrugs. "Your request was unusual."

It's three vials, two more than what I normally ask for. I took a risk asking him for as many as he could spare, but I tell myself this is the last time I'll need it, the last time I'll contact him, the last time I'll see him. There's no reason for him to get burned because of my choices.

Nick lays the money on the table. Another point we argued over last night, him paying for my tools of destruction. His winning argument was he can hide large withdrawals of money from his accounts. While it looks like no one has found my offshore account, it's a risk he's not willing to take.

We still have several more stops to make—a few more vets, the shooting range, Nick's blade guy, as he calls him, plus my first Krav Maga session—but something keeps my ass glued to the couch. We're in Doctor Joe's house. In the middle of the day.

"Nick?"

He gets up without a word and walks to the front windows, twitching the curtains out of the way. "Black Toyota three houses to the left. Wasn't there when we came in." He turns to the vet. "Any of your neighbors drive a black Toyota Rav4? Newer model?"

Doctor Joe frowns. "Three houses down, you said? That's the Hatfields. No Toyota."

Nick takes out his phone and nudges the curtain aside. "Peter? Dom. Need you to run a plate for me. California plate B37IX9Y. Black Toyota Rav4."

"What's going on?" the doctor asks.

I pull my gaze away from Nick. Joe's face is pale and growing paler, his eyes darting between the front door and Nick.

"Not sure yet." I note the sweat forming at his hairline. "Nick should know shortly."

The good doctor nods, his attention drifting to the front door once again. I scoop up the vials and tuck them into my bag, then slip my phone free of its pocket and thumb off the lock, keeping it hidden in the depths of my purse. One eye on the vet, the other on my phone, I type a quick message to Nick. *Doc's acting funny.*

Nick's phone pings twice in quick succession. His expression remains cool and blank as he reads the messages. His thumbs fly over the surface as he taps out a reply.

My phone buzzes in my hand a second later. *Car's not one of mine or Con's. Head for the back door. NOW.*

I tuck the phone into its pocket and zip my purse. "Doctor Joe? Do you mind if I get a glass of water? We've got a long drive ahead of us, and I'm a little thirsty." I paste on a sunny smile, forcing my lips wider when he glances over.

"Uh. Sure. Glasses are in the cupboard next to the sink."

"Thanks." I sling my purse over my shoulder and pick my way through the living room, dodging toys and small shoes. In the kitchen, I find the glasses, fill one with water, and sip it slowly as I scan the backyard.

Empty. It won't be for long.

Doctor Joe's yard backs up to someone else's yard, separated by a chain-link fence. Easy to climb, thankfully. The lot to the right has a wooden fence. Harder to scale, but doable.

I set the glass on the counter and ease open the kitchen door, careful to stay close to the house as I step outside. Gauging the distance between the back of the house and the fence, I adjust my grip on my purse and hurry across the lawn to the fence.

The first shout rings out as I swing my leg over the top. I drop to the ground and take off at a dead run for the wooden fence. My flats slip on the wood, forcing me back to my feet. Cursing, I rip off my shoes, toss them and my purse over the top of the fence, back up, and try again.

A splinter digs itself into the ball of my foot, but I manage to haul myself up. I lower myself to the ground, wincing when I land. The backyard I'm in is completely fenced, so no one can see me. I take a minute to yank the splinter free, then slip on my shoes as a gunshot shatters the quiet.

That's my cue to get the hell out of here.

The next house has a wooden fence as well, plus a two-by-four near the bottom where the boards are nailed. I use it as a toehold and poke my head over the top, pausing to look around.

A second gunshot follows the first, and Nick rushes into Doctor Joe's backyard. I boost myself up and over the fence, then head for the gate.

My heart's thudding loud enough it vibrates in my ears. I ease open the gate. The sidewalk out front is empty, but I'm more interested in the houses across the street. Heart in my throat, trying not to think about the shots, I lose countless seconds waiting for a curtain to twitch or a door to open.

The wail of an approaching siren breaks me from my stasis, and I slip through the gate and out to the sidewalk. Nick's nowhere in sight. Swallowing hard, I force myself to walk at a steady, normal pace to the end of the block, winding my way back to the car.

He's not there when I walk up. I fish my phone out of my bag, send him a short text, and lean against the hood of the car to wait. Ten minutes. If he doesn't show in ten minutes, I'll start walking.

The sirens grow louder. We might have been seen, coming or going. Nick might have been detained. I can't stay here. It's too close.

I straighten and turn away, ready to put some distance between me and whatever mess Nick left behind.

Where *is* he? Why hasn't he responded?

I glance over my shoulder one last time and see Nick at the end of the street. My relief's so great I forget all about being cool and composed and I run toward him. Seconds later, I'm in his arms, his mouth hot and reassuring on mine.

"What happened?" I whisper once he lets me take a breath.

Another quick smooch, and he eases back. "We need to move."

We get in the car, and he pulls away from the curb. He drives down streets at random, turning left or right every couple of blocks. He keeps up the silence and pulls into the parking lot of a small park.

Today must be our day for empty spaces because the park's deserted except for a woman and a dog, bounding happily after a stick. Nick and I walk to the swings and sit down, and I push off with one foot.

Ticking back and forth, back and forth, like a pendulum, I break the silence. "What happened?"

Nick sets his swing in motion. "Someone got to the doctor first."

"Isaiah?"

"He wouldn't say, but it's likely."

Who else would it have been. I pump a little harder. "Who shot first?"

"Nikos. He's dead."

"He's not on the list." Our ever-expanding list of names, men loyal to Isaiah.

"Because he was one of Constantine's. Isaiah must have gotten to him."

Or Constantine sent him. Where the hell did that thought come from? Nick's cousin has been nothing but helpful and concerned. All of this is on Isaiah's head, and no one else's. I ignore the niggling worry that I'm assuming too much. "And Doctor Joe?"

Nick doesn't say anything, and I tighten my hands around the chains of the swing. Some little kid's without his father now because of me. A lot of people seem to be getting in trouble because of me. "Maybe we should skip the others."

"Who are they?"

"I don't know," I admit. "Contacts of Turner's, people he's gotten supplies from in the past. None of them wanted to meet with me until I told them who's daughter I was." Doctor Joe's the only one I've needed before. Before I met Nick, my kills numbered nine. Nick would have been ten had I gone through with it. Three died by potassium chloride, one by heroin overdose, and the rest were death by knife.

I slow, and Nick reaches out and catches the chain on the swing, stopping me completely. I twist for a few seconds as the momentum spins out. "It's like I've become the Grim Reaper," I say softly. "I think I've killed more people in the last two months than I have in the last five years." I glance at him. "You remember the shoot-out in the garage?"

"Which one?" he asks dryly.

I scrunch up my nose. "The first one. That was the first time I've ever shot someone."

He stares at me. "First time?"

I nod. "I wasn't sure I could do it. Stay calm, remember what Turner had taught me." I shouldn't have worried. The way I slid into the mindset I used whenever I did a job was easy. Frighteningly easy.

Nick's continued scrutiny makes me antsy, and I stand, pace away from the swings. This fear, more than my need to please my father, is the one thing that has the power to smash my soul into the dust.

Every time I shut down to do what I'm paid to do, it's a little harder to come back. Taking Isaiah out for good, and all the chaos and bloodshed leading to it, might break me completely. It could cement what I've always wondered.

I'm not a good person.

I don't kill the bad guys.

I just kill people.

"Cassidy."

Schooling my face into a neutral expression, I face Nick on his swing. His face hasn't lost the intense concentration. "Talk to me."

"About what?"

He stands, the swing shuddering and jumping at the sudden movement, and strides toward me. He stops when he's within touching distance, and I have to tip my head back to keep my eyes on his.

"What's going on in your head?"

How do I tell him I'm afraid? As badly as I want to, I may never be able to walk away from this life because it's too much a part of who I am.

I curve my lips into a smile. There's no need to worry about this right now. We have other things to deal with, other things to worry about. "Nothing important." I take his hand, lacing our fingers together. "C'mon."

He dips his head, mouth brushing mine, the soft tenderness of the kiss jolting me out of the last dregs of darkness. "Ready when you are," he murmurs.

The remaining vet visits go off without a hitch. The fifteen vials of potassium chloride may not be enough, but I'm not in this alone. Nick and Constantine and the rest of Nick's guys are in this war as much as I am.

"How did Turner decide on vets?"

"What?" I snap back to myself sitting in the passenger seat while Nick winds through the streets of LA, heading to our next destination, a new knife for me.

"Veterinarians. How did he end up going to them for drugs?"

"They already have them on hand. Vets have to euthanize pets on a regular basis. Hospitals and clinics might have some in their pharmacies, but since there's so much scrutiny surrounding assisted suicide, the risk of drawing unwanted attention was greater."

We waste another half hour on random turns and half-empty streets. Nick parks in an alley somewhere in Culver City. It's clean, trash bagged up or in dumpsters, with a few cars parked outside back entrances. Strangely, it doesn't smell like an alley, either, as we step out of the car.

Nick leads us to an unmarked door and pushes a buzzer next to the frame. There's a click, and he opens the door.

The interior is dim. Fuzzy shapes flit around in front of my eyes as I adjust to the darkness. A set of metal stairs is off to the right, and Nick starts up them, the metal creaking and clanking under his feet. They'd make a good alarm—no way for anyone to sneak up without being heard.

The room at the top isn't much brighter. A lamp in one corner casts a pitiful glow within a five-foot radius, but it doesn't reach the top of the stairs. The room has no windows. On a battered couch is a painfully thin man. With his sunken cheeks and protruding eyes, he looks like he belongs in a hospice center. Thin tubing runs under his nose and over his cheeks, connecting to an oxygen tank next to the couch. Maybe my hospice observation isn't so far off.

Nick moves quietly to the couch, then bends to fold him in a careful embrace. "Elias. How are you?"

"He's about the same." At the sound of the voice, I whip my head around fast and hard enough for something to crack in my neck. A second man, much larger and healthier than Elias, is in the corner, perched on a stool. He nods once at me before his attention shifts back to Nick. "Your girl?"

"Cass, Theo. Theo, this is Cass."

Theo shifts to his feet and makes his way to a cabinet in the corner. He takes out a thick leather folio, brings it over, and lays it on the coffee table in front of the couch. I step closer, curiosity overwhelming my wariness.

"Kinda young for you, Dom." Elias's voice is little more than a rasp, painful to hear, and from the look on his face, painful to speak.

I ignore the comment and take in the steel in front of me. Most of what's laid out is meant for close work, thin blades tapering to sharp points, lengths varying from maybe three inches to almost a foot. I discard that one right off the bat; with the handle, the knife itself will be too difficult to conceal.

I focus on the ones in the middle, the blades ranging from four to six inches long, the handles slender. I pick up a few to test their weight and, dissatisfied, put them down again. Nothing in front of me will work. I miss my knife. If it survived the fire, I'll never know. The gas explosion incinerated so much; I haven't thought to ask Nick if it was worth going back.

I look up to find Nick and Elias both watching me, and I shake my head. "Nope."

Elias raises a brow. "No?"

I stifle a wince at his rasp. "No. You know this. It has to fit. None of these do."

Theo snorts out a laugh and scoops up the folio. "Told you, Elias." He puts it away and returns with a box. "If Dom's bringing someone by, he means it. Don't matter if it's a girl."

He opens the box, and I lean forward. Two knives gleam in old velvet, the fabric worn through in places so I could see the wood of the box beneath it. The blades are each about six inches long, about an inch at the widest point. One blade has a nick in it. The points themselves are about a quarter-inch taper, long and pointed enough to do some damage.

I pick one up and balance it. The handle is polished wood, smooth after years of use, with no chance of splintering. Curling my fingers around the knife, the hilt settles into my grip. I pick up the other, surprised when it slides just as easily into place.

I don't flip them. Don't spin them. My hands absorb their slight weight, letting them become a part of me. These are better than the knife I lost, on par with the one I lifted off Josef.

Elias has a blank expression on his face to counter the amused one on Theo's. I put the knives in the box and close the lid before getting to my feet. "These ones."

These blades will bring me Isaiah's blood.

Chapter 19

Krav Maga is nothing like Wushu. I lost track of how many times my back slammed into the mat last night. But the brutal offensive style will help me take down men larger than me, something I've never attempted to do in my past jobs. Coupled with the Taser Nick handed me last night, I'm better equipped than ever.

I hurt in places I didn't know existed. Whimpering, I manage to get out of bed and stumble my way to the shower. The hot water doesn't do much other than wake me up, and I resign myself to a day of sloth-like movement. If I'm lucky, the pain will mellow enough for me to go for a run this evening.

"Cass? You gonna be ready soon?"

I groan and turn off the water. No rest for the wicked. Emphasis on *wicked*.

After pulling on clothes, I beeline it for Constantine's kitchen and coffee. While Nick works, I'm supposed to pull as much information on the men Nick and Constantine believe are working for Isaiah and start tracking them to try to find the best place and time to strike. It's much like what I've done before, with one exception.

I'll know their names.

There will be names to go with the schedules and habits and residences and places of employment. There will be names to go with the faces.

I try to drown the nerves fluttering in my stomach with coffee. Nick's lounging against the counter, expression blank. "Okay?" he asks.

"I hurt." The coffee tastes like crap. "Did you make the coffee this morning?" I bring the mug to my lips and attempt to swallow more, but I can't. The scent of over-boiled coffee wafts up from the sink as I pour the contents of my mug down the drain. "Next time, stay away from the coffee maker."

"Brat," he mutters.

"Yeah, but I'm *your* brat." I work up a cheeky grin. He doesn't return it. I let it fall away and blow out a breath. "What."

"I know how you work, love. This isn't your normal. So I'm going to ask you again. Are you okay with the plan? Because I don't want you doing something that's going to break you." He sets his cup aside. "C'mon. We'll go find some real coffee."

Ensconced in the car, heading toward his office, I pick apart my response before answering. "You know what I thought the other day at the hospital? One of the nurses in the ER pointed out the restroom so I could wash my hands, and it occurred to me if I was anyone else, if I didn't exercise my capacity to kill, I'd probably curl into a ball on the bathroom floor and never come out. I didn't. I washed my hands and went right back to the waiting room."

Nick pulls into the lot of a cafe a couple blocks from Constantine's condo. "I don't know how I'm going to react once it's all done. It's scary," I admit. "All the bodies that have gotten in the way in the last few months, not a smidge of remorse. Don't know most of their names. Don't know if they have families and friends who miss them and curse my name every day.

"Marc…" My lungs squeeze painfully. "Marc is different."

We get out of the car. Nick comes around and cages me against the door. "Is it because you know his name, or because of how it happened?"

Good question, one I should have thought of myself. Steven is the only other man I've killed within the organization, and his name and face don't bring on the same gut-twisting guilt. "How it happened," I say softly, staring at Nick's chest. "Fuck, some days, if I let myself, I think I could fall so far down I'll never want to get up. He *wanted* to die. He was waiting for it. The resignation in his eyes, how hopeless he looked, yet he was incredibly peaceful about the whole thing. I just wish—" I choke on the words, and I suck in air. "I wish I knew for certain if he'd ordered the hit himself or if it was someone else, if someone wanted him to die."

He tucks a lock of hair behind my ear. "Does it matter?"

"To Isaiah? I doubt it. I wielded the knife. I took the job, I could have walked away, and I chose not to. To him, that's all that matters. To me?" I shrug. "I don't know. Maybe? It doesn't absolve me of anything. He's still dead, and I'm still the one who made him that way. But maybe knowing if he'd done it to himself would help." I glance over at the door to the cafe. "I don't feel much like coffee anymore."

Nick steps back and takes my hand. "I do."

The cafe is half full, mostly people standing around chatting or waiting for their orders. My stomach perks up a bit at the sight of the fluffy croissants piled high in the display case. Nothing like butter to cure a nervous stomach.

We get in line and wait in silence, listening to the clamor around us. The door jangles open at our backs. I sneak a glimpse out of idle curiosity and wish I hadn't because my stomach locks up tighter than Fort Knox. Tris steps to the end, two people between us, his gaze trained on the menu above the cash registers.

Dammit.

We have a plan. A workable one. Learn the schedules of all the men in Isaiah's circle and take them all out in a single day. It'll take a lot of planning, but the upside is no one gets tipped off and runs before we can catch them.

Unfortunately, it also means picking them off one by one is out of the question. So Tris gets to live and follow me around for another day.

We reach the front of the line, and Nick orders two coffees, despite my protests, a couple of croissants, and one of the giant chocolate cookies. "What's the cookie for?" I ask as we move to the other side of the counter to wait.

He kisses the top of my head. "You. You'll get hungry around mid-morning and come looking for me. When you do, I'll be able to placate you with a cookie."

I scowl up at him. "Placate me? Are you planning to piss me off?"

"You'll be pissed within a half hour of digging through names."

I swallow my growl and cross my arms over my chest. He's right. Unfortunately. The days I spent chained to the desk in his spare office, combing through old files, beat out some of the days I spent cooped up in the library, trying not to fall asleep as I read through dusty books, searching for scraps of information necessary to complete a paper. Nick had walked in more than once to my grumbling.

"It's so *boring*," I whine, barely resisting the urge to stamp my foot in protest. Nick just rolls his eyes and loops an arm around my neck.

Our order comes up, and he grabs the bag and the drink caddy before we head to the door. He hands everything to me once I'm in my seat, then rounds the hood and climbs in behind the wheel. "So. Tris."

"Yup."

Nick laughs, and the sound loosens a few of the knots in my belly. "Was he around on campus the other day?"

"Honestly? I have no idea. I was followed from your office to campus—black sedan, tinted windows—and it drove past when I pulled into a parking spot, but I couldn't see who was driving. I have no idea if he was in the car. Since I was being followed so obviously, I didn't think anything of it." There's no point in piling on more guilt. I'm starting to think if Isaiah wants to find a way to rattle me, he will.

"Any more attacks on your guys?" It's easy to forget the other side of Isaiah's vendetta.

"Not since Cory." His tone is grim, his hands gripping the wheel hard enough his knuckles are white.

He guides the car into the garage and parks near the stairs like always. We make it to the ninth floor without issue and split off to our separate offices.

I haven't been in this room since the stabbing. Didn't spend much time in it to begin with, only a handful of days, so the wave of hurt surprises the hell out of me. I sat at that desk and dug through file after file, culling information that might help me identify who was trying to kill me and Nick, when all along, my would-be killer sat on the other side of the desk. He joked with me, made me laugh, showed concern, and tried to look after me. It wasn't his fault that my guilt increased after hearing him talk about Marc. Isaiah's grief over losing Marc is a sucker punch in the gut every time I think about it because it's *real*. It might be twisted with this weird, sick need to push Nick off his pedestal, but his pain is genuine. The man cared about his cousin deeply.

Whoever said suicide is a victimless crime is a liar. The ones left behind are the victims.

I turn on the computer, spin the chair around to face the window, and stare blankly at the office building across the way. What would Denise say if she knew what I was planning to do? Better question, what would my father say?

Turner wouldn't say a damn word. He might nod, his eyes might glint with approval, but there'd be no words.

Denise would tell me to go to the cops, the FBI, or some legal authority. While Nick didn't bring it up when we were brainstorming the plan, the idea flitted through my mind more than once. If I go to the police, no one dies. I won't add to the blood on my hands.

But these are trained killers. They've played this game their whole lives, and they know what they're doing better than I could ever hope to.

To get the police to take action, and take it quickly, there would have to be irrefutable evidence.

They're not stupid enough to leave evidence behind.

Nick won't run. He may have gotten a boost from his father, but I don't doubt he worked his ass off for it. He's already made it clear he's not leaving it for me. And maybe someday we'll reach a point where I don't want to be a part of this world, and we'll break up.

The thought makes me scowl at the window. Our best option is to kill everyone who wants to cause me or Nick harm. I will serve life a million times over if I'm ever caught.

Obviously the solution is to not get caught.

I spin back to the monitor and pull up the server portal I used the last time, then search the drawers for a pen and a notepad. My phone pings as I shut the empty bottom drawer, and I scoop up the phone to check the message on my way to Nick's office. He'll have something I can use, and I can steal the bag of croissants while I'm there. Birdies, meet stone.

The text is from a number I don't know, but I recognize the picture immediately. Neese and Charlie are entering the emergency room, the shot clear enough I can make out the worry on Denise's face.

Fear steals my strength, and I have to lock my knees to keep from falling. Isaiah knows where to hit. All the cool and grace I've exhibited under pressure flee at the thought of losing my best friend.

I have to get her to leave. Today, if possible.

I hurry to Nick's office, knock once, and slip inside before he has a chance to answer. He's on a call, and he arches a brow in question. I shake my head and sit in one of the chairs facing the desk, phone clenched between my fingers.

He hangs up, and I set my phone in front of him. "I know she's my weakness. It's why Isaiah's digging his dirty little fingers into the wound. He knows it'll mess me up." I suck in a breath, blow it out, imagining some of the tension draining away with the exhalation. "Can you help me get her and Charlie to Colorado today?"

He studies the photo. "This was taken the other day?"

"The day Scott was shot," I confirm.

Seconds drip down into a minute, two minutes, and Nick's gaze never wavers from mine. "What does Turner have to say about weaknesses?"

I sneer. "Eliminate them. The man doesn't exactly practice what he preaches, though. My mother's his Achilles heel. He'd do anything for her." I don't even rate a close second. The familiar ache swells and retreats.

He taps the phone. "If Denise is out of the way, who would he go after instead?"

Turner. He'd never get close, though. There's a reason I didn't need more than a few jobs to establish a reputation; I was trained by one of the best. "My mom, probably. But Turner can handle anything thrown at them."

He nods. "I can pull a few strings, get them on a flight out tonight if they can get to the airport."

"Thank you," I whisper, pathetically grateful. I pick up the phone and return it to my pocket. "Can I borrow your keys? I'll head over there right now and talk to her." I can't tell her the truth. I can't risk making her a party to my sins. I *can* tell her someone's targeting me, and to rattle me, they're going after the people I love.

He pulls his keys out of his pocket and hands them over.

"What do you do? With your weaknesses?" I ask.

"Protect them by any means necessary." His eyes glint with fury and determination, and more of the tension fades. I'm safe. If I'm safe, I can move and protect the ones I love.

But who protects him?

Rounding the desk, I drop the keys on the surface and cradle his face in my hands. "I am so glad I didn't kill you like I was supposed to."

He laughs. "Same here."

Chapter 20

The Westwood apartment I shared with Denise is nice, but Charlie's is nicer. Of course, his parents pay his rent, so it would be. Whenever I visited in the past, though, the place was neat, but still had a thin layer of boy-clean over it. Clean yet not clean.

Denise moving in has made a huge difference. The vacuum lines are still visible in the carpet. There are *coasters*. More than that, I see pieces of Neese everywhere, from the bright orange throw pillows on the couch to the fluffy chenille throw puddled in a nearby chair, its bright purple color cheery against the faded brown fabric.

"Um. Wow. Would it be totally inappropriate of me to tell you how much better Charlie's apartment looks?" I drop my bag by the front door.

"I won't tell if you won't." Denise leads me to the couch, and we sit. "Charlie will be back in a few minutes. What's this about? Is Scott okay?"

"I think so. I haven't had a chance to call him. Nick was able to find out when he was released." I link my fingers together in my lap to stop myself from tugging at my shirt hem. "When do you leave for Colorado?"

She shifts on the couch, grimacing when the cushion squeaks under her. "Spring," she says at my questioning look. "There's a couple broken ones. We're getting a new couch when we get back. We're not leaving until Christmas Eve. It was cheaper, and that way we can spend some time with my family too. So don't worry. We'll still be around for your birthday." She flashes a grin at me.

I'd completely forgotten my birthday is in a few days. "About that." My throat's as dry as toast. "I haven't been honest with you."

The open, expectant look on her face folds in on itself, leaving behind the careful mask she showed me at El Dorado. I hated it then, and I hate it now. "This is about Nick," she says.

"Not entirely." I'd give my right arm for a glass of water. I swallow, trying to wet it and failing, almost choking on the lump forming. This admission is going to destroy what's left of our friendship. "You were right about the wounds to my stomach and my throat. They weren't random or coincidences. Someone attacked me, and before you go blaming Nick, he hasn't done anything. It's what *I've* done. He's caught in my backlash."

Her brows draw together. "I don't understand."

And I don't know if I can make her understand without telling her the whole truth. I rub my lips together, staring at the wall over her shoulder. There's a picture of Denise and Charlie, grinning like the fools in love they are. It's almost identical to the first picture I'd been sent. My heart seizes, and I get up to study it in more detail.

The picture's not quite the same. The halo of light is missing, and there's a palm tree in the background. But the way they look at each other... They're each other's *it*. There will never be anyone else for either of them. There is no doubt in my mind Charlie will do whatever it takes to protect Denise, and he'll love her fiercely until the end of days. "There's too much I can't tell you." Plausible deniability. She has to have it. "Just know that it's dangerous, highly illegal, and there are people who would hurt you because you know me." Gathering my courage, I face her, willing my fisted hands to relax. "I need you and Charlie out of the city by tonight. Nick can arrange to get you to Colorado early so you don't have to change your plans."

There's no color in her face. None. Denise has gone paper-white, blue eyes glassy and wide. "Neese?" I hurry over and drop to my knees in front of her. "Denise?"

The second I touch her hand, she jerks, violently enough she kicks me in the thigh as she falls back. "How—why—?" She shuts her eyes and draws in a breath. "You're involved in something illegal."

"Yes." I rub my palm over my thigh.

"And you won't give me any more information other than it's dangerous? God, Cass, I could have figured that out for myself. You were stabbed! You almost *died*. And you expect me to believe this doesn't have anything to do with Nick?"

The accusatory look she shoots me hurts more than any of the wounds I've received so far. Why? I've been lying to her for years. I knew if I said anything it would change our friendship.

I don't want to do this. I don't want to be Cass the Assassin with her, all ice and emptiness. But to get her out of harm's way, I don't have a choice.

The shift inside me has never felt as physical as it does this time. I stand while I consider her point. "It doesn't," I say coolly. Isaiah would have come after me sooner or later. Hooking up with Nick just gave him new angles to play with. "If anything, Nick helped. If he hadn't found me in the parking garage, I would be dead." I glance at her, and my resolve falters at the shock on her face. "Are you going or staying?"

That's where Charlie finds us a few minutes later—Denise staring into space from her spot on the couch, me standing a few feet away, waiting for her response. "Babe? You okay?" He glances at me as he rounds the couch, brows raised in question. He sits next to her, the cushion giving way, and she slumps toward him on a gasp, face crumpling.

I manage to stay upright by imagining a steel rod where my spine is. Is she feeling anything like I am? Like someone's taking a spoon to my insides and scraping it out, bit by bit? Having to deal with the fear of the unknown at the same time? She'll be out of my reach. There's nothing to prevent Isaiah from sending men to Colorado to track them down, other than it expends unnecessary energy.

"Cass?"

I blink and meet Charlie's eyes. "You both need to leave the city tonight." I give him the same speech, minus the painful hesitations I gave Denise. I like Charlie. He's got a calm, practical side that keeps Denise from flipping out too badly, and I'm counting on that side to get them through this.

His face pales, lips going white as he flattens them. His hold on Denise tightens, and she turns her face into his neck. To his credit, though, his question is thoughtful and logical. "How do you know these men won't follow us?"

A question like that deserves honesty. "I don't. I can tell you Isaiah's attention is already divided, so the amount of effort it would take, plus man power, wouldn't make it worth his while. With you and Denise gone, he'll turn his attention to my parents most likely." He won't get through Turner, though he'll sure as hell try.

And Dad will love watching him fail.

Charlie nods, then whispers something to Denise. They get to their feet and leave the room, disappearing down the hallway. Instead of following them, I take out my phone to call Nick. The lump in my throat is back. My voice will shake. It'll crack, and everything will come tumbling down.

Isaiah could follow them to Colorado. Chances are he won't, but there's a *chance*. Not a guarantee. I need as close to a guarantee as I can get.

Nick answers on the third ring. "Well?"

I pinch my stomach to distract myself. "Charlie's talking to her. I think they'll go."

"Car will be there in an hour." He hangs up, and I slip the phone into my pocket.

Denise walks out of the bedroom a moment later, her eyes still haunted and frightened. "I think you should come with us, but Charlie says no."

She *would* be worried about me. I smile. "Charlie's right, Neese. Me going with you will ensure someone will come after you. The safest place for me is with Nick. I know you don't agree," I continue, holding up a hand to cut off her protests. "It is, though. Nick will do whatever he has to do to ensure my safety."

She screws up her mouth and narrows her eyes, her expression all doubt and no confidence. I suppose it's too much to ask that she trust Nick, and if I take a minute to look at it from her side, she has no reason to. Since I've met him, it's been nothing but gun fights, car chases, explosions, and blood, some of it mine. She doesn't see the lazy evenings on the couch or the teasing I endure from him and Constantine while I make us dinner. She doesn't hear the murmured conversations we have in the dark, cozy and safe under the blankets. Nick's love looks nothing like Charlie's.

But it's the love I want.

"Come on," she says at last. "Charlie says Boulder just got snow. He keeps trying to get me to pack fleece."

"There's a reason for that, California girl." I follow her into their bedroom. The bed's made and while there's clothes strewn all over it, that's the only place they are. I hold back a grin. Definitely *it*.

The next hour flies past as Denise packs for cold weather, giving Charlie the death stare whenever he tries to get her to pack the fleece still sitting at the end of the bed. He finally rounds the bed and holds her close, cupping the back of her head as he tells her she *will* freeze because she's a pansy about cold weather, and he means that in the most loving way possible.

She flips him off and stuffs the fleece into her suitcase.

I'm standing at the window watching the street for the car Nick's sending while Denise hurries around the apartment snatching up various power cords and chargers. The knock at the door cuts through her nervous chatter, and the three of us stare at the door. Charlie's building has a secure entry. You have to be buzzed in, and the buzzer hadn't gone off.

I wave at Charlie and Denise and point to the kitchen, the room partially blocked off from the living room. They hurry out of the room, and I peer through the peephole. The tension drains from my body as quickly as it came on, and I flip the locks.

It takes all of my willpower not to fling myself at Nick. If I do, I'll never let go. "Hey." The greeting comes out flat, and he lifts a brow, reaching for me. I back away. "Don't," I whisper. A little longer until Denise and Charlie are gone, and I can relax. Fall apart, even. Not until then.

He studies my face, and for the first time in weeks, I drop my gaze to his chest, unwilling to meet his eyes. As he walks past me, he picks up my hand and presses a kiss to the palm. "Denise? Charlie? Car's waiting."

Denise sticks her head out of the kitchen, eyes wide. "Um. Hi."

I don't bother shutting the door; Nick's already picking up their bags. The four of us march out of the apartment, down the stairs, and through the rear entrance to the alley. A boring blue sedan's parked in the middle of the narrow street, and Nick pops the trunk. He and Charlie place the bags inside while Denise and I stare at our feet, hands in our pockets.

She's coming back. When this is over, she'll be back. They both will. They have to. There's a whole semester to get through before graduation.

In danger of never coming out of the cold, empty space inside me, I grab Denise and wrap my arms around her. "I'm sorry," I whisper. "I'm so, so sorry." The lump's like a jagged rock, scraping at my throat.

She whispers something at me, but I can't hear her. A long, long moment later, she's climbing into the backseat of the car and I've banded my arms around my stomach to hold in the shakes. I won't be going with them to the airport, even though she begged. It's safer I don't know where they are.

I hurry to Nick's car parked a few blocks away and get in. Streets blur together as I struggle to keep the tears inside. My phone rings. I ignore it. Blocks and blocks and blocks, dotted with palm trees and parked cars, office buildings and tiny houses crammed together. The hazy sun sinks lower in the sky, shafts of sunlight piercing the windshield to blind me. I find a parking spot, get out, and start walking.

It hasn't changed. There's a comfort in that, knowing this slice of Santa Monica Beach is the same. Seagulls wheel overhead, screeching for the trash that beach goers leave behind. The wind blowing up from the ocean is cool, and I pull up the hood of my sweatshirt. I settle into the sand and watch the waves roll in, breaking over one another. My phone rings again. I silence it.

Letting Denise walk away without knowing when I'll see her again is more than I can handle, and I was lying to myself earlier, thinking it'd be all right to fall apart after she was gone. The only way to see this through and put aside my emotions is to forget I have them. When footsteps crunch softly over the sand, I fight the need to turn toward the sound.

"Smart choice, getting your best friend out of the city."

I keep my eyes on the water. "I thought so." I'm relaxed. Loose. He's to my left; most people would run to the right. He wouldn't expect me to run toward him. "I guess you'll have to find someone else to taunt me with."

Isaiah drops onto the sand beside me, close enough we can hear each other, far enough apart I'd have to lean over to touch him. "You've just proven how important she is to you. But you're right. Not worth pursuing. Too much to be done here."

"Good to know." Don't engage. *Don't* engage. If I sit here long enough, maybe he'll tell me what he wants.

The sun becomes a brilliant orange strip of light, the edge of the ocean glowing. Sometimes I think you can really fall off the end of the world, topple right into the glittering pool of sun on the water. A seagull flaps around on the wet sand, hopping along, wings fluttering as it dodges the water.

"Why do you come here?"

He doesn't deserve the answer. Not the one I gave Nick. "It's peaceful. Hasn't been a lot of peace lately."

"There hasn't," he agrees. "Most people would pick a less crowded place."

I shrug, glancing at him through the encroaching dusk. "Seems stupid to drive for hours to find an empty beach when this one's big enough for everyone."

The last of the glow fades, leaving behind deepening shadows. I stretch my legs out in front of me, the strap of my ankle holster rubbing against my skin. I sharpened the blades this morning. People are starting to desert the beach. A while longer, and it'll be empty enough I can make my move.

"I've underestimated you."

I allow myself a smile. "Don't worry. You're in good company."

He ignores the jab and continues like I didn't even speak. "You're losing Dom a lot of money. Surprised he hasn't cut you loose."

This is interesting. I assumed everyone in the family had guessed by now how much I mean to Nick. Constantine certainly gave me that impression. "Does Nick often choose money and the family over his women?"

Isaiah doesn't respond. I don't need him to. If he believes Nick's simply waiting for this all to go away, that's his business.

"Are you familiar with how parley works?"

I squint against a gust of wind, daring to close my eyes to keep the sand out. "I know it's not something that's been used since the nineteenth century."

"It still is. We just use other words to express the same idea."

"Interesting." *Get to the point.*

He sighs, the sound swept away by the crashing of the water. "I didn't expect to like you, Cass. Like you or respect you. My men respect you. You've proven to be clever and smart."

"Oh, stop, Isaiah. You'll give me a big head."

"A parley. To negotiate terms. I'm offering you the chance to choose who dies." The sand crunches as he leans over and kisses me on the cheek. "Make it easier on us all," he murmurs. "Do this for Dom."

It would take a second to loosen the blade strapped to the inside of my forearm. It's a second too long. "You think the solution to this problem is for me to decide which of my loved ones gets to die?"

He stands and brushes the sand from his jeans. "Think about it." Then he walks away, leaving me with a knife in my hand and no one to plunge it into.

Chapter 21

This will never feel right. Guns are not my thing. The way the grip presses into my palm, the reverberations racing up my arm, the *noise*. I brace my hand and squeeze the trigger, the hole in the target obscured in the bright light.

I lay the gun on the ledge in front of me and hit the button to bring the target forward. I squint at the pockmarked sheet. Pretty much what I expected. My shots are scattered around the chest and shoulders, and I missed. A few hit the upper stomach area. If Nick's going for distance, this is the wrong gun for it.

I clip up a fresh target and send it back, replace my glasses, and adjust the oversize ear protectors. Sweat dribbles down my neck. The target practice is Nick's idea. Since he insisted on a new gun, it's a smart one and has the added bonus of providing me with a ready-made distraction.

The thing about paper targets is they're poor approximations of the warm bodies you're going to be aiming for. Bodies on the other end of a gun don't tend to stand still and wait for you to line up properly and shoot. But he's right on one count—don't bring a knife to a gunfight.

My modus operandi insists I don't engage in the fight to begin with. The report of the gun kicks up my arm, my shoulder aching from overuse. A blister's popping up on my palm from the constant rubbing.

Nick doesn't understand my reluctance. "Guns are impersonal," he said. Efficient and more accurate than a blade or trusting that the potassium chloride will be enough.

I empty the clip into the target and bring it forward, then strip off my gear. Guns aren't impersonal. They're loud, for one. It's too easy for something to go wrong. And most of the time, you'll be facing your target. You'll get to see the surprise, anger, defeat, sadness on his face as he realizes it's all over. Life as he knows it is done.

Knives *force* you to be accurate. You have to disconnect. It shoves you into a slim space so confining that if you don't move with frightening precision, you will screw yourself over and likely end up dead yourself.

No, Nick doesn't understand. He may never understand. That's fine with me. I still have hope that once this is done, I can back out of the life. Take on some new role at Nick's side where my hands aren't covered in blood.

I can be a teacher and share a bed with a mafia king, right?

The indoor range is only half full, every other lane empty as I walk past. Gunshots crack and echo in the cavernous space, and I quicken my step, eager to get out. I've spent too long familiarizing myself with this new weapon. I need a shower, food, and quite possibly a nap.

Nick's leaning against the hood of the car as I make my way out of the building into the parking lot. I lift a hand to shield my eyes against the hazy winter sun. It feels good on my skin. The last few days have been cooler than usual.

He straightens once I'm within earshot. "Well?"

"Still don't like them. It's a decent fit, though. Gave me a blister." I hold up my hand.

He frowns. "We'll try something else." He pops the trunk and takes the case from me, stows it inside, and shuts the lid.

"Please don't. This one is fine. Guns are not my thing. They will never be my first choice. As long as it's not obscenely bulky and I can hold my hand steady while firing, I consider that a win. I don't think we'll be able to use them as much as you want," I say softly. "We want quiet, and gunfire will only draw attention to us."

The waiting is driving us both crazy, but we're still gathering information. "Add anyone to the list today?" I ask, dropping into the passenger seat. Nick and Constantine have been meeting with Andreas and Anton to go over the men who've been placed under Isaiah's command. They've pulled phone records and made discreet inquiries among the rest of the rank and file of the organization. It's tedious work, but doing it now will make it easier to pull off our plan.

He closes my door, walks around the hood of the car, and slides in behind the wheel before answering. "No. I think we're hitting the edge of Isaiah's inner circle. Peter's working on pulling schedules. Should be able to start surveillance soon."

"Goody."

The car rumbles to life, and he pulls out of the parking lot. I squirm a little in my seat, my shirt sticking to me in places. We've got at least a forty-five minute drive to get back to the city.

Ten minutes later we haven't hit the freeway. "Um, I'm pretty sure we're going the wrong way."

Nick grunts in response and continues heading west. The unfamiliar terrain zips past, all palm trees and brown and green rolling hills, scrubby grass and asphalt. I spot a sign for the Pac Coast Highway. I didn't realize how close to the ocean we were. The gun range Nick took me to isn't one I've used before. "I've told you I'm not a fan of surprises, right?"

He picks up my hand and presses a kiss to the palm, the car slowing to a stop. The ocean spreads out in front of us, peeking through the traffic of the highway. "I think you'll like this one."

I free my hand from his. "As long as you remember I have a knife and know how to use it, sure."

I catch his grimace, and he pulls onto the highway, so I settle back in the seat, trying to ignore my sweaty, sticky clothes. The sun's sinking lower in the sky, painting it in garish, vibrant reds and purples. Normally I'd insist Nick pull over somewhere so I could watch. Some people prefer sunrise. It's a new day, another chance at life.

For me, each sunset means I've survived another day.

The only thing I want today is a hot shower and some El Dorado, and the bastard's taking me farther away from both. I try one more time. "Nick, please. Whatever you've got planned, I'm not in the mood for it."

"Take a look at it first. You don't like it, we can go back to Con's." He turns off the highway and starts driving up the rolling hillside into Malibu. A few minutes later he's pulling into a lot in front of a squat, stucco building, the red-tiled roof shadowed by the setting sun. A discreet sign gives me the name of the place: Oceanview Inn and Spa.

The Oceanview Inn and Spa.

Denise and I tried to get up here for her twenty-first birthday last year. All we wanted were a couple of facials, maybe a pedicure. A fantasy for a few hours. We knew it was popular and appointments were hard to get, but we figured two months out would be enough notice.

Nope. They were booked out for four. Then they got featured in *InStyle*, and we said buh-bye to the idea of getting pampered at one of Southern California's most famous spas.

"If you tell me I'm getting so much as a pedicure here, I'm going to call you a liar." I stare out the window at the place. It's not much to look at from the front. Beige exterior, an arched, covered walkway leading to a shadowed front door. I know it extends down the cliffside. Every room has a view of the ocean.

Nick gets out of the car, comes around, opens my door, and tugs me to my feet. "Okay. You're not getting a pedicure." I glare at him as he grins. "You're getting a massage." He shuts the door and starts walking toward the entrance. I trip over my feet and stumble after him, willing my brain to catch up. We're here. At the Oceanside. There are bad men trying to kill us, and Nick's apparently decided I need to relax. "Our room should be ready. You probably want a shower first. You'll have to hurry, though."

He spins around and clasps my waist, cutting off my protests with his mouth. "Happy birthday, love," he murmurs against my lips.

I melt. There's no other way to describe what those words do to me, melt my insides along with my brain, the warmth of his mouth turning everything gooey. All day I pushed myself from one training exercise to the next—a trail run along Topanga Canyon with Con and Nick, a modified Wushu routine, sharpening and cleaning my knives, inventorying the rest of my supplies. I put off calling my mother because I didn't want to be reminded how different today was from my past birthdays. There'll be no celebration with my parents and Denise and Charlie today. No dinner at El Dorado, no bad bar karaoke with Scott. Caught up in the swirling mess my life had become, I figured I'd let today pass like any other day. I'd just be officially one year older.

I draw in a shaky breath and let it out. "I think this surprise might be okay." He grins, kisses me again, and leads me inside.

I barely have time to take in the sleek black slate of the bathroom before I'm rushing through my shower to make my appointment. Face down on a heated, padded table, dim lighting beckoning me toward sleep, the masseuse digs her elbow into the meaty part just beneath my shoulder blade and banishes any thoughts of a quick nap.

She finds muscles I didn't know I *had*, the knots crunching under the pressure. When she's done, I feel like I've been pounded with a meat tenderizer, and I want to curl up on the table for that nap.

I make my way out of the spa and to the room, two levels down. Nick's on the balcony. His gaze trained on the view, he doesn't turn toward me as I step outside. The sun's gone, stars obliterated by the light pollution. The moon's out, though, and streetlights dot the hillside below. I stand next to him so our arms brush against each other. "This time last year, I was probably laughing at something Charlie said, trying not to snort beer out of my nose."

Nick reaches for my hand and curves his around mine. I ignore the tingling in my nose and sniff hard. "Denise would have thrown a napkin at his head, my mother would have chastised them both, and Turner would have been stone-faced at the end of the table, one eye on the door, the other on the table."

He rubs his thumb along the back of my hand. "No smiles from your dad?"

I shake my head. "He rarely smiles in public. Not even at my mother." The tingling increases, and my eyes start to burn. "There is this bar that has karaoke on Friday and Saturday nights. It's always packed, and since it's so close to the university, they let people underage in, stamping their wrists so they can't buy alcohol. We went there for my birthday freshman year, and went back the next two. Last year was the first year we didn't have to get stamped, and Scott insisted it was my duty as the birthday girl to get plastered. I had the worst hangover the next day. Couldn't get out of bed. Haven't been that wasted since."

"You were drunk that first night at the condo."

"Trust me, it wasn't nearly as bad." Looking back, that first night in the condo when I dumped my beer over his head was the first clue I had that Nick was more than interested. Sometimes I wish we hadn't lost so much time between his initial denial and my long recovery. I drop his hand and tuck my own inside the sleeve of my robe. "Anyway, freshman year was the start of a tradition. Dinner with Denise and my parents at El Dorado, karaoke with Scott and a couple other friends. It feels weird to be doing anything else."

Shivering once in the rapidly cooling air, I go up on my toes and kiss his cheek. "Thanks for the massage. I didn't realize how much I needed that."

He wraps an arm around my waist and steers me inside. "I hope the change in your birthday plans isn't too horrible."

I drop my head onto his chest for a moment, slipping my arms around his waist. "No," I say softly. "Honestly, with everything that's going on, I planned to ignore it. Thought I might call my mother this evening, maybe Denise and Scott if you say it's okay, but otherwise, I just wanted it to pass." A sudden thought hits me, and I tip my head back. "How'd you know today was my birthday, anyway?" I didn't tell him. Hell, I don't even know when *his* birthday is.

"Same way I found out when your theater class met." He drops a kiss on my nose at my scowl. "Denise told me as well when I took them to the airport and threatened bodily harm if I didn't A—get you enchiladas with mole sauce and B—find a way for her to call you tonight. So there's enchiladas on the table and a secure line waiting for you. She's going to call in about an hour."

The tingling becomes painful and tears well. If I had doubts about his feelings, any doubts at all, everything he's done in the past few hours erased them and then some. I rest my head against his chest as I wait for the tears to recede.

It's official. If Nick leaves me, I will be devastated.

I lift my head, and he kisses the corner of my mouth. He busies himself warming the food while I wash my hands.

He's on the phone as I step out of the bathroom, and he points to the table and the plate of food. Delicious, delicious mole sauce, all for me. I glance at the other plate and smirk. Nick still hasn't learned his lesson about the mole sauce. He opted for the tomatillo sauce.

Next to my plate is a small flip phone. I poke it with a finger, then cut into the enchilada. The first bite is chocolaty perfection. He looks up and grins at my groan before moving back out to the balcony to finish his conversation.

I'm halfway through my food when he comes inside, phone in his pocket. "Business won't wait, huh?"

He sits and cuts into his once-again cold enchiladas. He grimaces at the first bite. "Mexican, no matter how good it is, should not be eaten cold." He gets up to stick the plate in the microwave on top of the minibar. "Business, as you put it, doesn't care if we're dealing with internal family shit. Deals need to close, money needs to be made, and projects still have to be finished on time. We're pushing out a new app in a few weeks, and I haven't been keeping as close an eye on it as I should have been."

Do you have any idea how much money Dom's losing? I drop my gaze to my plate. I haven't told Nick about my little visit with Isaiah. Telling him would only give him more ammunition to fuel his worry, and since Isaiah didn't actually *do* anything, I figure Nick doesn't need to know. I cut off another bite and stick it in my mouth. "I know you've been worried about me, but if you need to spend more time at the office, I can find ways to entertain myself," I say after I've swallowed.

"This is an unexpected setback. Cory was in charge of the project, and his assistant has been doing a good job of keeping up, but the whole team's shaken and slowed by Cory's death." He takes the plate from the microwave and sets it on the table, closer to me than he was before. He scoots the chair over and sits. "Tell me about Tori."

It takes me a minute to remember who he's talking about. I take a sip of water before answering. "I met her the same day you did. She was covertly fangirling you before you came over." I grin. "She was relatively calm after Scott was shot, dialed 911 after a little prompting, and came by the hospital even though she'd never met Scott before." Turner asked me to do this on occasion, formulate opinions based on what little information you could glean from a first impression. He wanted to look for weaknesses, but I have a feeling Nick's not interested in those. "She kept her head and had the compassion to check in on a stranger and stick around until she knew he'd be all right. I'd want to take a closer look. Are you thinking of hiring her?"

His smile is slow and wicked. "Have I ever told you how much I love your brain? There's a few internships available at some of my companies. I'd like her to apply."

The next hour passes in a blur of Mexican food and beer and Denise's voice happy and relaxed on the other end of a phone line. My phone, my actual phone, rings right as I hang up with Denise, and I catch Scott's name on the screen. Nick gives me a thumbs up to answer the call, and I manage to pick it up before it goes to voicemail.

He's telling me more about Tori when Nick's phone goes off again, and he moves away to answer it. From the way his expression goes from thunderous to dangerously blank, I know the news isn't good. I hang up with Scott after a promise to get together with him and Tori in another day or so and turn my attention to Nick. "What's wrong?"

"You're going to need to get dressed. Someone's hacked into the mainframe and released a virus. Peter's trying to contain it, but it's eating away at the app scheduled to launch. If he can't stop it soon, we'll have to start over."

This is new. Isaiah's gone after loved ones, taken out key employees, but he has yet to attack the legit side directly. "He wants you to lose everything," I say, heading for the bag Nick brought with him. I pull out clean clothes, drop the robe, and hurriedly drag on pants and a long-sleeve shirt.

"Seems like it. I've texted Con. He's on his way in. He's not as good as me or Peter, but he should be able to help slow it down."

The last of my pleasure sluices away. I know someone who can stop this from destroying everything Nick's built. I turn to him, tugging at the hem of my shirt. "Do you trust me?" At his frown, I sigh. "With the app. Your business. Do you trust me?" He nods slowly, and I pick up my phone. "I'll have Turner meet Constantine there."

Chapter 22

"Your dad *repairs* computers." Nick says this like it'll convince me to call Turner back and tell him never mind. It didn't work the first three times he said it, and it won't work now.

"Turner works with computers. Full stop. He repairs the hardware and knows his way around the operating systems like he's designed them himself. Considering he *did* create one himself, that's not exactly a stretch." I pull my gaze away from the night-dark freeway and turn toward him. "Seriously, what's the big deal? You want this problem solved quickly. If anyone can find a way to stop the virus from killing everything, and Peter hasn't already figured it out, Turner can."

A muscle in his jaw jumps, and I lean across the center console to kiss it. "Nick. What's wrong?"

His grip on the steering wheel tightens, and he checks his blind spot before merging the car into the next lane. "Every time you see him, you shut down," he finally says. "It fuckin' pisses me off because I can't do anything about it, and even if I could, I don't know what that would *be*." He shoots me a glance. "You really think he can fix this?"

I'm not some naive little girl who thinks her daddy is a superhero. I know my father's skills. But Nick's right. Seeing him tears open the wounds, and I don't know how to close them permanently. I don't know if that will ever be possible.

I take his hand from the steering wheel and fold my own into it. "I think if your guys can't fix it, and Turner can't fix it, no one will be able to." My phone buzzes in my pocket, and I boost a hip off the seat to dig it out. I hold it up after reading the name on the screen. "It's Constantine. Turner's there and setting up."

Nick's hand squeezes mine before he puts it back on the wheel. "Another fifteen minutes. Let's hope this doesn't go any further."

I push the phone back into my pocket and fold my hands in my lap, inching closer to shutdown the nearer we get to Nick's office. I don't want to. I wish it wasn't a necessity. It's the only way I can get through this, though.

Nick parks in the underground garage and takes my hand in his as we head for the stairs. There's enough left of the Cass who loves him not to shake off his hold. I want to. I want so badly to close down completely, fall into the empty, blank space inside. It's a safe place. A familiar one.

One growing more familiar every day.

The stairs are quiet, nightlights illuminating the vacant stairwell. Our progress slows to a crawl once we realize the motion sensitive lights aren't brightening like they should. They're designed to be energy efficient and come up as someone walks past. They're not doing it. He nudges me behind him and starts to climb.

The only thing louder than our footsteps is our breathing, but I strain my ears anyway, on alert for the tiniest sound, ready to vault over the railing to the staircase below. Guns out, eyes scanning the dark corners, we arrive at the eighth floor without interruption, and Nick lets us out of the stairwell.

While there's a small server room on the ninth floor, most of the servers are on the eighth, taking up about a third of the floor. Cold air rushes out as we walk in. Peter's already there, a thick cable dangling down to a laptop balanced on his knees. Constantine's on the near side of him, fingers racing across the keyboard of his own laptop.

Standing at the terminal is Turner. The faint light from the screen reflects off the glasses he wears for close work and reading.

For the first time since Nick told me he had to get to the office, I'm uncertain about my role here. My skills aren't up to Constantine's level, much less my father's. I know how to cover my tracks well enough I can't be found by anyone who doesn't possess hacker skills, but dismantling a hacker's attack, stopping a virus from eating away at a program? I'd just get in the way.

"Cassidy." My gaze snaps back to Turner. "We'll need water and food."

If I weren't already so far removed from this, I would be pissed at his dismissal. As it is, it's a little flicker of annoyance, because he's right—I'm good for being the coffee girl at this stage. "Back in ten."

Nick places a hand on my arm. "Cass—"

Now I do shake off his hold. "He's right," I say quietly. "Get to work, Nick. I'm not much use at this stage. Too advanced."

The twelfth floor break room has all the best goodies. After losing a full minute to listening for out of place noises in the stairwell, I climb the stairs and ease open the door. The floor sounds as empty as the stairwell, but I muffle my steps as best I can anyway and tiptoe into the break room for supplies. I find a reusable shopping bag stashed in a cupboard and fill it with a couple of water bottles and some protein bars, constantly checking the shifting shadows for sudden movements.

My paranoid vigilance proves necessary when I step out of the break room and catch a glimpse of a man ducking into the stairwell. Setting the bag down with a muffled plop, I draw my knife from the sheath at my ankle and follow him.

The landing's empty, and thanks to the disabled motion detectors, I have no way of knowing which way he could have gone. The stairs only go up two more flights to the roof, so I check that way first. It's empty, and the door is closed and locked.

Which leaves down.

My breath shallow, I creep down the stairs as quickly as I can. He could be almost to the bottom by now. By the time I reach the eighth floor, I'm calculating the worth of trying to track the guy down or checking in on the men's progress.

Checking in means Turner will want to know where his precious water is.

A faint squeak from below makes up my mind for me. My sneakers will do the same on the polished concrete, and I'll slip in socks. I yank off my shoes and socks and race down the stairs barefoot, my feet slapping against the cool surface.

Footsteps clatter below me, and I risk breaking my neck to peer over the railing as I fly down the stairs. A dark head flashes in and out of view two levels down. I'm fast, but not that fast. I won't be able to catch him before he reaches the bottom.

A shot cracks the quiet and pings off the railing. I flatten myself against the wall. Rookie mistake. There's no point in wasting bullets if you can't see your target. I crouch on the step and inch toward the railing, sprawling on my back when another bullet zips past. I flip onto my belly and slither up to the landing above.

There's two options: let whoever it is go, or wait him out and swing over the railing to the next flight of stairs in an attempt to make up some distance. I'm not wearing shoes, the drop is several feet and awkward, increasing the chances I'll hurt myself, and since this guy has proven himself to be a dumbass with a gun, I could end up getting shot for my troubles.

On the other hand, if he's the one who fed the virus into the system, he might be able to get it out faster than we can.

I slip the knife back into its sheath and draw my gun. Holding my breath, I scoot to the top of the stairs and shift forward to balance on the balls of my feet. It's awkward, moving like this, but it makes for a smaller target. I turn sideways and place my back to the wall, stepping down one stair at a time. At the landing, I slide forward onto my stomach and belly crawl to the railing.

Another shot, this one barely over my head, and I curse my decision to go after this guy and lift my head to line up my shot. The report of the gun kicks up my arm, and I drop my head, bracing myself for his answering bullet. I press my cheek to the cement as his curses drift up through the stairwell.

"Cass?"

No point in being all stealthy, I guess. "Eighth floor landing. He's got a gun, and he's stupid enough to use it," I call out.

Footsteps, thunderously loud, and they stop abruptly on the landing above. "Why are you lying on the floor?"

"Gun. Bullets flying. I'd rather not get shot again." More footsteps, this time from below. "If you're coming with me, you might want to hurry."

Nick descends the stairs, back to the wall, and kneels beside me. "He's not going anywhere." I arch a brow when he grins. "Doors at the lobby level and the garage levels are locked." He places my shoes and socks next to me. "You might want these."

* * * *

He reminds me of a scared teenager. Face pale but set, hair damp with sweat, blood seeping from the wound on his arm where I managed to graze him with my shot, but there's a defiance in his eyes warring with the fear.

Nick cuffing him to a chair doesn't help matters.

Turner and Peter are still in the server room, desperately trying to eradicate the virus. After the standoff in the stairwell, the guy had taken off running for the ground floor. I took my time putting on my shoes and socks while Nick backed up and took the elevator to the garage, keying himself in through the door at the bottom. Trapped between the two of us, gun swinging like a pendulum, Nick relieved him of his gun when he stupidly turned his back.

Constantine hasn't joined us, which is surprising. This information affects him as much as Nick.

The room isn't overly bright. There's a standing lamp in the corner and another on a nearby table. Nick sets his gun there instead of holstering it, so I place mine next to his. "Nick?" I bend over and draw the knife from its sheath. "Is Constantine joining us?"

"No," he murmurs absently, studying the guy in the chair. Chair guy's eyes cut to me, and his gaze catches on the knife in my hand. Nick glances over and nods once at the blade. "Good idea."

I'm not sure why I'm holding the knife, other than it felt logical after setting down the gun. From the way our captive is staring at it, though, and Nick's blank face, I come up with one quickly.

I'm just surprised Nick is actually letting me participate.

I flip it, end over end, light flashing off the blade as I consider what questions to ask. We might not have the time for me to find out why Isaiah is so intent on killing Nick. What matters is determining if this man is here because Isaiah sent him, and that Isaiah is the one behind the virus.

I want him alive. I want him to give Isaiah a message because I am tired of this game we can't refuse to play.

Turner's training included many, many things. Knowing the points of the body that would bleed a lot but not fatally was one of them. I doubt he intended for me to sit in on an interrogation, much less conduct one. He only wanted precision.

But I might as well make myself useful tonight.

The knife is a perfect fit in my hand, elegant and deadly and balanced. I hold it up. "There's two ways to do this. The first is you tell us how to stop the virus and we let you go. The second is you refuse, I carve little pieces from you until you give us the information we need, and we let you go. It's up to you how much blood you want to lose."

For the first time since he was forced into the chair, the guy smirks. "I know how this works. You'll kill me anyway."

I shake my head. "Not true. We didn't kill Demetrios. He wasn't going to talk no matter how much pressure we put on him, and there wasn't any point in killing him, either. He was just unlucky enough to get caught in the crossfire. You, on the other hand..." I run the tip of the knife along his thigh. "You *have* something we want."

"How do you know I installed the virus?"

Good point. "We don't. If you can make me believe you, we'll let you go. We'll just pin our message to your chest so Isaiah gets it." I step behind him and place the edge of the blade at his throat. It moves as he swallows hard, his breath hissing out when it presses into the skin. "Now. Did you install the virus?"

"No."

I shrug. "Okay then." I shift the edge, feel it bite into the side of his neck. "Cass."

I've never heard that tone from Nick before. Is it worry? Resignation? Does he finally realize what I figured out? That as long as I'm with him, I can't leave this life behind so I might as well embrace it?

"If you think he knows something and he's not speaking up, this is the time to tell me," I say to Nick. "Torture isn't really my deal."

His gaze flits to the man in the chair. "She's giving you an out you don't deserve."

The prisoner barks a laugh. "She doesn't have the balls to go through with it."

I do. If he doesn't say something to save his own ass, he'll find out soon enough, too late to do anything about it.

He's an amateur. If he was seasoned by Isaiah, he wouldn't be sweating so much. I lean forward and speak directly into his ear. "You're the brains, right? The guy Isaiah turns to when he needs to worm his way past firewalls. You stay behind, safe in your office, while the rest of them are out running the streets and enforcing rules with violence."

A strangled noise breaks free of his chest. I slide the blade down to his collarbone. It won't hurt much, certainly won't bleed much, but it'll get the point across. "How do we stop the virus?"

"I don't know what you're talking about." His voice has already lost some of its bravado. Then he whimpers, a high, pathetic sound, as the knife cuts through skin.

"How do we stop the virus?"

"I don't know what you're talking about." Softer this time, and it earns him another slice along the inside of his bicep, deep enough to reach muscle. It'll bleed, and it'll *ache*, worse than the sharp burst from the initial cut because it'll linger.

I ask the question three more times, each time resulting in another wound. Down the line of his sternum into the fleshy part of his belly. The outside of his thigh. A shallow nick into the delicate flesh where his jaw meets neck, close enough to vital arteries he screams and babbles out instructions.

Nick dashes out the door, and I reach for the towel on the table, wiping my hands.

"What's next?"

His voice is tired, resigned, and I flick my gaze over his body. The knife did its work. Blood drips down his neck and arm, seeps through his jeans, splotches the middle of his T-shirt. So ugly compared to my usual work. Ugly and messy.

I finish wiping my hands and move on to the knife handle, gingerly mopping up excess blood from the steel. The nubby fabric isn't the best for it, but I don't have the proper materials, and I can't let it dry. "We send you back to Isaiah. I'm not sure how that part works. That's up to Nick. But you'll live, and provided you seek proper medical attention, your cuts won't get infected. You'll have scars." I meet his eyes, the distance between us wider than the few feet separating me from him. I've sunk so far inside myself, I feel I could ask him his name, then stab him in the heart and not care.

Nor would I come back from it. So I don't. I put the knife aside and fold the towel. "What's his plan? Besides killing me?"

He works up a sneer. "I'm not stupid."

"You were stupid enough to get caught," I point out. "Stupid enough to give up the instructions on how to stop the virus. Chances are Isaiah will kill you anyway. You might as well tell me what you know."

His mouth trembles and clamps shut, and I sigh. "Tell Isaiah I'm tired of this. I'm not going to choose someone to die in my place. If he wants me to suffer, he should just kill me and get it over with." Nick walks into the room, and I peer over his shoulder, expecting Constantine at his heels. "It's done?"

"Done. Half the programming is a loss. There's holes in the firewalls that your dad and Peter are patching now."

A frown tugs at my lips. Still no Constantine. "You're going to take care of this guy yourself?"

"Con's running through the security footage." Nick unlocks the cuffs, drags the captive to his feet, and recuffs him. "Tell Isaiah to stop fucking around," he growls and shoves him toward the door. "Back in a while. Text if you leave with Con."

I make my way up to the eighth floor and find Turner hunched over the terminal. "Cassidy. Water."

Nice to know some things never change.

Chapter 23

I can't stop rubbing my hands together. I dry wash them, over and over, watching the streetlights flash past. The dead space inside shrinks as seconds speed into minutes, each block taking us closer to Constantine's condo and the shower.

I am going to lose my grip before we get there. This has *never* happened. I don't let it. Cass the Assassin is only peeled away through ritual. I clutch that self to me and force myself inside, flexing my muscles and stretching my limbs until it's me, and there's no trace of Cass the College Student.

It's like I can feel it flaking off. There's no beach, no sugar rush, only a shower awaiting me. Nick asked about the beach. I told him no. I need the shower more than anything. If I can scrub away the blood and disgust, I can hold it together. I won't need the ocean.

My body is vibrating with anxiety by the time we pull into the garage. I tuck my hands in my pockets to keep them away from Nick. The moment we clear the front door of Constantine's condo, I toe off my shoes and kick them aside, then shrug out of my hoodie and toss it in the direction of the living room couch.

His hand stills mine on the hem of my shirt. "Cass?"

"I can't," I whisper. No talking. Not now. I pull my hand free and spin around, stride down the hall as I pluck and twist at the hem of my shirt. Nick follows me into the bathroom, shutting the door behind us. I flip on the shower and shed my clothes, conscious of how frantic my movements are, how jittery I am. The not quite warm water hits my skin, and I pick up Nick's bar of soap because it's the closest cleaning implement.

I can't scrub hard enough. I want to rip into my skin, shred it, and grow a new one. It reddens and then fades under bubbles of soap, the warm scent of cinnamon drifting under my nose. When my hair falls into my eyes, I rake a hand through it. The sharp sting on my scalp as I tug hard is oddly calming.

The shower curtain snaps open, cool air surging into the steamy enclosure, and Nick steps in behind me. He pries the bar of soap from my hand. "Something wrong?"

Breath stuttering in and out, I take him in, water streaming over his bare chest, a concerned gleam in his dark eyes. Yes, something is wrong, but I can't find the words to tell him what it is.

Our first kiss was because he couldn't think of any other way to break me out of the ice. I want him to do it again. But not in the seductive and seductively gentle way he did it before. I don't want *gentle*. I want to be taken. I want all those times where he's held himself back for fear of hurting me.

My step into him, my hand trailing up his body, is the only soft, sweet part of this I'll allow. I don't want to reach a point where violence equals sex, where sex is what takes away that edge a hit leaves behind.

Tonight is different. It wasn't a hit that did this to me. It was the interrogation, the casual dismissal from Turner, the interrupted birthday celebration. It was everything and nothing, and I want to erase it.

I might have gripped the back of his neck a little too hard. I might have nipped a little too sharply into his lower lip. But he doesn't say a word, doesn't back off, just launches his own attack. Lips slipping against one another, tongues gliding and tangling, I'm wrapped around him and arching away from the slick, cool tile before I realize he's stolen control from me.

His hands are busy roaming my skin, fingers dragging over my hip, his mouth swallowing my gasp as he pinches a nipple tight enough I feel the blood rushing back when he releases it. The sting ripples outward, tingling, and I scrape my teeth up his neck, silently begging him for more.

"Cass."

How is it possible for a single word to express so much? Lust. Worry. Love and need and *tell me what's wrong so I can make it right*. One word. My name, and the weight of it threatens to crush me. I sink my fingers into his hair and kiss him. "Don't talk," I mumble against his lips. "Just do whatever you want with me."

He groans low in his throat and eases away, lowering himself to kneel in front of me. Water pounding his shoulders, hair dripping onto his forehead, he tips his head back to look at me, love writ harsh and fierce on his face. That look steals the air from my lungs. We're past the stage where sex is nothing more than a good time and a release. I'm a fool to try to push us backward.

Somehow, despite being on his knees and the shocking tenderness between us, he knows how to give me what I'm craving. He grips my thigh hard enough to make me yelp and spreads me open for his mouth.

I hit my head on the shower wall. There will be crescent impressions in Nick's shoulders from my nails digging into his skin. Already hypersensitive, he's taking full advantage and pushing me faster than I've ever gone. I curve my leg around his neck, keening whimpers bouncing off the tile, ending in a scream as he nips into my clit.

"Again. Nick. *Again.*" Undo me. Destroy me.

He thrusts two fingers into me instead. Rising from his knees, fingers buried deep inside, I taste myself on his lips as his thumb presses down hard on the throbbing bundle of nerves.

The orgasm rolls over me in a quick, fiery burst, and I shriek again as he digs his fingers into my hips, boosts me up, and plunges through tissues still pulsing with aftershocks.

"God." He drops his forehead to my shoulder, and I want to pound on his back. There's another orgasm hovering beyond my reach, and he's keeping me from going after it. "Never get used to this." He pulls back and snaps his hips forward. "So *hot*. You burn me alive."

Then he shuts up and kisses me like his life depends on it, and maybe it does. We become a writhing, blurred mass of limbs, speed increasing with each panted breath. An ache blooms low in my belly, growing in weight and demanding all the while to be fed. "Can you come for me?" he rasps, dark eyes intent on mine. "Like this?"

Can I? The only friction I have is where his cock rubs me on each thrust, and as I bite my lip and strain toward the ache, he tilts my hips and rubs against a new spot. My eyes go wide as the ache expands. He groans. "Fuck. You like that."

"Yes." Dear sweet Jesus, I love it. "Nick." Release is a wire winding tighter and tighter, and I'm going out of my mind. It keeps expanding, the ache ramping higher. This has to break somewhere.

It's like standing under a wave as it crashes down. It sweeps everything away, sound drowned by the roaring in my ears. I am molten fire. I'm surrounded by him, swamped by him, by what he's done and how he pushed me under until I am drowning.

Opening my eyes, I blink away the water stinging them and wonder how I'll make it out of the shower because I don't have a bone left in my body. "What," I pant, "was that?"

"*Le petit mort,*" he whispers. "They got it wrong. There was nothing little about that. I don't know that I've ever made a woman come that hard."

Somehow I manage to find the strength to move my head. "What did you *do* to me?"

He lowers me to my feet, taking my mouth in a slow, sweet kiss that threatens to mushify my already hazy mind. "Exactly what you asked for."

I lift a shaking hand to my hair and push it off my face, catching Nick's hand as he lifts his own. Pressing a kiss to his palm, I lay my head on his chest, uncaring that the water's starting to chill.

He strokes his hands down my back to my hips, then nudges me away. Picking up the soap, he motions for me to turn around, and I shut off the cold tap to let the rest of the hot water through.

"One of the first things I loved about you was how open you are when we're making love." His voice is quiet, his touch gentle as he rubs soap into my skin. "You just throw yourself into every part of it. It's kind of incredible."

I peer over my shoulder at him, sighing when he brings his hands around and begins to glide the soap over my breasts. "You make it easy to do," I whisper. "I feel like you could talk me into anything, and I'd do it because you'd make it feel good." The statement comes dangerously close to my reasons for going bare with him, and I hold my breath, hoping he doesn't notice.

He suckles a kiss at the curve of my jaw. "I could talk you into anything, huh? That's a dangerous thought."

Tell me about it.

The water's really cool now, so we hurry through the rest of the shower and dry off. I drag out the hair dryer I bought and never used, plug it in, and use it to get the worst of the damp out.

Still restless despite the sex and the shower, I pull on a pair of sweats and a sweatshirt, find a pair of sneakers, and go in search of Nick and his car keys. I find him at the kitchen bar, bottle of whiskey in one hand and a glass in the other. His keys are on the far end, and I walk past him and pick them up. I curl my fingers around them. "I—" Why is this so *hard?* I swallow and try again. "I need to get out of here for a while."

He sets the glass on the counter with a clink and holds out his hand for the keys. When I don't, he says, "Cassidy. Give me the keys."

"I can't." My hands are shaking, whatever afterglow I hung on to gone. This is worse, a thousand times worse. The man's anguished cries echo in my head. We never got his name. I didn't care. I *don't* care. We got what we needed, probably couldn't have gotten it any other way.

Probably. Definitely. I don't *know*.

He leans over and snags the keys, then my hand, drawing me to him. "Come on."

The street's basically dead when we pull out of the garage. Nearing midnight, and there's clearly no nightlife in Constantine's neighborhood. I spot a McDonald's up ahead and point. "Can we hit the drive-through?"

He complies in silence, only quirking a brow when I correct him from a Diet Coke to a regular. Back on the road, he doesn't head west; he heads north. Back toward Malibu. The top creaks on my cup, threatening to pop off as my hands clamp around it. I don't think I can wait until we get there. Something's alive and crawling under my skin.

Guilt. It's got to be guilt. Or regret. The same thing practically. What happened with the programmer didn't have to. I could have let Nick question him. I *should* have let him.

A half hour later, I've finished the soda, crushed the cup in my hands, and we're driving past the beach at Santa Monica. Anywhere along here would be fine. The place is quiet. The tourists have all gone back to their hotels for the night. "We can stop anywhere around here."

"Another couple minutes. I've got a place in mind." He takes the cup from my hands and places it in the cup holder.

"The place" is an even quieter section of beach, backed up to a shadowy stretch of land covered in scrub brush. I think it's part of a state park. He swings into the parking lot, and I'm out of the car before he's got the engine shut off. He catches up with me as I sprint toward the ocean.

I'd fling myself in if I thought it would help.

Arms tight around my waist, he pulls me down onto the sand. "Talk to me."

I shut my eyes and breathe. Cinnamon, creosote, and salt mingle and clash, waves roaring in to break into tiny droplets. Nick's strong and warm beside me, his arm anchoring me to the sand. "How do you do it?" I ask. "How do you keep it from breaking you?"

He shifts around so I'm between his legs, and when my back comes into contact with his chest, I sag against him. "Didn't figure this would be a problem for you." His breath tickles my ear. "You'd gone cold. I figured you were fine." He takes my hands and wraps his around them, tucking them close to my stomach for warmth. The brush of his thumb along my knuckles sends a prickle of awareness up my spine.

"It's conditioned into us," he says. "You demonstrate a certain aptitude early on, so the old guard starts working on the new guard to take over. Con and I started sitting in on those meetings and summits when we were sixteen, and at the point, we'd known for a while what our family was into. We *wanted* it. We knew we'd get it once we'd proven ourselves.

"That guy got off easy tonight. He shot at you. Tried to destroy months of work that could have cost us millions of dollars. He bled, but not enough. We were raised on power," he says quietly. "We were told from the time we could walk that we could have whatever we wanted if we proved ourselves worthy.

"And part of that is recognizing an innocent when we see one." His thumb stills, and I half-twist to look at him, see the anger on his face. "You fooled me back there, Cass. I should have known better. That's not your game. You need the quick and easy out, the ability to walk away without the conversation lingering in your ears. I *knew* that, and I didn't make you leave."

Nick knows me better than I thought. He's right. I shouldn't have been in that room tonight. I should have left it to Nick who knew what he was doing, had been trained to chain it down and tighten the screws. I sink deeper into his arms and rest my head on his shoulder. The moon's out. The cold, clean glow has never been all that appealing to me until now. I like the sterility. It makes me think I can brush tonight aside as an anomaly.

"Tell me about your relationship with Turner."

I snap my head up. "What?"

He lets go of my hand and grips my chin, turning my face toward his. "You have this tendency to dodge the question whenever he's the subject. You don't get along." I shake my head, the movement truncated by his hold. "So why do you do what he wants anyway?" he asks.

I jerk my chin free of his fingers. "Isn't it obvious?" The bitterness in my voice should be a big freakin' clue.

"Not gonna fly this time. Talk."

I chew on my lower lip, staring out at the water. The moonlight ripples over it, turning the ocean a glimmering white. "We had a great relationship until I was about seven or eight. Typical dad and daughter relationship. Something happened right around then, and he became…well, the guy he is now. Only shows affection for my mother, and rarely in public. I didn't understand what had happened. All I wanted was my dad back. By the time I was thirteen, I found a way to get it, or some of it. He'd never made it a secret he practiced jujitsu and tae kwon do. I told him I wanted to, too. It became a pattern. I noticed something new, and I'd ask to tag along, ask him to show me how to do it."

He'll get it. I won't have to say it. Nick's a smart guy. Picks up on a lot of things without a word from me, and I've just drawn him a map.

"How long has it been?"

Too long, I suspect. "I was sixteen when I completed my first hit." A wave rolls in, dangerously close to our feet. "We should move, or we'll end up soaked."

We stand and brush sand from our clothes, avoiding each other's eyes. Not hard to do, really, since Nick seems to have no interest in actually looking at me. He takes my hand, and we start up the beach, following the water, tripping away as the tide creeps in. "I don't think I'll ever get back what I lost." I kept my voice quiet, so I'm not sure if he hears me over the noise of the ocean. "But I can't seem to stop myself from trying."

He stops and turns into me, wrapping his hand around my hair and tugging my head back. The kiss he gives me is quiet and soothing. "You know where I stand." His gaze is hard and intent on mine. "You want out, I won't force you into taking a job. People will come at you as long as you're with me. With Isaiah after you, it's getting around who you are. As long as you're with me, though, I'll do whatever I can to let you be a college student. Maybe a teacher."

He remembered. Something mentioned once or twice in passing conversation, and he remembered.

Can I stay with you forever?

Instead of asking the question, I nod and shut my eyes. I don't know about forever with him.

Forever looks like a prize I'm not sure I deserve.

Chapter 24

The light in the guest room is bright and full when I wake the next morning. I roll over to peer at the clock. It's after ten. I blink, uncertain I'm reading the clock right. It's definitely after ten, and the other side of the bed is empty and cold.

Nick should have woken me. He *always* wakes me. Brain still mostly asleep, I push my hair away from my face and kick away the blankets. While I'm hunting for the sleep tank and boxers Nick stripped off me last night, I listen for any indication Nick or Constantine are still in the condo.

Nothing. Nothing aside from the usual faint noises of the street below.

The silence puts me on edge, and I palm one of my knives. Nick's been reluctant to leave me alone since the stabbing, so it doesn't make sense he'd do so today. The click of the door is ear-shatteringly loud, making me wince. The hallway is empty. The door across the hall, Constantine's office, is open. I duck inside and do a thorough scan and find nothing.

The living room and kitchen are both empty. Constantine's bedroom door is shut, and I stand in the middle of the living room, knife balanced in my hand, staring at the door. It *sounds* like the condo is empty. It *sounds* like Nick and his cousin left me to sleep while they went into work.

Assumption is also the mother of all fuckups.

I tiptoe across the living room and place my hand on the doorknob. Aside from the day I swiped his car keys, I've stayed out of Constantine's room. I nudge aside the vague itch of guilt over invading his space and turn the knob.

My cell rings from somewhere else in the condo, and I jump away from the door. When it doesn't fly open, I walk backward into the kitchen and retrieve my phone. It's stopped ringing by the time I pick it up, and I see the caller was Nick.

I call him back. "Why didn't you wake me?"

"Good morning to you too," he says dryly. "You were exhausted. You don't remember slapping me earlier?"

"No," I mutter. "Are you going to come pick me up, or should I find my own way there?"

"Stay. You need a break, Cass."

"I don't need you making decisions for me. I'm fine."

He sighs, and there's rustling and muted conversation before I hear the distinct noise of him shutting a door. "You need a break." His tone says don't argue, but I prepare one anyway. It dies on his next words. "You almost fell apart last night because I wasn't smart enough to pull you out. Take the time off. I'll be home in a few hours. We'll go see a movie or something."

A movie? In the dark where anyone could sneak up behind us? "Are you sure that's a good idea?"

"Maybe not a movie," he concedes. "But I'll be home in a few hours, and we'll go out."

"Like on a date."

"I believe that's what young people still call it these days, yes."

"Did you just make an age joke?"

"I have no idea what you're talking about. Finish checking the condo and go back to bed or something."

I stick my tongue out even though he can't see me. "How'd you know I was checking the condo?"

"Because it's what I'd do in your situation. Go. I'll see you soon." He tells me he loves me, and the words send a thrill up my spine. Part of me hasn't quite accepted that *he loves me*. Eleven year age gap and all, Nick loves me.

I set the phone aside, flex my fingers on the knife, and check Constantine's bedroom before making my way to the guest room. I lock the door behind me and head for the shower. I'm too awake to fall back asleep, but an extravagantly long shower is enticing.

Warm water slides over my skin, the heat in my face growing the longer I stare at the tiled wall of the shower. Last night replays in flashes. I don't think I've ever abandoned myself like that. We've been sweet and tender and greedy and teetering on the edge of violence, and he's right— I've been open to whatever he wants to try. We've come so far in a few short weeks, and he's given me things I didn't even know I wanted. He's broken me out, shown me how powerful sex is. How powerful *love* is. But sometimes, like last night, the way I just throw myself into it without any thought other than *gimme gimme gimme* shocks me. Eventually I'll stop being embarrassed by what he does to me. Today is clearly not that day.

I dry off and wrap myself in a towel, then spend far too long pawing through my clothes in an attempt to find something to wear. A date. An actual date. When I start debating which top is more date-like, I groan. This is *Nick*. He's seen me with blood in my hair. I could wear a paper bag, and it wouldn't matter.

I'm nervous. There's no doubt in my mind we're in a relationship. We've been out in public together, holding hands, kissing, all the things normal couples do. We've just never gone on an actual *date*. The one time I accompanied him as his date, the restaurant exploded in gunfire and screaming. I pull on a cranberry three-quarter sleeve sweater and a pair of skinny jeans. There. Date attire.

Pushing my hair behind my ears, I grab my boots and head for the living room. There's got to be some awful daytime TV to distract me from these ridiculous thoughts.

That's where Nick finds me two hours later, curled up on the couch and thoroughly engrossed in a completely unrealistic yet strangely captivating soap opera. "Cass? What the hell are you doing?"

I hold up a hand and lean forward, intent on the screen. When the show cuts to a commercial break without following through on a promised payoff, I blow out a frustrated breath. "Now I know why these shows are addicting. Seriously. That guy, that evil guy? I *know* he's about to screw the blond chick, and she's totally going to be into it, but she's already suspicious of him, and I *have* to see her face when she finds out what he's been up to!"

Nick pries the remote from my hand and shuts off the TV. "Obviously, I never should have left you alone. Watching soap operas? You? Who are you and what have you done with Cass?"

I peer around him at the blank screen. "But—"

He grabs me around the waist and tosses me over his shoulder, scaring a yelp from me. "No 'buts.' We're leaving."

Despite the great view of his ass as he carries me out of the condo, I keep up a string of protests, going so far as to smack him in the middle of the back, demanding he put me down. He finally does when we reach the stairwell, trapping me against the wall with a fierce kiss.

For once, he doesn't try to lose an unseen tail as we drive out of the parking garage. I slip on the Oakleys Nick insisted on buying me and settle back in my seat. "Where are we going?"

"Thought I'd take you to one of my favorite places since you've shown me one of yours." He reaches for my hand and laces our fingers together. "Quiet, good food. There's a back patio. I called ahead and reserved a table."

Not just a date, but a semi-fancy one. I fight the urge to squirm in my seat, softening when he brushes his lips over my knuckles. "I'm tired of hiding," he says quietly.

The statement could mean a few things. We've been hiding from people in his own organization. In some ways, we've been hiding our relationship. By taking a direct route instead of our usual circuitous one and sitting in plain view of everyone and their uncle, we're killing two birds with one stone.

I tighten my fingers around his, the nerves in my chest fluttering harder.

The restaurant is on a quiet, unassuming side street in Hollywood, the one place I never would have expected quiet or unassuming. The worn brick building has huge windows in the front, a small, dark green awning hanging over the door, and the name of the restaurant, Fiddleheads, in gold script across the front.

The reception area is small, holding only a few hardback chairs and a dark wood podium. "Dominic! So glad to see you!" The host, a short, slender man with dark red hair slicked away from his face, hurries forward with a hand outstretched. "Your usual table is ready." He gives me a discreet once-over that's mostly concealed by his warm, friendly smile. "Welcome to Fiddleheads. I'm Gary."

"Cass."

Gary grabs a couple of menus and leads us through the restaurant to a set of French doors, flung open to the unseasonably warm day. We're seated at a small table in the far corner of the patio, a bottle of champagne nestled in a silver bucket of ice.

I study the wine. "Are you *trying* to make this the best date ever?"

Nick pulls it free of the ice and pops the cork. "Consider it a continuation of your birthday. Got you something." He shifts around and digs into his pants pocket. He drops a key on the table in front of me.

I pick it up. It's an ordinary house key, the silver shiny and new. "What's this go to? Did you find a place already?" We've been too busy for Nick to go house hunting, but maybe he squeezed it in somehow. Disappointment tugs at me that I didn't get to go with him. It might have been fun.

He shakes his head and fills my glass, the bubbles rising in steady streams. "I'm not sure if I want to stay in Santa Monica any longer, and once I buy a house, then I've got to buy all the shit that goes *in* the house, and I don't have time for it." He points to the key. "It's for your new apartment."

My new— I stare at the key in my hand. I mentioned in passing I wasn't sure I wanted to go back to the apartment I'd shared with Denise, and with Isaiah staying down the hall, it's not even an option anymore. And I knew I needed to figure out the whole housing situation before the next term started.

But Nick went over my head, behind my back, and took care of it all by himself, without any input from me. "Oh," I say quietly, placing the key on the table. Then I push it across to him and leave it. "Thanks, but no thanks."

"Cass."

I hold up a hand to silence him, willing my anger to recede enough I can speak without yelling at him. "I know I'll need to find a place to live, and I'll need to do it soon before the next semester starts, but *I* was going to do it. And I was going to ask you to come with me."

Clenching my hands into fists, I draw in a breath, let it out, and lift my gaze. "I love you. I know you love me, and I know you're worried about my safety. That does not give you the right to just…completely take me out of the equation when it comes to where I'm supposed to live."

He pushes the key back toward me. "It's a one bedroom on the fifth floor out of seven, stairwells on both ends of the hallway, no balcony, with a separate key for the front entry. It's close enough to campus you can walk. Quiet street, opposite end of campus from your last place."

"That's nice, but I'm still not taking it." I probably can't afford it, and there's no way in hell I'm going to let him pay my rent. I push the key away.

He ignores it. "You haven't even seen it."

"Would you feel better about me rejecting it if I see it first? Fine, we can go by after lunch." I snatch up my champagne and drain the glass. I want to fling the key in his face. "Whenever you do something like this, I have to fight off the doubts. I am really, really tired of doing that."

His brows draw together in a frown. "Doubts?"

For a thirty-two-year-old man, Nick can be pretty clueless. "I wonder if you're with me because you want to be or because you feel responsible for me."

I pick up my menu. Nothing sounds appetizing, and I no longer feel like celebrating. Aside from those few hours at the spa last night, it's been a waste of time.

A finger appears at the top of the menu, hooking on and tipping it down. His dark eyes are sober as he studies me. "If I didn't want to be with you, you wouldn't be here."

"And I get that. It's just hard to remember when you pull this kind of shit."

He takes the menu out of my hands and lays it on the table; then he gets up and comes around to crouch next to my chair. Something about seeing him at my feet kicks my nerves into gear, and they rev higher as he clasps my hand. "Since we've hooked up, you've been shot at, assaulted, stabbed in the stomach, and died on me—twice," he adds. "We've been chased, and someone set my house on fire while you were in it. You've also amazed me and surprised me and proven that you can handle almost anything thrown at you. The longer I'm with you, the more I love you. I am not going to lose you because I didn't do enough to protect you."

Some of my anger fades. "Then *talk* to me about it. I don't want to worry you, and believe me, that's a lot less likely to happen if you make me a part of this." My free hand shakes as I lift it to push a lock of hair off his forehead. "You pull shit like this, it makes me want to go behind *your* back and put my own plans into place, and then not tell you until I'm acting on them."

"For fuck's sake, Cass, *don't* do that. Then I'll have to handcuff you to my desk." Catching my hand, he presses a kiss to the thin skin of my inner wrist. He works his way toward my palm. "Actually, that's not a bad idea," he murmurs, and when he looks up, the worry's been replaced by desire, warm and designed to make me melt. "I'll make you a deal. You see this place, pick out a few others, and if one of those meets both your specifications *and* mine, I'll get out of the lease on this one."

As compromises go, it's a good one. "Deal." I kiss him to seal it, whimpering when he refuses to let me break it. One hand cupped at my nape, tongue flirting with the seam of my lips, he threatens to take a simple kiss to indecent territory until I remember we're supposed to be having lunch.

He smiles against my mouth and plants a quick smooch on my lips before he eases back. "Do you think you could get up now?" I ask. I wave a hand at him. "You're making me a little nervous."

The smile becomes a smirk, a very smug one. "When I propose, it'll be when you least expect it."

My heart skitters to a stop, slamming into my rib cage. *When*. Not if, when. "You're awfully confident," I manage.

The weirdest expression flits over his face, as though he just realized what he said, and now he's not sure if he means it. Logical me doesn't expect him to. We're fine now. But the few months we've had aren't a strong enough foundation for me to start building my fairytales on.

I do it anyway. I see a house on the beach and Nick chasing a little boy with his dark hair and charming smile. I see me surprising Nick at work, and nights out with just the two of us. I see a church and flowers and my dad looking sharp and cool in a tux, Nick waiting at the end of the aisle.

I see a lifetime in a handful of seconds, and I want this beautiful, impossible dream more than anything. I block it out and work up a smirk of my own. "Who says I'll say yes?"

The rest of lunch flies by, and Nick's right—the food is delicious. He doesn't mind me scanning Craigslist for apartments while we eat, and I show him a few listings. Only two pick up when he calls and let him schedule appointments for that afternoon.

"What are your requirements for my apartment?" I ask, pushing the last bit of pasta around in my bowl. Someone at a nearby table has a strawberry and chocolate dessert that looks fantastic, and I tried to save room. I didn't do a very good job.

"Easily visible exits and accessible stairwells. Quiet street, no parking garage."

I lift a brow.

"If I could, I'd never let you walk into a parking garage again," he growls.

"Yet we keep using them."

He flips me off, making me giggle. "Multiple floors, though the building would have fewer than forty units. Preferably fewer than twenty five. Windows and doors that can be reinforced. You?"

"No balcony," I start. "Within walking distance to campus, a decent size kitchen. Everything you've already mentioned. Washer and dryer in unit, but if I can't have that, I'll settle for laundry facilities on the same floor." I point my fork at him. "Something I can afford on what's left of my loans." I meet his scowl with a bland look. "Not budging on that one. I'm paying for it."

"Half."

"All of it."

He leans in. "Half. I'll be spending as much time there as you. We'll split the rent." Our waiter appears with a plate covered in chocolate and strawberries, and Nick's scowl fades into a smile. "Hope you saved room for dessert."

Chapter 25

I'm standing in the middle of an empty living room when it hits me: this is absurd.

It's strange, unreal, an alternate reality that makes so little sense I'm dizzy. I'm looking at apartments. I'm looking at apartments with *Nick*. Like we'll be *living together*. Me, who hasn't had a steady relationship with a guy since I was seventeen.

I can't do this.

The apartment's decent. It's small, but bright, and it's a corner unit. The bedroom is tiny, and the bathroom isn't big enough for a tub. The kitchen is okay, though, with plenty of cabinets to make up for the lack of counter space.

I pull out my phone to re-check the listing for the rent. I can afford it. Barely. If I dip into my savings to pay for everything else. And only stay until the end of the next semester.

"What do you think?" Nick's face is neutral. A little too neutral, to be honest. Which either means he hates it, or it meets every one of his criteria and he wants me to sign on the dotted line.

"I can't really afford it," I admit.

Nick turns to the property manager, an older, craggy-looking guy in a loose plaid shirt. "Could you give us a moment?"

He shoots Nick a skeptical look, but shrugs and shuffles out of the apartment, shutting the door behind him. "You're only paying half," Nick reminds me.

I am *not* paying half. He can just forget about that right now. I wander over to the window. "This feels weird." The street below is lined with parked cars on both sides so parking will be a bitch. "There's an order to this sort of thing, and we're skipping around."

"What are you talking about?"

The street is also completely void of people. Not a single, solitary soul outside, walking a dog or hurrying to one of the cars. "This. All of this. Talking about living together like it's a given. We *just* went on our first date. Aren't we supposed to go on the date, *then* move in together? In like a year? Or more?"

"Convention dictates that, yes, that's how it's supposed to go. We're not conventional, Cass."

"Maybe I want to be," I whisper.

The only way I know he's behind me is from the increased heat at my back. "Turn around."

I do as he asks and stare at his chest. When he slips two fingers under my chin and tips it up, the anger in his eyes surprises me. "I could give a flying fuck about convention. I *like* coming home to you. I want you to steal the covers from me and complain about how bad my coffee is. I don't *have* to find a new place to live right now. If Con kicks me out, I'll stay with one of my sisters, or my parents, or, fuck, a hotel. I want to be wherever you are, Cass. If that means sharing a shitty apartment with you while you finish school, I'll do it. And I *will* pay half."

His little speech should have made me feel better, but it has the opposite effect. Heat blooms and spreads across my cheeks, and I tilt my head away from his hold.

"What?"

I shake my head, and he captures my face in his hands. "Talk to me."

"I feel stupid," I blurt. "Okay? Stupid and embarrassed and *really* showing my immaturity."

His expression is so much like a parent searching for patience I pull myself free, thoroughly mortified. "It's been a while since I've been in a relationship. A *long* while." I edge around him. "Forget it. Let's just go. This place won't work."

Our phones chime simultaneously. Before I can open my text, Nick spins me around and kisses me. Hard. The kiss is all anger and frustration and heat and, within seconds, I want to climb him like a tree. He breaks the kiss on a growl. "I am getting tired," he says, voice a low, menacing rumble, "of having you doubt me."

I shut my eyes and point at my face. "See? Stupid and embarrassed and immature." I sigh, peering up at him through my lashes. "I don't doubt your feelings for me, Nick. I'm just... I've never done this before, and what if we're going too fast?"

Another quick kiss, and he releases me. "Then we'd better buckle up."

A hot lick of fear tickles my belly, and I smother it. Later. We'll talk about this later. After I've had some time alone to sort through the chaos in my head. I check the text I received, and fear roars back to life, threatening to set everything ablaze.

It's a picture. A proof of life, I think they call it. There's a copy of today's *LA Times* visible in the bottom quarter of the picture. Something that shows, yes, we mean it. The background of the photo is indistinctly gray and industrial.

The woman in the picture is my mother.

Gagged. From the position of her shoulders, her wrists are bound behind her. A bruise is forming on her right cheek, and her hair's come loose from its twist, scraggly locks hanging around her face.

Isaiah has my mother.

Always, before, it's been a conscious effort to slot myself into the headspace I need to kill. Not today. Not with my mother's face staring defiantly at her captor. I slip in and then breathe out as the cool, efficient emptiness stretches over me.

I hold up my phone. "We need to get to a computer. I can't make out the details on a screen this small."

He holds up his phone in response. "Your father hasn't reported to work today."

As quickly as it came on, the emptiness threatens to break wide open and flood me with despair. But this is Turner. He can take care of himself. Mom... I hate thinking of my mom as a damsel in distress. She won't be sitting around, waiting for her husband to rescue her. She's smart too. Smarter than all the guys in that room probably.

Turner would tell me to go after my mother.

"Mom first. Computer?"

"Shoot it to Con. He'll get started on the analysis. I don't have my laptop with me, so we'll have to wait until we get to the office." Nick strides across the room and opens the door.

My finger hovers, refusing to lower over the button to forward the text to Constantine. Nick's cousin has proven helpful in the past. He's stepped up and given me a place to stay when he didn't have to open his home to me. He sat next to my bed while I was recuperating in the hospital, sometimes holding my hand when the pain became too much and Nick wasn't there.

Constantine has proven himself, over and over. So why are my instincts telling me no?

I shove my phone into my back pocket. "Not yet," I say, hurrying for the door. "Unless we reach a point where neither of us have made any headway, I want to keep Mom's kidnapping to ourselves. Can you see if he can track Turner, though? He's probably looking for Mom, and if he manages to find her before we do, having someone on him would help *us* because Turner won't ask for backup."

The manager's still in the hallway. Nick stops briefly while I head for the stairs, probably to tell the guy we won't be taking the apartment. He catches up when I hit the ground floor, edging in front of me to check the street before we hurry out of the building and into the car.

It's so perfectly, blandly *gray*. I enlarge the photo on my phone, tuning out Nick as he coolly relays orders to someone who isn't Constantine. Gray, gray, and more gray, and if I blow up the photo any more on this small screen, it'll pixelate.

Unwilling to give up, I shift the picture around, scanning the pipes over my mother's head. More gray. There's no one else in the photo. Not even a finger from whoever's holding the newspaper. Isaiah's good. He's very, very good. Nick or I may be able to see some minute detail once the picture's on a larger screen, but on my phone, I can't distinguish jack shit.

"How do you know Turner didn't show up for work?" I ask, setting my phone in my lap. Nick takes a turn a little too fast, and I grab the door handle to keep from careening into him.

"One of my guys, Easton, says he didn't check-in this morning, and he hasn't seen him anywhere around his office. He's on his way to your parent's house with Peter. I had people on both your parents. Isaiah's got me spread thin, though, which was the point. Your dad made it a little easier for me by checking in every time he arrived or left. He wanted more people on your mom."

Turner's weakness. His one soft spot, one you wouldn't have to dig very far down to find. "He's not there. He would have gone to Mom's office first to talk to her paralegal and the receptionist, and if they didn't have any useful information, he's probably holed up in one of his safe houses, plotting out a way to get to Isaiah."

"Know where any of these safe houses are?" Nick roars into the parking garage, tires squealing on the polished cement as he turns into his parking spot.

"No," I admit. "I don't even think Mom knows. Plausible deniability. Worst case scenario, we'd both be able to legitimately say we don't know where he is."

We climb out of the car, Nick doing his best to surround me as we make our way to the stairwell. Once inside, I dash up the first couple of flights, Nick at my heels. By the time we reach the fifth floor, I'm breathing harder than I'd like. On the seventh, my muscles are starting to burn. Eighth, they're going rubbery, and he's literally right behind me, ready to push me up the stairs.

Now's a *fantastic* time to learn that my recovery is not going as well as I thought.

We make it to the ninth floor, and I brace a hand on the wall beside the door as he checks the hallway. He jerks his head, and we slip out of the stairwell, barely making it to the empty office I'd been using without being noticed.

Without a word, he boots up the computer and logs on. He hands me a cable to plug my phone into the computer, and I shake my head. "Already e-mailed it to myself," I murmur. He stands and moves aside so I can take the chair, and I bring up my e-mail account, the one I use for jobs. His noise of approval barely registers, and I click on the picture.

The larger screen only serves to show the tear tracks on her cheeks. I shut my eyes, defeat threatening to overwhelm me. I didn't bother to text Isaiah back because he wants a reaction, and I won't give him one. Not yet. Unless there's a distinguishing mark or three in the background, we'll be forced to turn to Isaiah for more information.

"Up." To punctuate the command, Nick grasps me gently by the elbows and lifts me to my feet.

He shifts the picture into a different program, a small box off to one side running a constant string of commands. "What are you doing?"

"A search to match the picture to any others we've already got in the database. If Isaiah's smart, he won't use any place known to the family." Nick scowls at the screen. "Maybe we'll get lucky and he slipped up."

His phone buzzes, and he swipes it awake, turning it on speaker. "Kosta."

Constantine's frustrated voice growls out of the phone. "Caleb Turner hasn't been by his wife's office in several days. Got the security officer to show me the lobby and the elevators to see if he might have slipped in sometime today without anyone noticing. Man's in the wind."

"You won't find him unless he wants to be found," I say, leaning on the desk. "He's fine."

"Nothing on the security footage from his office?" Nick asks.

"We're still trying to get it. Easton didn't report any unusual activity outside the building this morning. I'll call you if something turns up." Constantine disconnects the call, and Nick turns away from the computer.

"There's a possibility the two disappearances are connected. If you let me tell Con, we'll have that many more eyes who know what to look for." He crosses his arms over his chest, glancing at the monitor when the computer beeps quietly.

My belief in Turner and his abilities is so absolute it hadn't occurred to me to connect the two until Nick said something. The man's a ghost and knows more ways to kill someone with his bare hands than he does with a weapon. Nick has a point, though, and I weigh it against what I know of Turner. "I don't think so. The only way—the *only* way—someone could have taken Turner is if it were multiple someones and they'd managed to incapacitate him from a distance."

Nick blinks once. "Tris is a trained sniper. SWAT."

A sniper. Isaiah's one step ahead of us. Again. "How does he find time to do police work in between following me around?"

The computer beeps again, and Nick spins the chair to face the monitor. "Multitasking. We all do it. Can't be criminals all day long." He clicks on a photo and layers it over the one of my mother, hits a few keys, and sits back. "Possible match. Should know in a second."

I peer over his shoulder. "You're going to have to teach me this. Too useful to pass up."

Nick yanks open a drawer in response, rifles through it, and unearths a pen and a scrap of paper. "Warehouse out in Long Beach." He scribbles the address on the paper and hands it to me with a frown. "Too easy."

Exactly what I'm thinking. I stare at the address in my hand. She could be out there. It could be a diversion, and she's somewhere else, somewhere Nick wouldn't know about. I don't want this to get out, to get back to Constantine, because my gut's still muttering that he's not what he seems.

I have to get to her. Somehow. I will not take any chances with her life. "Send someone else," I finally say.

He picks up his phone and dials, his eyes on mine as he holds it to his ear. "Bas. I'm texting you an address. Get your brother and check it out. Might be hot, so go in careful." He hangs up and tosses the phone on the desk.

"Where would you take her?" I circle the desk and begin pacing, one foot in front of the other. "If you needed to go somewhere no one knew, where would you go?"

"If I didn't have anything readily available, I'd start with properties owned by people who owe me favors. It'll take too long to pull together a list of people who *might* owe Isaiah something, but searching for recent real estate transactions is easy enough. Should have thought of it sooner." Mouth set in a grim line, he punches a few keys and pauses. "Go back six months, or longer?"

"Better make it a year to be on the safe side. Marc has been dead a year, and that gives Isaiah a long time to plan." He's likely taken advantage of it too. Everything he's done so far has gone off too smoothly for it to be anything less.

Nick goes quiet, and the small office fills with the sound of my feet walking back and forth, back and forth, keys clicking along. There has to be *something* I can do to help. Right now I'm doing the equivalent of twiddling my thumbs.

My phone buzzes as he motions for me to come over. I pull it out as I step around the desk. He taps his finger on the screen. "Three new properties on the first sweep. He didn't do much to cover his tracks on these purchases. He flipped two, kept one. A house out in the Valley."

Lines of code roll up on a small box in the corner of the screen. I point to it. "Another search?"

"Not a very good one. It's pulled all property sales in LA, Orange, and San Bernardino Counties, and it's programmed to run against a separate database of known aliases and shell companies. We've been working to update it once we found out about Isaiah, but he caught us with our pants down." He glares at the monitor. "Fucker's been playing us for too damn long."

"So we're stuck here for an indefinite period of time." I chew on my bottom lip, turning my phone over in my hands. Line after line of code sprawls across the little box, seconds ticking away as my mother sits in some anonymous space, bound and gagged and furious. From what Nick's said, the query is doing most of the work. "If you had an extra set of hands and eyes, would it go any faster?"

He shakes his head, staring at the screen. My phone buzzes again, and I almost drop it. I forgot I'd taken it out for a reason.

The emptiness, the cool, precious emptiness, threatens to flood with rage. With fear. With everything I can't afford to feel right now.

You're not cooperating, and I'm bored.

7058 Huntington.

Attached is another picture of my mother. There's blood on her face, and her eyes are swollen shut, her hair matted and sticking to her forehead.

The background's the same, industrial gray. Either he's playing with us by taking the time to manipulate the photo so it looks like it's been taken somewhere else, or my mother really is in the warehouse in Long Beach and he's just texted me the address.

My lungs are on fire, and my phone falls to the floor with a clatter. The room's too small. There's no air. I grope for the desk, the rage creeping in. "Nick."

He spins toward me and grasps my wrists. "Cass. Breathe."

Breathe. He reaches up and cradles my face, dark eyes intent. I gasp in air, and the burning eases some. His gaze is steady, calm, bringing me back to the cool emptiness. Another breath, and I nod. "Is this the address of the place in Long Beach?"

After another long minute, the burning fades completely, and Nick scoops up my phone, right as the computer beeps behind him. He glances at the monitor. "Shit."

Chapter 26

"The photos don't match," he says, scanning the accompanying code. "We would have caught it eventually. I don't know if there's enough left in the footprint to recover the original background."

The likelihood the warehouse in Long Beach isn't the address I just received increases a thousand-fold. "Does it really matter anymore? He's sent us an address. *Isaiah's bored.* Boredom doesn't bode well. Even if there's no one there, there's something he wants us to see. We need to go." My hands are trembling. I fist them and push them into the desk.

Isaiah's getting what he wants. He's snapping all my constructs one by one, dismantling the very structure that enables me to kill without compunction. *Don't let your emotions dictate your actions, Cass.* Turner's voice in my head, telling me to hold on. Stay calm.

The most effective way to help my mother is to keep that shit locked down.

Nick shoots me a look that says *are you done?* And strangely, it helps. The faint condescension and derision mean so much more than any platitude he could offer. "If I can uncover the original background of the photo, that may give us a starting point when we search whatever building this is. It'll take a little while, but I can use that time to find the property, possibly building schematics, or blueprints."

I nod, and Nick passes over his phone. "Call Con and tell him to get in here."

I ignore his phone and use mine, scrolling through my contacts until I find Constantine's number. Nick's muttering to himself, his fingers racing over the keyboard, so I circle the desk and sit in one of the chairs on the other side.

Constantine answers on the second ring. "Cass. Still trying to locate your father."

I'd forgotten neither of us had bothered to tell him it wasn't worth the time. "If he wants to be found, you'll know. Sorry to waste your time. I need you to come in. Isaiah's taken my mother, and Nick needs some help." Nick grunts and stops typing long enough to flip me the bird.

"I'm in North Hollywood. Give me twenty minutes." He hangs up, and I lower my phone to my lap with a frown. North Hollywood. Turner's office isn't anywhere near there, which makes me wonder what Constantine's doing in that neighborhood. Instinct sits up and kicks me in the ass, telling me to pay attention, but Constantine's whereabouts aren't of primary concern.

The computer beeps quietly, though Nick's fingers don't stop moving. "Address is north. Encino."

I can't do anything with that information. Not yet. Frustrated, I pull out my phone and call Turner. Unsurprisingly, it goes straight to voicemail, and I disconnect without leaving a message.

The waiting is this insidious, toxic sludge, seeping in through unseen cracks. The longer I sit here, unable to *do* anything, the wider those cracks get. There's no doubt in my mind I'll be able to kill Isaiah on sight or that anyone who steps into my path will end up dead.

I'm just afraid I won't be able to stop.

That I can feel fear, that I'm pacing and jittery, that I'm *anything* other than a sleek, efficient machine is disturbing. It's like there's a glitch in my system, and I can't reset it. I get to my feet and resume pacing. It's better than nothing.

Constantine arrives, muttering something about traffic. Nick hasn't stopped working and merely nods in response to his cousin's greeting. Constantine sets a laptop on the desk, pulls up one of the chairs, and logs into something with a few keystrokes, officially making me completely and utterly redundant.

It's fifty steps from one side of the room to the other. One foot in front of the other, over and over. Fifty steps. Turn. Fifty steps more. Turn.

I've never worked with a partner before. Never thought to use anything other than what I could readily access without digging beneath the top layer. Nick's methods might work for him, but mine have yet to fail me. If I wasn't so focused on trying to keep myself from raging out of control, I would have remembered that sooner. Encino. I have an address, a vague location. I take out my phone, type the address into Google, and click on images.

The address—7058 Huntington—is a house. A large, rambling house, sprawling across the property with little thought to efficient planning. I enlarge the image as much as I can, note the side entrance and the alley running behind the house. It's in the middle of the block, the houses on either side neat and tidy, at least in the picture. I need to get out there. I do my best work on the ground. I have to see for myself what I can use and what I should avoid.

I have an address, a location, and a picture, and they're sitting over there with their computers dicking around for information we don't actually need. Nick keeps a spare set of keys to the car in his desk drawer. He locks everything, but locks are easy to pick.

"Cass?"

I fight the urge to shove my phone into my pocket like a kid caught with her hand in the cookie jar. "Yeah?"

Nick waves me around the desk. "Managed to uncover some of the background."

I lean into the monitor. The picture Isaiah sent of my mother is blurred and pixelated in places. Small patches of some dingy, indistinct color are interspersed with the gray of the warehouse. "A basement?"

"Possibly. Either a basement or a space with little light. Those patches would be brighter if there were uncovered windows." He minimizes the picture and brings up a map. "Street doesn't see much traffic during the day. I haven't located the county records yet." A muscle jumps in his jaw, brows drawn tight. "They should have come up first thing. Either they've been scrubbed or buried deep enough that locating them will take time."

"What's in the records?" I have to get out of here. Now.

"Usual information—placement of gas and sewer lines, previous owners, and sale prices. Some will have the original builder's floor plans. That's what I'm hoping for."

He can keep his floor plans. The images I have might not be complete, but they're enough to go on for now. I nod and step back from the desk. "I'm going to get some water. Need anything?"

"I'll take one." Constantine doesn't look up from his computer.

Nick closes a hand around my wrist. "Another ten minutes," he says quietly. "Fifteen, tops."

That's ten to fifteen minutes my mother might not have. I shake my head. "Now. We go now, Nick. I don't need any of this information. Neither do you. We don't have time for an elaborate rescue set up. Whatever information I can't pull off Google Earth, I'll get when I'm in front of the house."

His grip tightens as I try to pull free. "That additional information could save your life and your mother's. Floor plans will tell us if the house has been modified in anyway, if there's any entrances that we might not be able to see from the street, and if we can get to them without being seen. Ten minutes," he repeats. "You go into this without a firm plan in place, you could end up incapacitated or dead. I want to help you get your mom. I *need* you to stay alive."

"None of that *matters*. You can see all of that from the street. We split up, approach from different directions. We know he's expecting us, so we're not completely blind."

"Actually, we are."

I glance over at Constantine. He shoves a hand through his hair. "Someone expects you to show up, you have to be doubly cautious. He could have the entire house rigged to blow. He could have his men hiding in places we don't know about, ready to kill on sight. This isn't your standard recon mission, Cass." He scowls down at his laptop. "Though if we don't find more information soon, we may have to do what you're thinking and go in anyway."

"If they're public records, you should have been able to find them by now, right? Unless they aren't online?"

"In theory."

Theory's good enough for me. "Nick, if you don't hand over your keys right now, I'm calling a cab."

The computer beeps, and he ignores it, his hand still around my wrist, dark eyes intent. Some unknown emotion flits across his face, then settles into resignation. "C'mon."

Finally.

The drive out to Encino drags on, made longer by stoplights, heavy traffic, and construction on one of the main routes, necessitating a detour. Almost two hours have passed since Isaiah's text, and I'm all but vibrating in my seat, ready to spring out of the car and attack.

One good thing from all the work Nick and Constantine put in, the street really is as deserted as they said. Nick parks several blocks away, and the two of us slink down the alley running behind the house while Constantine positions himself between two houses, standing in the alley that bisects the other side of the block. Even with a pair of binoculars, he still has a less than stellar view of the front door. I expect sirens any minute; a strange man standing in an alley with a pair of binoculars would give anyone cause for alarm.

Nick's Bluetooth earpiece blinks a steady, even blip, and his murmured "Got it" is low enough I wonder if Constantine heard him. "No movement in the front of the house that he can see," he says. We're coming up on the neighbor's garage. We pause behind it, and he turns to me. "You ready?"

He insisted I use the gun. I pull up my shirt and unholster it from the small of my back, check the clip, and flick off the safety. Nick creeps forward until he's reached the far corner of 7058 Huntington's garage, peeking around the corner. I force myself to stand there and wait for him to signal me to move toward him.

The yard is empty. So empty I expect to see tumbleweeds bounce past. I brush past him and walk onto the porch, the steps squeaking under my feet.

When the back door swings open at the barest touch of my hand, I slide to the edge of the doorway and duck, prepared for gunfire. There isn't any. The kitchen is as empty as the yard, only instead of tumbleweeds there's a thick layer of dirt and dust over every surface. Thick enough I can make out a set of footprints leading away from the door.

I follow them from the kitchen and nudge open the first door I come to. It's a small bathroom with mold spots on the wall and rust stains in the sink. It's also empty. Maybe the whole place is, and we've been played.

The next room is not.

It's the dingy, closed-off room in the photo, what little light there is sneaking in around the edges of the blackout curtains hanging on the window. Mom's tied to a chair in the center of the room, dried blood on her face and a thick piece of duct tape over her mouth. Her eyes have swollen shut. Strands of hair trail across her cheek, sticking to the tape.

There's no way to get the tape off without causing more pain, so I grab a corner and peel it away, ignoring her moan. I glance at Nick, standing in the doorway, and re-holster my gun to free both hands. "Mom?" I whisper, brushing the hair off her cheeks. "I'm here. We're leaving."

"Cass." My name is barely a sound, and I lean in closer. "Your father—"

"He's probably fine. Looking for you." I move around to the back of the chair and pull the knife from its sheath. They used those zip-tie things on her wrists, tight enough the plastic digs into her skin. I grit my teeth as I slice through it, nicking her arm in the process. "Sorry. Can you stand?"

Her head lolls to the side, and I come around to cup her under the elbows. "Your father's here." Soft words, pushed out through raw, bleeding lips.

They must have really messed her up if she believes Turner's here. "He's not, Mom, but I am. Nick and I can help you out to the car."

She shakes her head with a sudden violence, hissing in pain at the movement. She sits down hard. "*He's here.* They brought him in to see me. I heard him. He's here, Cass."

The first surge of fear rushes into the blank space, my hands trembling with the force of it. I slip the knife back into its sheath and reach for my gun. Catching Nick's eye, I jerk my head to my mother. "Get her out of here."

I slip past him and out into the hall, not bothering to muffle my footsteps as I approach the living room. There's no point. If there's anyone left in the house, they already know we're here, and they didn't stop me from going to my mother.

Which means Mom isn't the target.

Turner is.

He's tied to a chair in the middle of the living room, arms twisted behind him, his legs bound to the chair. Isaiah has a gun to his head and a sick, sick smile on his lips. "Glad you could finally join us, Cass."

I drop my gaze from that smile to Turner's face. Blank. Even outgunned and facing his own death, he won't show emotion. "Cassidy. Go to your mother." Cool, calm, like nothing unusual has happened. A typical Turner reaction.

My feet have turned to cement. They got him. They got the drop on my dad. On Caleb Turner. The Ghost, the man who couldn't be taken, couldn't be caught, who is *feared*. "Turner?"

"Cass. *Go.*"

I stare at him, his blue eyes hard and cold. The gun bumps against his head, and he winces.

Winces. Turner doesn't feel anything. Doesn't show anything. "Dad?"

Click. Cool metal presses against my temple, and I jerk away. An arm wraps around my waist, holding me still. Like I'm going anywhere. I can't get my feet to move. I can't lift my arm to fire at Isaiah's head. He's *right there*, ripe for the plucking, and I'm paralyzed.

"Cass." His whole face softens, and for the first time in over a decade I see the father I loved when I was a little girl. "Cassidy, *leave. I love you.*"

An explosion.

A spot of red, blooming in the middle of Turner's forehead.

More red, running down his face, covering his nose, his mouth, his eyes truly blank.

Screaming. Lots of screaming.

My father slumping forward.

"*Daddy!*"

Chapter 27

Nature's a cruel mistress. It should be overcast, slightly chilly, with some rain thrown in to make it interesting. Instead, the sun's shining like a spotlight, and the temperature's climbed to an unseasonably warm seventy-five degrees. A sick joke made all the more ironic for the cold, remote nature of the man we're burying today.

Mom's a mess. In the week since we found her at the house in Encino, some of her injuries have started to heal. The swelling around her eyes has gone down, and her lips are no longer chapped. But she's not sleeping or eating, and the swelling's been replaced by dark circles and heavy bags, bleeding into the hollows carving out her cheeks.

Her black dress hangs on her like a garbage bag. I went shopping for it without her and got the wrong size. She's refused to leave the house until today. Funeral arrangements, phone calls to the insurance company and Mom's firm, dealing with Turner's coworkers has all fallen to me.

I can't call him Dad. He's Turner. He's been Turner for years.

That single, horrifyingly bittersweet moment is always there, every time I shut my eyes. I hear it as I'm falling asleep, as I'm waking up. *I love you.* It whispers to me throughout the day. Every time I hear it, another piece of Cass the College Student crashes and shatters into a million pieces.

I am not her. I will never be her again.

"Ashes to ashes, dust to dust…"

No casket. Practical Turner, outlining what he'd wanted. Cremation, and his ashes to be spread out in the Joshua Tree National Park. Mom's barely upright, leaning on me so hard if Nick wasn't on my other side holding me up, I'd be sagging under her weight. There are far more mourners than I expected. Denise and Charlie are somewhere toward the back, along with Scott. Tori's with him, and that makes me smile, despite everything. Lia and a tall guy with dark red hair and brown eyes. Noah, most likely.

Andreas and Malena. Constantine, his parents.

Tris, lurking behind a nearby tree.

And Isaiah. He's waiting in the distance, giving me this chance to say good-bye. He knows I won't kill him here. The arrogant motherfucker.

He walked right out the front door because I'd been too busy screaming and begging my dad to come back to life, and Nick had already escorted my mother out of the house. Constantine claims he saw Isaiah but couldn't get to him in time.

"Caleb's daughter, Cassidy, will say a few words."

Nick steps behind me and takes hold of my mother, freeing me to join the minister next to the headstone. He's a grandfatherly type with a kind face and a round belly. Give him a beard and a red furry suit, he'd be a perfect Santa. I owe the man far more than he could understand. It's his calm, quiet generosity that guided me through this whole process.

Small comfort.

I meet Nick's gaze and hold it, needing the connection to both parts of me to get through a speech that's part truth, part lie. "Dad was a hard man to know and harder to understand. He had these...ideas of right and wrong that didn't allow for much deviation. We didn't always get along," I admit, thinking of the last year, "but I never doubted he loved me." The first lie. The biggest lie, the one I tell for my mother in hopes she'll hear it. "He was also a man of absolutes. His family was everything to him." *Mom* was everything to him. "He didn't deserve to die the way he did."

I love you.

"I like to think he's in a better place where he doesn't have to worry." He'd tell me revenge isn't worth it. It will only twist me up and spit me out, worse off than I was before. Killing, the way he did it, the way I do it, isn't about revenge. It's a business transaction. I drop my gaze to the urn on the small table in front of me. "I'll miss you, Dad."

Daddy!

My heels sink into the grass as I walk back to my mother. She doesn't acknowledge my presence, just sways on her feet and stares at the urn. She hasn't cried. I think she's spoken maybe twenty words, tops, in the week since Turner was murdered.

As there's no casket to lower into the ground, the service breaks up after that. A neighbor comes up to Mom and leads her away toward a car waiting to take her home.

"Whenever you're ready," Nick murmurs, tucking a strand of hair behind my ear. If he's noticed my lack of enthusiasm for his affections, he's doing a damn good job of hiding it.

The part of me that yearns to lean into him, let him wrap his arms around me and promise me everything will be all right, is closed up and chained shut. I don't know if I'll ever let her out again. She feels too much. She's too easily hurt.

I am always cold.

"I need a moment."

He nods, kisses me softly, and heads into the crowd, rounding them up and shuffling them away from the gravesite. Denise starts for me, and Nick cuts her off. I've been avoiding her since she and Charlie returned home a few days ago. I didn't want her to come. Not with Isaiah still alive. But she ignored my pleadings and Nick's outright order, and here they are.

The minister helps round up the stragglers, leaving me alone with the urn. Nothing ornate, just simple, polished copper that'll still look good as it oxidizes. Better than a metal box. I run my fingers along the edges. I know he can't hear me, but I can't keep the words inside. "Why Joshua Tree? What was that place to you?" I'd been once on a school trip, but never with my parents. What had he found in the rocks and sand and heat?

I close my hands over the top of the urn, shutting my eyes against the day. "*Why?* Why couldn't you have said it sooner?" Like Mom, I haven't cried. I have no tears now, but the pain and the rage burst to the surface, threatening to explode. "You're *Turner*. You're invincible. *You are not supposed to be here*." A container full of ash, instead of flesh and bone and blood, ready to hunt in the shadows. We could have done it together. If he'd unbent slightly, if I'd *begged*, he might be here, and it would be Isaiah's headstone I was standing in front of.

A mere suggestion of sound, and I dig my fingers into the urn. Of course he wouldn't wait for me to come to him. He has to get his final dig in, invade this now-sacred space and taint it. "Isaiah."

He stops behind me, close enough I catch his aftershave drifting on the breeze. "Cass." Another step, and I force myself to relax my fingers. "It was business."

Nick's father, Andreas, said something similar to me on the night I met the rest of the family. I've used the justification myself. Death is part of the business. It's my only business. "Is that the lie you tell yourself so you can sleep?"

He sighs. "It *is* business, Cass. It's how my world works. You take something from me, I take something from you. We call it even. Everyone goes about their lives and does their best to put it behind them."

He lays a hand on my shoulder, and it's all I can do not to tense up. "If it's any consolation, the debt has been paid. Your mother is safe. So are your friends. I won't be coming after you unless you continue to ally yourself with my cousin."

Nick. Beautiful, amazing Dominic Kosta, who refuses to leave me to fight this on my own. "You think you can take him out, take over his position?" There's much I don't understand about the Kosta family and all the action they control, but I understand enough to know that between Nick and Constantine, losing one or the other will cause a rift so big the family may never be able to cross it.

The hand on my shoulder squeezes gently. "Your faith in Dom is admirable. He will fall, Cassidy." He slides his hand down my back, onto the dip in my waist, nudging me around. His dark eyes, so like Nick's, full of concern and sympathy, lock with mine. And to think I actually found him attractive once. "He'll fall, and if you stand with him, so will you. Think of your mother and what that will do to her."

He doesn't know. He can't. He wouldn't be this close if he knew I wasn't following his rules. This parley is a farce. I let the knife I have tucked up my sleeve slip down.

"How?" I ask. "We know there are men loyal to you, but it's not enough. Or are there more that we've missed?"

Stupid, complacent Isaiah, with just Tris to watch his back. Stupid, trusting Isaiah for thinking I'd follow his rules.

I won't kill him here. It's not time for him to die. There's a lot of work to be done first. But he will bleed. It's only fitting he do so here. The angle's a bit tricky. I'm right handed, and although I've trained to use the knife in either hand, my left will never be my strongest.

I don't need it to be strong.

Isaiah shakes his head. "The organization's had problems since before Dom and Constantine stepped up. All we're doing is cleaning up the mess." He lets his hand drop to my free one and raises it between us. "You want out," he says quietly, "this is your chance."

"Don't worry about me." The handle fits into my palm, and I drive the blade into his belly above the belt. His eyes widen with shock before pain and fury take over. I free the knife and my hand and step to the side. "You should get that looked at quick. It's not fatal. *Yet.*"

I tuck the knife into my sleeve and weave through the headstones to the drive where Nick's leaning against his car.

He straightens as I approach. "What'd Isaiah want?"

"The usual. It's business, consider the scales balanced, blah blah blah." I hold up the knife. "Cleaning supplies?"

"Glove compartment, as requested." He opens the door, and I drop into the passenger seat and rummage through the glove compartment. I pull out the cloth. He climbs in behind the wheel and starts the car. "I take it he had no idea?"

"Nope. He won't die if he gets it stitched up quickly. It'll hobble him. We've got a little time." The blood smears on the cloth. "He's gunning for you. Said something about problems before you and Constantine took over and now he's cleaning up the mess? I think he might have more men inside that are waiting for the next stage."

I rub a small amount of oil into the metal and take out the whetstone.

"We didn't think it would be that easy to end this," Nick says, the scowl evident in his tone. "We'll start on a new list tonight." He reaches across the car's center console and takes the knife from my hand. He sets it in my lap. Closing his fingers around mine, he lifts my hand to his mouth and brushes a kiss across my knuckles. "We'll take him out, Cass. We'll get rid of the problem."

I stare at the knife in my lap, allow myself to feel the warmth of Nick's hand on mine. Together. He will help me if I let him. We are stronger together, smarter together. Better. Whole.

I don't know if I'll ever be whole again.

Meet the Author

When she's not plotting ways to sneak her latest shoe purchase past her partner, Amanda Byrne writes sexy, snarky romance and urban fantasy. She likes her heroines smart and unafraid to make mistakes, and her heroes strong enough to take them on. Amanda lives in the beautiful Pacific Northwest, and no, it really doesn't rain that much. Visit her website at Amandakbyrne.com, find her on Facebook at www.facebook.com/authoramandakbyrne, on Goodreads at www.goodreads.com/Byrneafterreading, and follow her on Twitter @amandakbyrne.

If you haven't read Amanda's first book in the Game of Shadows series, it's a must read for more of the same sexy, edgy thrills.
On sale now.

Game of Shadows

The girl next door just got deadly.

On the outside, Cass Turner looks like any other beautiful California college girl. But besides studying at UCLA, she's hiding a shocking secret: she's a highly trained assassin with multiple kills under her belt. After a year spent avoiding the family business, she takes what she hopes will be her final job and winds up saving her target's life and getting way more than she bargained for…
As a lieutenant in LA's largest crime family, Dominic Kosta is determined to find out who wants him dead, and he's convinced Cass can help him find out. But the longer they search for the truth, the more questions arise…and the deeper their attraction grows. Nick has his own reasons for wanting to resist Cass, but it's a losing battle. And together, they're free of secrets and lies. Still, getting involved with Nick has put a target on Cass' back—and in this game, it's either kill or be killed.

Chapter 1

I should have said no.

Even as I walk down the street, hands tucked in the pockets of my hoodie, I'm arguing with myself. So many things about this job are off. The lack of information. The lack of movement. The compressed timeframe. The late deposit on the heels of the rush request. I don't need the money, though it's always welcome. I should be home, trying to finish my essay on sociological theory's roots in Marxism.

I haven't pulled a job in almost a year, which is why I took this one. Practice or a need to prove I can still do this, take your pick. Whoever wants the hit completed took the time to research how I work. I prefer to operate on a "keep me in the dark" basis. I don't need to know whether they're good or evil, whether they're guilty or not. I'm not judge or jury, just the executioner. All I need is a photo and a bare bones schedule, and I can pull it off.

But I didn't have a lot of time to do my recon, and that's the current argument kicking around in my head as I hurry down the darkened street to the site. The e-mail gave me a place and a time along with a picture.

He's why I'm here. I might as well admit it now while I can.

He has this presence that captivates me, even in a photo. Dark hair, dark eyes, a nose, cheekbones, and a jawline that look like they belong on a Greek god.

I'm young and female. Last time I checked, I was alive, and my hormones were functioning on a normal level, thank you very much. I think my reaction was well within the accepted range for someone presented with a visual they found compelling.

It's not so much that he's attractive, though. It's that combined with something else. He looks as dangerous as me. Or the "me" that Turner insists I'm capable of being.

Thoughts like that lead to sloppiness and distraction.

Focus, Cass. Lock it down.

The entrance to the restaurant is on a tiny side street, narrow and cluttered with cars and garbage, clumps of people dotting the sidewalks. The buildings are crowded together, some flush, others with dark cracks barely large enough for a body between them. Those cracks are perfect for my needs. Heading for the alley, I skirt the light pouring from the restaurant entrance onto the sidewalk and slip into a narrow passage beside the restaurant. If there's a back entrance to this place—and there should be—I could very well end up screwed. Just because the entrance is in the front doesn't mean that's the one he'll use.

I poke my head into the alley. Not only is there a back entrance, there's two guys hanging around it, smoking and chattering in Spanish. The alley's so narrow the busier cross street at the end is almost obscured. No wonder the dumpsters are out front. The dark is deeper here, no streetlights or businesses to break it up. Keeping one eye on the two men, I edge into the alley. One building over, on the opposite side of the alley, is another skinny break, much like the one I just left. It empties onto another crowded street. Perfect for disappearing.

The target's supposed to enter the front of the restaurant at nine PM. I pull out my phone, hunching over to block out the glow of the screen. Ten till. Ten minutes to find a decent place to hide, ten minutes to figure out how to pounce.

This is the shittiest job. I should have said no.

I head back to the front of the restaurant and scan the few cars parked along the curb. None of them are large enough to hide behind. I weave through the crowd to the other side of the street, searching for a shadowed nook, an empty doorway, something that will serve as a disguise. Finding none, I pull out my phone again. Almost nine.

Time to walk away. This isn't worth it.

Frustrated, I push my hood from my head and study the street one last time. If I had more time to prepare, I might have been able to make this work. Crowds are actually easy for me—lots of camouflage. Quick jab of the needle and off I go, let the poison do the rest. It's good for knife work, too, though not as reliable. Hanging around to see if the wound I made was fatal could be the difference between walking away and getting caught, so I don't.

The street's too narrow. That's the problem. Not enough room to move, and the shadowed spots are out in the open. A litany of excuses run through my head as I search for a place to hide. Turner would be able to make it work. His voice echoes in my head, a stream of chastising statements, disapproval lending them weight. I glance over at the restaurant one last time. Maybe I missed something.

I did. *Him.*

He's striding toward the entrance of the restaurant, all dominating and alert. He's tall. Built. People stop what they're doing, follow his progress as he walks down the sidewalk. Cars slow.

Cars.

The black SUV rolls along behind him, stopping when he pauses outside the restaurant. I wasn't told there'd be men with him. Newbie mistake, assuming he'd be alone. I can't finish this job. I won't be able to get close enough.

The front passenger side door cracks open, the snub-nosed barrel of a gun barely visible in the light stretching into the street.

Follow your gut, Cass. Your gut will get you out of trouble.

Turner's words have never failed me before, and neither has my gut, as he calls it. My gut says that gun isn't for protection. They wouldn't be tailing him in a car if they were meant to guard him.

I'm not about to let someone else take my payday before I have a chance to decide if I want it. The target's still outside the restaurant, so I dart across the street, shedding my hoodie as I go. Little changes to fool anyone who might have noticed me before. I try not to wince as I think of the syringe I just abandoned, tucked in the pocket of my sweatshirt. "Hey, baby!" I throw my arms around his neck and bounce up, hoping like hell he's a fast thinker.

His hands cradle my ass, his face inches from mine. There's no trace of surprise. Only a slick, sinful smile that ties my tongue into a giant knot. "Who the hell are you?" he murmurs.

I suck in a breath. Mistake. Oh, big, big mistake. He smells incredible. Like cinnamon. He squeezes hard, and I stifle a yelp. Bastard. "I'm assuming you noticed the SUV crawling after you?" He flexes his hands in response, loosening his grip. I widen my grin. "Unless they're yours, I thought you might want some help getting out of here."

His gaze flits down to my mouth and back up, his smile changing to a smirk. It stings, that change, as though he thinks there's no way I could be of any help, and my conviction wavers. Why did I think this was a smart idea? He's a job. The more contact I have with him, the harder it'll be to go through with it. I unwind my legs and slide down his body. He catches my hand in his before I can walk away and leads me into the restaurant.

All the tables are full, the noise level a high hum, punctuated by the clatter of plates and laughter. He slides a hand into the back pocket of my jeans and bends down, his breath tickling my ear. "Help away."

I *really* should have stayed home.

"Back entrance is through the kitchen. We can cut through the alley to the next street." He shifts his hand to my hip and squeezes once. I hope that means he understands.

We're halfway across the dining room when the front door to the restaurant opens. I quicken my pace, pulling free of his hold, winding around the last few tables.

The first shots are loud. It's a spray of them, *crack crack crack*, and I abandon my oh-so-casual stroll to the back door of the restaurant and lunge through the entrance to the kitchen, slipping on the greasy floor. He's right behind me, his hand grasping my elbow before I can go down. The cooks mill around, exclaiming in Spanish and English, getting in the way as we race for the exit.

There's a vise on my lungs. My heart's beating so hard I'm positive I've broken a few ribs. We tumble out into the narrow alley as the next gunshot rips through the chaos of the kitchen.

It's a few hundred yards to the next break between the buildings and the relative safety it represents. Adrenaline churns in my stomach as I sprint for it, banging my elbow on the unforgiving brick as I dart through the opening.

Dark. So very, very dark. The pavement is broken and cracked, and I twist my ankle in my haste to get to the other side. *Fuck.* Pain shoots up my leg as I put weight on my foot.

"You gonna keep going, or you gonna let them find us?"

I ignore him and limp forward, gritting my teeth with every step. He swears, and I swallow a squeak as he grabs me from behind and tosses me over his shoulder in a fireman's carry. "What the hell?" I hiss.

"Moving too slow." He jogs to the next street and sets me on my feet as he pushes out into the open. "You're going to have to walk. We'll draw too much attention if I carry you."

Nodding, I put my foot down, wincing as pain vibrates up my shin. "I'm parked about ten blocks away." He stares down at my feet, and it hits me—we don't have to stick together. "You know what? Never mind." I wave a hand at the street in front of us. "Go. Disappear. Watch out for black SUVs with super tinted windows."

A bullet zips past, leaving behind a burning line of pain along my right thigh. He curses, scoops me up, and runs down the street, dodging people trying to get away from the gunfire. He veers off through the nearest door. It's a bar, and all I can say is it's dimly lit and not even half full. "Back entrance?" he barks. The bartender silently points to the far wall, and my target—for one fleeting second I wish I knew his name—dashes through the bar to the back. He eases the door open, and I stick my head out to scan the alley.

Some of the gunmen are at the far end, facing away from us. Likely searching the street to see if we'll pop up there. I withdraw my head. "Opposite end of the alley. Four of them."

Shouts from the front of the bar push him through the door, catching it before it can slam shut. He keeps close to the building, using the shadows as cover, pausing at the next door to try the knob. It doesn't budge. He moves from doorway to doorway, each second that passes with us out in the open bringing us closer to a date with the wrong end of a gun.

We're running out of doors. He tries another doorknob. It twists easily under his hand. He nudges it open with his foot, and we slip inside as shouts sound in the alley.

When he puts me down, my ankle throbs in protest. Bright spots flash in front of my eyes, pain streaking down my leg. This fucking hurts. Blood seeps through my jeans, soaking the heavy fabric.

He fumbles with the doorknob, muttering under his breath. "See anything we can put in front of the door?"

I shake my head, too distracted by my ankle and the bullet wound to my thigh to notice much of anything. Turner would be telling me right about now to push through it. I swallow hard. "I can walk. I'll find some place to hide out for a little while." The faint wail of sirens sends a wave of relief through me, weakening my knees, and I slide to the floor. Sirens mean cops. Cops mean whoever those bastards with guns are will be clearing out.

Derision's clear on his face as he looks down. "You can walk?" He leans over, grabs my hands, and hauls me to my feet. "Maybe if we're lucky this place has a first aid kit we can use."

The sirens scream closer. It's a comforting sound, which is strange. It's never been a comfort before. I grip his arm as I limp forward. "Looks like some kind of storeroom."

He doesn't respond, just guides me through the dim hallway. We find a small room off to the left, outfitted with a busted couch, a table, and a few chairs, lit by a bare bulb that sputters a couple times before staying on. "Go lie down. On your side. Take your pants off first."

The fog of pain lifts for a minute. Attractive as he is, I'm not letting this guy see me without my pants. "How about not? If there's a first aid kit around, fantastic. I can clean myself up. You can sneak out or whatever."

He levels his gaze at me. "Take off your pants."

The temperature in the room rises about ten degrees. "I can take care of my own injuries, thank you. Your concern is touching but unnecessary."

The button on my jeans is undone in a blink, his fingers lowering the zipper, inch by inch. What the fuck? I swat at his hands, pull them away. "Stop it."

"Pants off, love. You're going to need some help with that bullet graze." He brushes his fingers over the exposed skin above my panties, and the heat of his touch, one simple touch, blanks my mind. He peels them over my hips, working his fingers into my pant leg to pull the fabric from my skin where it's sticking with blood. Embarrassment catches up with me as he kneels to untie my sneakers and free my ankles of their denim bindings. The hottest guy I've ever seen is taking off my pants, and the only reason he's doing it is because I can't bend over and take care of it myself.

The offending clothing item is in a heap at my feet, and he picks me up again. The couch makes an ominous creaking sound as he lays me on my side. "Thought I saw a sink nearby."

I'm half naked. Cold. Cold and getting colder, the adrenaline rush draining from my body. He's prowling the room, probably searching for the elusive first aid kit. Those things are damn hard to catch in the wild. I bite down on my lip to keep the giggles inside and listen for the sirens. They've stopped. Hopefully that means the police are out on the street, rounding people up.

The target holds up a white box. "Found it." He opens the kit and sifts through the contents. A packet of gauze, an Ace bandage, some tape, what looks like a couple of wipes, and a tube of ointment end up on the table next to the box. After washing his hands, he dampens some paper towels from the holder over the sink in the corner and returns to my side, kneeling next to the couch to wipe the blood from my leg.

The first touch stings like hell. I dig my fingers into the couch cushion. What's that phrase? Lie back and think of England? Think of something else. Anything else. The e-mail to send to the client, declining the job. The conversation I've been putting off with Turner. The research paper on nineteenth century poets I haven't started. That stupid sociology paper. "What's your name?" I gasp.

"You can call me Nick." His focus never wavers from my thigh.

Crap. I didn't actually mean for that question to come out. "Nick." Knowing his name will make it harder to kill him. Fantastic. "Thanks for this. You really didn't have to stick around."

"Right. Do I look like a monster? Those men would have eaten you alive. Besides, I owe you."

I don't have an answer for that.

He tosses the used towels on the floor and gathers the stuff he set out. He squeezes the edges of the wound together and reaches for a bandage. Warm. Way too warm, his hand on my leg, the rest of him close enough I can smell him. Cinnamon. Unusual. Intoxicating. "Do you think we'll be able to get past the cops? I mean, if they're still out there? I've got a paper to finish." Maybe if I focus on my assignment I won't notice how good he smells.

"A paper?" He glances over, our eyes locking for a brief moment. "You're a student?"

"Yeah. I'll graduate in the spring."

He smooths the first of the butterfly bandages over the wound. "UCLA? USC?"

"UCLA." I shut my eyes, giving in to the fatigue and pain clouding my mind.

"Thought you looked young," he muttered. "What's your name?"

Ow. Ow ow ow ow *ow*. The wound burns more the longer he pinches the edges together. He can't get those bandages on fast enough. I open my mouth to lie, and the truth falls out. "Cassidy. Cass. I go by Cass."

"Cass." He strokes a hand down my leg, closing it around my swollen ankle. "Shift onto your back for me, and we'll get this wrapped." He lifts his head enough to meet my gaze. "Then you can tell me how a college student gets through a gunfight unfazed."

www.ingramcontent.com/pod-product-compliance
Lightning Source LLC
Chambersburg PA
CBHW031428250626
47155CB00004B/1660